SABERJET ONYX

"Deceptions have consequences."

NOVA PUBLIUS

© 2011

SABERJET ONYX

ONE

The wind – more like a gaseous ice pick – cut through his rain-soaked jacket as if it were so much tissue paper. Wet tissue paper. Cold. The early December storm had left the low Sonoran desert enveloped in a fresh, semi-sweet aromatic blanket of wet creosote and mesquite. In the pre-dawn hours, the temperature drop accelerated as the rush of clean air scrubbed over the terrain.

Off to the right, on the far horizon, the first faint suggestions of the approaching dawn licked at the bottom of distant stratus clouds, turning them a dim smudge of pewter-peach. He adjusted the volume on his iPod and dialed up "*Imagine*" in the earbuds. He opened the scope eyepiece cover and peered at the lime green night vision image – a pickup truck with a camper shell – over a mile away. An unfortunate casualty of a backroads hunting trip gone awry, and on a gunnery range yet, he thought. Tragic. He released the weapon's safety and wondered: how had it come to this?

***

She shivered as the wind bit at her ears, hissing like an irritated sidewinder jolted out of hibernation. The fragrance of wet creosote and mesquite filled her lungs as she squinted through the scope atop the McMillan TAC-50. The advancing air-glow on the undersides of the distant clouds from an even more distant sunrise allowed her to dampen the scope's night vision mode. The image was clear, even from a mile away: the chilling clarity of digital imaging, she thought. She twirled up "*Sweet Home Alabama*" on her iPod Shuffle and released the safety.   And she wondered: how had it come to this?

***

Neal stretched in the cold, narrow confines of the F-250 pickup bed, pulling his sleeping bag closer around him and repositioning himself on the air futon mattress. The camper shell had helped shield him from last night's drizzle; but not from the cold. He reached over to the side of the cavity, turned the valve to the propane tank on and pressed the piezo spark igniter. The muffled 'whooooSH' of the external burner signaled that the fuel was doing its job and that the fan-driven heat exchanger would soon be pumping warm air into the shell. And he wondered: how had it come to this?

TWO

One Week Earlier

Rossiter sat at the third table on the left, by the window. He glanced around the room to see if the contact – he'd be wearing 501 Levi's and a black U2 fan shirt – had arrived. Not yet. He was uncomfortable. Starbucks was not exactly the chain he frequented with any regularity, especially in Georgetown. Oh, maybe an occasional mercy stop in an airport, when forced to fly commercial when both of the firm's Gulfstream III's were down, but other than that, no. He much preferred the Mayflower. Superior ambiance. Linen tablecloths and napkins. Sterling. Refined.

A figure wearing the designated uniform opened the door and stepped in. He was tall, almost lanky, with short-cropped walnut-tan hair and a single stainless steel stud imbedded at the end of his left eyebrow. It matched the stainless steel of his rimless glasses. He began a quick sweep of the patrons, then locked on Rossiter, who acknowledged the recognition with a small upward bob of his chin.

Grant walked over to Rossiter's table – clumsily bumping into a waiter on the way... the only Starbucks in town with waiters – and sat down. Neither offered the other a hand salutation.

"You're Grant?" Rossiter asked.

"Yeah." He leaned slightly forward in his chair. "And I guess you don't need a last name, do ya?"

Rossiter shook his head. "No. Better that way."

Grant smiled. "Yeah. Better."

A waiter appeared, not the one he bumped on his trip from the door, to take their orders: a cappuccino and a double espresso.

Rossiter looked over toward the door, then back at Grant. "So... Grant... how is your little part of this... fandango... coming along?"

Grant tossed a few furtive glances at his surroundings –
left, toward the door of the café; right toward two Georgetown
students "studying" in a back booth – then looked over the lenses
of his wire-framed glasses, darting back and forth between
Rossiter's eyes: "Good. Really good."

Rossiter nodded approvingly. "Some details, please?"

Grant allowed a small grin and returned the nod. "Well, for
openers…" he paused and tilted his head to the left, "…my part of
this, what do you call it… Saberjet Onyx thing… is now actually
ahead of schedule…. by about, oh, maybe… two weeks …"

The conversation was briefly interrupted by the waiter,
returning with the coffees, one in front of Rossiter, and Grant's
espresso, opposite the cappuccino. He disappeared as quickly as
he had appeared. Rossiter took a quick sip, gauging the
temperature of the liquid.

"Two?" Rossiter hissed-whispered, his eyebrows peaking.
He put his cup down. "*Two weeks?* That's significant…"

"Yeah," Grant concurred, sipping his liquid, his napkin
absorbing some excess fluid at the corner of his mouth. "We were
finally able to get DOHS security clearances for two janitors and
one waiter for the commissary. So that made the task easier. A *lot*
easier." Another sip of espresso. "But I gotta tell ya, security over
there at National Archives is almost as tight as at Langley… but,
hey, it's done." He lifted his cup and sipped again. "Had to pay
off a couple of the existing janitors and, well, get one of the
security guards into a 'compromising situation'" emphasized with
double air quotes, "… but like I said, it's done."

"Compromising situation?" Rossiter asked.

Grant shot him a quick yeah-duh-squint-frown. "Dude,
yeah … you know, like, one-way mirrors and … stuff… down in
Southeast?"

Rossiter circled the rim of his cup like an orbiting satellite.
His fingers and hands bore the scars of decades of brutal "K"
Street lobbying: evenly tanned; liver-age spots bleached into the

background epidermis; nails symmetrically trimmed, shaped and buffed as only a $400 an hour manicurist for the well-to-do could manage. Rumors abounded in the "K" Street community as to what his feet looked like.

Rossiter stared into his cup, then constructed his best, patented sneer onto his lips. "Grant… let me ask you something."

"Yeah?"

"Is the money that gets eee-eff-teed into your bank account each month from Grand Cayman in any way defective? That is to say, have you been able to access it and spend it all right? Immediately? No problems?"

Grant frowned. "Nah… the loot is great… great. Half of it went last week for that yellow 'Vette across the street." He smile-frowned. "What do you mean, defective?"

"And you'd like those infusions of money to continue, I presume?"

Grant first nodded, then shook his chin back and forth. "Where's this going?"

"I knew you'd ask. I have your answer. And, please, listen closely, because I *hate* repeating things once clearly stated." He fixed his gaze on the café's front door, out toward the Corvette, but he spoke directly for the benefit of its owner. "If ever again you address me as 'dude' or show the slightest degree of flippancy about what's going on here… and what is at stake… or cough up sarcasm as a substitute for some clarification I might request…," he shifted his fovea to Grant's left eye, "… you will deeply and permanently regret it."

Grant said nothing, but slowly lifted his cup to his mouth again and took another, longer sip, still looking at Rossiter's hazel stare, then glanced back over at the "students" in the far booth.

"Are we clear on that?" the lobbyist asked.

Grant exhaled into his cup. "We are."

Rossiter sat back in his chair. "Good. Great." A glance at the waiter and a raised cup shortly brought another cappuccino; he smiled his "K" Street "I-am-*so*-superior-to-you-you-struggling-loser" smile for the waiter's benefit, then turned his attention back to Grant.

"There is a meeting taking place next week." Rossiter said.

"The Chicago meeting?" Grant responded.

"How do you know about that?"

Grant nodded. "Saw it in an e-mail that was mistakenly copied to me." He saw Rossiter's accelerating frown. "Not to worry. *Sheesh,* du… just chill, will ya? All I saw was 'Chicago' and 'meeting' and I double-deleted it anyway when I saw who the other recipients were."

Rossiter's attention twitched rapidly back and forth between Grant's eyes, like that I-hope-you're-telling-me-the-truth ordeal he'd used so often on congressional staffers when he wanted something done, *now*. The Ivy League just wasn't putting out the quality of people he'd seen – and used – in the past.

"Really," Grant said. "I double-deleted it and did… not… read… it. All I saw was the subject line, not the text. And you know you gotta scroll down anyway to see the text in these things… and there were no attachments." He leaned back in his chair.

Rossiter nodded. "OK." He stopped his visual assault on Grant's eyes. "The various pieces are all coming together, from here, from there." Some cream into the hot cappuccino. "Your part, or at least the pieces part, has to be completed not later than the end of next week." A sip. "Can that be done?"

Grant generated a combo-frown/nod. "Absolutely. With time to spare."

Rossiter chuckled. "Time to spare… that's good." He smiled at Grant. "Like they say, never waste a crisis."

Grant repeated the nod. "No, I mean with *lots* of time to spare…"

Rossiter allowed a small frown to creep over his forehead. "And by that you mean…?" he let the question trail off, inviting an answer.

Grant swallowed the rest of his espresso, as if taking a shot of Chivas. "By that I mean, Bob… umm, can I call you 'Bob'… *Mister* Rossiter…. or do you prefer 'Robert'…?"

Rossiter could feel his jaw clenching. "Why are you… trying to provoke me…?"

"Hey, Bob... nah… that's harsh. I'm hurt." He cradled his chin in his fists and leaned forward on the table. "You see, I'm just trying to impress on you that, for whatever reason you and your crew are skulking around this town and whatever it is you're up to, I don't care. What I *do* care about is that you understand that I've got the assignment done. Now. And I can deliver the paper. Now. That's what I mean when I said that the task *was made* a lot easier once we got the janitors and the security guard taken care of." He grinned. "And did I say 'was' like in, past tense? And did I mention…. it's *done*? Also past tense?"

"Are you telling me…?"

"What I'm telling you… Bob… is that the… items… you ordered are secured. Now. Not next month … not next Wednesday. Today."

"Today?"

Grant leaned back in his chair and grinned. "You know, I never noticed that echo in here before. Yeah, Bob… today… ummm…. with the expedite surcharge, of course…."

Rossiter's mouth and lips evolved from the clenched jaw into a silent, ferocious slit, the pink around his mouth blanching white as the pressure forced the blood out of his capillaries. He squinted at his target. "Expedite surcharge, eh? And that would be…?"

"Well," he exhaled, "since you guys seem to really *really* want these items a lot… and since I know that as soon as I deliver, there's probably been an 'accident' arranged for me, … so I'm gonna need to disappear from *everyone* pronto… and you don't want to know how much I had to pay the archives security guard and that photographer…. Yikes."

"What's the tag on your 'expedite' fee?"

"Two K K."

Rossiter shot glances back and forth again between Grant's pupils. "Two million dollars?" He frowned deeply. "Are you kidding me? You've already been paid over two hundred K… and now you're trying to extort *more*? *Two million dollars*… for…"

Grant raised his left hand and extended his index finger. "Stop. Stop."

Rossiter stopped.

Grant leaned toward the lobbyist. "Did I say two? Two? Stupid me…, my bad. *My* bad." He tapped his chest. "My mistake…. it's four. Four." He tilted his head slightly. "And the next time you balk at the fee, it'll double again." He drank the rest of the espresso in a single gulp and firmly set the cup down on the table. "Wanna go for eight, Bob? Do ya? Huh?"

Rossiter's jaw clenched so hard that his cheeks began turning white.

Grant tilted his head farther to the left. "Look, from all the things I've been reading lately, I know that there's a growing concern over your guy's tenure… ahhh, yes, the pitfalls of office. And what did the bard say: 'oh, what a tangled web we weave…'?"

"Four million dollars? You think he's four million dollars concerned?"

Grant smiled. "C'mon, Bob… you're makin' me nervous. Like you guys can't afford it? Are you *kidding me*? That's, like, what, fifty… sixty seconds of spending in the new budget he just proposed. Just be glad I'm a believer, or the next time you balk at the number, it *could* go to eight. Or more." Grant grinned at him. "Do the math…."

Rossiter's slit tightened even more.

"So….., Bob… look at it this way, exactly how much has he spent so far on suits and ladies of the night like you fighting disclosure in court? Huh? More than zero, yes?" Grant leaned forward slightly in his chair and nodded again. "Look, I voted for the guy too, and I still support him… for what reason, I'm beginning to wonder. But I still do. So consider this my 'preferred client,' discounted fee.

"Look, if it had been the other guy askin' for help, the expedite tariff would have been three times bigger. You know the risks I've taken to get the paper you guys demanded? You know, I'm thinkin' you should be sayin' to yourself, 'whew… I thought it would be more…' But, hey, I'm not greedy. I'm just cautious. Gotta be cautious, these days. Four million, EFT'd to the account… the *other* account in Grand Cayman should do it. *Not* the account in George Town. The one in Bodden Town." Grant glanced right, then left, then back at Rossiter. "Four million, that is…, unless I detect another balk…."

Rossiter slowly shook his head. "When?"

Grant raised his eyebrows. "Like I said, the delivery can be made today, if I get confirmation from Bodden Town on the deposit today. Tomorrow's OK, but… today would be… better… for both of us." Grant looked at his watch. "And we're in the same time zone anyway, so we've got… what…, another two hours of business window…." He let the observation trail off with a nonchalant shrug.

Rossiter fixed his gaze on the extortionist as he pulled his iPhone from the left inner breast-pocket of his suit. He flipped through a few apps, tapped it… waited… tapped it… waited… then texted: "for immediate action, transfer from Saberjet Onyx operating account… four million dollars (U.S.) for deposit to the following account in Grand Cayman…," then looked at Grant. "And the account number would be…?"

Grant gestured for the iPhone; Rossiter complied. He tapped in the account number and handed it back.

Rossiter spoke as he texted: "bank routing number is..." then looked up at Grant, who peeled a yellow sticky-note from his wallet and handed it over. Rossiter alternated between the note and the iPhone, tapping... checking... tapping... checking... send..."

They each sat back in their chairs, not unlike a pair of boxers nearing the completion of a round, still nurturing a simmering, mutual contempt for one another and sizing each other up in an attempt to decide whether it was worth one more sucker-punch or whether it was better to wait for the bell and prepare for the next round. Clearly, neither fighter had knocked the other one out... or even down. A few hits, but that was about all. They were startled by the shattering glass of a water pitcher that a waiter had dropped on the concrete floor of the café, and then... the vibrating buzz of Grant's iPhone went off. He pulled it out, tapped it... then nodded.

Rossiter mirrored the nod. "And now?"

Grant smiled. "Now... we go to my car."

Rossiter jerked that involuntary "you-gotta-be-kidding" twitch that pops out when unexpected news unfolds.

"You're kidding, right?"

Grant shook his head. "Bob... I normally don't kid when someone has paid my expedite fee on two minutes' notice... and without needing to check up the food chain for permission..." As he stood up from the table, he looked over both of his shoulders, as if he were checking for bystanders before telling a racial joke.

"Ummm... look, maybe it's none of my business..."

"Very likely true..." Rossiter agreed.

"Ahhh... against all of the stuff we've been reading lately, what..., exactly, do you guys need... with blank strips of parchment from The Articles of Confederation?"

Rossiter finished his cappuccino then wadded the paper napkin into the spent cup. "You're right. Expedite fees aside, that's none of your business." He raised his eyebrows slightly to emphasize his next remark: "And if you know what's good for you, you'll never even *think* of asking anyone that question again. Could be unhealthy…. toxic, even…"

Rossiter removed two ten dollar bills from his clip and dropped them onto the table, then stood up and began walking toward the door. "Coming?"

Grant ran his index finger around the lip of the cup and stared at the checkerboard parquet of the tabletop. It reminded him of a chess field; the upper ten dollar bill sat face up, Alexander Hamilton staring past his left shoulder, up at the ceiling. He stood, walked toward Rossiter and gestured for the lobbyist to exit first. He did.

THREE

Neal clicked open the e-mail folder on his iPhone. Spam. Delete. Spam. Delete. Spam, cruise ship weekend special, spam, spam. Highlight, shift, down, down, down, delete. E-mail re: F-86 Onyx. Double click. Arthritis acting up... pop an Aleve with some flat Diet Coke.

"urgent. just learned of change in scheduling of the oral arguments in locke. imperative that your work be completed and delivered by tomorrow, no later than 4 am. confirm to me asap... now... can this be done? correction: this must be done."

He frowned and clicked "Reply."

"Why?" he tapped. "The deal was that I had until next week and it is already near midnight. That is a very tall change order on very short notice."

Send. Seconds, seeming more like minutes, passed. Message received.

"tall order or not, the task must be completed. ch at ca shop needs time to format the text and complete the transfer by noon for delivery. the transfer is by hand cursive and that is what takes time."

He exhaled. "I can do it, but it's going to take me a while to get back to Georgetown. I'm in Baltimore right now and the laptop is secured at my condo." He hesitated, then decided to offer the sarcasm. "And, BTW, have you ever heard that haste makes waste?"

Send. Seconds again. Message received.

"do not spit bromides at me. and do not lecture me on things you know nothing about. and stop wasting time. repeat, the text must be delivered to ch at the ca shop not later than 4 am in order to get the finished product done and to the loc by noon. the

14

shop needs at least seven hours to finish its work, leaving only a one-hour cushion. we will not be able to keep the press at bay past then and we've scheduled a cover press conference at 1 to buy even that little additional time."

Pause. Another message received.

"there are many… many things in motion here which you know nothing about. be thankful for ignorance. the pieces must be coordinated for max impact and there is approximately zero room for error. ZERO. all you need to know is that if the task is not at a stage for delivery to the shop by 4 am, the potential for bad things happening … REALLY bad things…. increases. exponentially. so do it. create and improvise, but get it done. that's what we're paying for, isn't it?"

This was serious. He had never used capitalization in his messages before, and now twice in the same paragraph. Neal remembered – why, at this point, was baffling – the comic strip his grandfather always reminisced about from the 20's, Archy and Mehitabel. Archy, the cockroach with a literary flair, and Mehitabel, the alley cat who claimed to have been, in one of her prior lives, Cleopatra, were inseparable friends who expounded their collective wisdom as commentary on the passing scene.

Mehitabel would tell her friend what to write, and Archy would pounce down as hard as he could on the keys of an ancient Royal typewriter (or was it a Smith-Corona?), one letter at a time, to activate the mechanical keys and produce their literary tomes. He remembered especially that Archy's prose came out all in lowercase (and normally without punctuation) because he was neither heavy enough nor limber enough to simultaneously depress both the shift and letter keys to produce a capital letter. In that one respect, at least, Ellis differed from the literate cockroach. This *had* to be serious.

Reply. "Understood." Send.

***

Neal removed the Mac from the safe and plugged in the transformer. Once warmed up, he opened Outlook. Password: • • • • • • • • • • • •. He went to the Thomas website via bookmark, found the table of contents for The Federalist, then minimized the page. Drafts. Saberjet Onyx.

He opened the document and read through to where he had left off on Monday.

"To the People of the State of New York.

"When last the multitudinous issues attending the completion of the collections of these papers were addressed, through your humble servant Publius, but with the sage counsel and confidences of the like-minded, yet not without the trepidations customarily and normally attendant upon matters of such gravity, the singular issue of the qualifications and eligibility of the Chief Magistrate and President of the United States was considered, a series of later-perceived questions and issues surfaced. These issues, originally thought to have been adequately addressed and adumbrated in prior letters, are nonetheless of sufficient concern to warrant modest, albeit likely unnecessary, clarification to the end that such confusion and inexactitude of purpose as might be argued as extant within the plan of the convention, but anathema to the plan itself and any of its ancillary propositions as well as to the ultimate objectives of a true republic, are here further explored and elaborated upon."

He placed the cursor to the right of the end quotation mark, set the paragraph alignment format at "left" and began tapping:

"To that end, some preliminary observations would appear to be in order. And although manifest in their importance, these observations and conclusions need neither be lengthy nor of a convoluted nature, as it is understood that the prior essays heretofore presented to The People of the State of New York implicitly confirm that which hereinafter shall be articulated with specificity."

He clicked "Save" then moved the cursor over to the minimized copy of The Federalist Papers he had extracted from the Thomas website. 4:00 AM? What kind of an idiot would try to rush something as important as this to completion in… he looked at the lower right corner of the screen: 2:32 AM … eighty-eight minutes? He positioned the cursor and again began typing.

"When first this nation was conceived, much as would be a child in the womb of its mother, the womb of the experiment took the form of the minds of those who had witnessed first-hand the potentials as well as the pitfalls of the Articles which were the subject of the first thirty-six of these essays, and in particular No. 15 outlining the insufficiency of the then-extant articles of confederation to preserve the Union."

He took a long swallow from the now-tepid to-go cup of Seven-Eleven concoction and glanced again at the digital time on the screen: 2:57 AM. He shook his head to himself, then locked his eyes at the bottom of the screen. That's it. Improvise, huh? OK, improvise it is. Back to minimized icon to maximize the digital copy of The Federalist. A few clicks into it, a highlighting of some selected text, a click of "copy," then back to the Word document. Insert an internal quotation mark, then hit "paste" and up popped:

"It will be forgotten, on the one hand, that jealousy is the usual concomitant of love, and that the noble enthusiasm of liberty is apt to be infected with a spirit of narrow and illiberal distrust. On the other hand, the vigor of government is essential to the security of liberty; that, in the contemplation of a sound and well-informed judgment, their interest can never be separated; and that a dangerous ambition more often lurks behind the specious mask of zeal for the rights of the people than under the forbidden appearance of zeal for the firmness and efficiency of government. History will teach us that the former has been found a much more certain road to the introduction of despotism than the latter, and that of those men who have overturned the liberties of republics, the greatest number have begun their career by paying an obsequious court to the people; commencing Demagogues, and ending Tyrants."

That looked good. Same stilted, archaic syntax. And having the added virtue of being real Federalist language. He nodded to the screen: this could work. He began again and thought: what would Publius have next said? A quick detour into some Internet sites, search for "Acton" and "Liberty Bell," good... then he thought: how 'bout...

"That such pernicious temptations have proved the undoing of innumerable prior experiments of like character as here proposed is a matter of common knowledge, giving the famous recognition by Sir John Dalberg-Acton, Lord Acton, *viz.*, that 'power tends to corrupt, and absolute power corrupts absolutely' peculiar relevance to the matters at hand. For ever since in the Year of Our Lord 1774, when first the Liberty Bell rang out in proclamation to the world the independence of a new gathering of Peoples assembled as the First Continental Congress, the central concern of those who have pledged their fortunes and lives has been the perfection of a plan ensuring that the Chief Magistrate and President of the United States shall be one bearing absolute, unfaltering and unquestionable fealty, allegiance and dedication to the nation and People he will be sworn to preserve and protect from all enemies, foreign as well as domestic."

Another swallow of even cooler coffee. 3:18 AM tumbled into view on the screen; he fought to return to a Publius frame of mind, then typed.

"As a part of the process of ensuring that such qualities as will tend, if not inescapably guarantee, that the Chief Magistrate and President is possessed of the qualities most critical to the furtherance of the plan to ensure service of undivided loyalties and allegiance to this nation, and none other so long as he shall so serve, and as noted elsewhere in these essays, the individual shall be ineligible to the office unless he shall have, on or before the date of first taking office, attained the age of thirty-five years. The Constitution manifests very particular attention to this object. By excluding men under thirty-five from the first office, and those under thirty from the second, the Legislative body, it confines the electors to men of whom the people have had time to form a judgment, and with respect to whom they will not be liable to be deceived by those brilliant appearances of genius and patriotism, which, like transient meteors, sometimes mislead as well as dazzle. In addition, he shall similarly be deemed ineligible to the office unless, on or before the date of first taking office he shall have been a lawful resident of the United States for fourteen years."

The coffee had become totally unpalatable.   3:26 AM.
Back to Thomas for some additional filler.

"The executive authority, with few exceptions, is to be
vested in a single Magistrate. This will scarcely, however,
be considered as a point upon which any comparison can be
grounded; for if, in this particular, there be a resemblance
to the king of Great Britain, there is not less a resemblance
to the Grand Seignior, to the khan of Tartary, to the Man of
the Seven Mountains, or to the governor of New York."

Think Publius… think Publius.

"Thus, a third condition of eligibility to the office, and one
over which the individual would have no control, but which
unquestionably will serve and promote the objective of
ensuring undivided loyalty and allegiance, must be that of
being a natural born citizen or a citizen of the United
States, at the time of the adoption of the Constitution."

A quick return to the Thomas digital Federalist… highlight…
copy…minimize… paste… edit:

"As to the differing standards between the States regarding
naturalization and the bestowal of rights of citizenship, the
new Constitution has accordingly, with great propriety,
made provision against them, and all others proceeding
from the defect of the Confederation on this head, by
authorizing the general government to establish a uniform
rule of naturalization throughout the United States.
Accordingly, to the question of what qualities such a
natural born citizen would possess, and particularly one
who would have no control over his parents' allegiances
and loyalties, such matters, it is submitted, are better

reposed neither in the judicial nor legislative branches, but rather in the hands of the People themselves as expressed in the process of the periodic elections and deliberations of the electors contemplated hereunder. Thus, as to questions of whether one or both of the parents of the Chief Magistrate must also themselves be natural born citizens, as distinguished from native born citizens, or whether one alone will suffice, particularly where such is the mother, and whether when born, should the father have previously demised, leaving only the mother, would or indeed should such disqualify the Chief Magistrate, will be removed. Can it be persuasively argued that the candidacy of the Chief Magistrate to the office would not be subjected to the most thorough and complete scrutiny of the People prior to any election? Such a process, it would seem beyond peradventure, would be more thoroughly exercised through the People than through either the judiciary or the legislative branches, since the election by the People of the President is, at bottom, the quintessential characteristic of the nation being proposed. Such political questions are, without serious contradiction, better entrusted to the sound judgment of those who will be governed by the Chief Magistrate. In the course of the examination of candidates for Chief Magistrate, it cannot seriously be contemplated, much less persuasively argued, that every aspect of the person's loyalties and allegiances to the nation he would lead would be anything other than exhaustively revealed by and to the People, such that upon election of the Chief Magistrate to the office by the popular vote of the people, confirmed through the electors, the Magistrate will become, to utilize Blackstone's Latin, *res ipsa loquitur – the thing speaks for itself* – such that the election alone will confirm and ratify the president's natural born citizenship."

Hit save. 3:36 AM. He returned to the top of the document and entered the final edits:

"The Federalist No. 86   June 8, 1788"

Word count: 1321. Not enough. *Too* short. The assigned target was a minimum of 1900, and the folks at CA knew how to do a word count better than anyone in the administration. Back to Thomas and The Federalist digital copy, maximize... search for "magistrate." Good. Federalist 68... highlight... copy.... 3:47 AM... back to text, position cursor, and:

> "It was also peculiarly desirable to afford as little
> opportunity as possible to tumult and disorder. This evil
> was not least to be dreaded in the election of a magistrate,
> who was to have so important an agency in the
> administration of the government as the President of the
> United States. But the precautions which have been so
> happily concerted in the system under consideration,
> promise an effectual security against this mischief. The
> choice of SEVERAL, to form an intermediate body of
> electors, will be much less apt to convulse the community
> with any extraordinary or violent movements, than the
> choice of ONE who was himself to be the final object of
> the public wishes. And as the electors, chosen in each State,
> are to assemble and vote in the State in which they are
> chosen, this detached and divided situation will expose
> them much less to heats and ferments, which might be
> communicated from them to the people, than if they were
> all to be convened at one time, in one place.
>
> "Nothing was more to be desired than that every
> practicable obstacle should be opposed to cabal, intrigue,
> and corruption. These most deadly adversaries of

republican government might naturally have been expected to make their approaches from more than one quarter, but chiefly from the desire in foreign powers to gain an improper ascendant in our councils. How could they better gratify this, than by raising a creature of their own to the chief magistracy of the Union? But the convention have guarded against all danger of this sort, with the most provident and judicious attention. They have not made the appointment of the President to depend on any preexisting bodies of men, who might be tampered with beforehand to prostitute their votes; but they have referred it in the first instance to an immediate act of the people of America, to be exerted in the choice of persons for the temporary and sole purpose of making the appointment. And they have excluded from eligibility to this trust, all those who from situation might be suspected of too great devotion to the President in office. No senator, representative, or other person holding a place of trust or profit under the United States, can be of the numbers of the electors. Thus without corrupting the body of the people, the immediate agents in the election will at least enter upon the task free from any sinister bias. Their transient existence, and their detached situation, already taken notice of, afford a satisfactory prospect of their continuing so, to the conclusion of it. The business of corruption, when it is to embrace so considerable a number of men, requires time as well as means. Nor would it be found easy suddenly to embark them, dispersed as they would be over thirteen States, in any combinations founded upon motives, which though they could not properly be denominated corrupt, might yet be of a nature to mislead them from their duty."

OK, go back to cut and move the natural born citizen part to make it the final, concluding paragraph…

"Accordingly, in all debatable questions relating to the eligibility of the Magistrate to become a candidate as well as to thereafter serve, if having been first elected, but in particular with respect to questions relating to the person's loyalties and allegiance to the republic as implicated by the third criteria, *viz.*, that of being a natural born Citizen, it is seen that these are matters properly reposed in the People alone, and nowhere else."

Now, add the signature: Publius. 3:55 AM... no time for a final read, he thought, but that's what the formatters at Custom Alterations do for a living. He rationalized: if Congress doesn't read the stuff that it votes on, what's the difference? Word count: 1,893. Seven words short. He indulged in a mental grin: close enough for government work.

Save as: Saberjet Onyx.

To:custalterCH@tangello25.com; RE@tangello25.com.

Subject: final draft

Message: "The draft essentially meets (.9963) the volume parameters set by RE and has been spellchecked against the 1852 Webster's database, the most recent one I have on my laptop. Have your formatters use Samuel Johnson's database and 1788 spellchecker to cross-check for contemporary jargon or vernacular. I have not had time to do that or do a final proofread given the new deadline from RE." He hesitated. "This pig is now yours to glamor up. Improvise. Good luck."

He pushed "Send." 3:57 AM. Minutes to spare... minutes. And he thought: where's the problem?

FOUR

Rossiter shoved the S-600 Benz into "park" and adjusted the intermittent wipers to twenty seconds; the rain had lightened, but still continued in a thin cascade of microdrops. He looked into the rear-view mirror at the figure in the back seat.

"Senator, I've got to tell you, the argument in *Locke* did not go well."

The senator nodded. "S'what I heard from my CoS. But he wasn't there. He got the word second-hand. Hearsay, I guess they call it."

Rossiter nodded. "Well, in this case, you can take it to the bank. The argument did not go well for us. Not well at all."

"Because?"

"Because all but two of the justices were flat out not buying the argument that the plaintiffs lacked standing. And after Locke's attorneys rammed their decisions in *Flores* and *Lujan* up their nose... and hot-shot Cassini absolutely imploded in his attempt to distinguish those two cases... it was pretty much all free-fall from there. And it didn't help when Cassini admitted that he had taken exactly the *opposite* position now argued for Boalt than that which he had taken when he was with the Solicitor General's Office in *Lujan*." Rossiter shook his head slowly. "If they find standing, the golden goose could turn to lead... or something worse... overnight."

The senator glanced out the window, which was fogging up. "Standing... schmanding. What, exactly, does that mean?"

Rossiter slowed the interval on the wipers again. "It's just a legal gizmo they use when there's no other good reason if they want to punt on making a decision. The legal question could be the most significant one you could imagine or the most trivial. Doesn't matter. If the Court doesn't want to touch the issue being presented, it can always punt the ball by 'finding'" he twitched the double air-quote gesture "that the plaintiffs lack a 'stake in the outcome' of the dispute that is different from anyone else."

"And?"

"And then, their case can be labeled not 'justiciable' or doesn't present a legitimate 'case or controversy'" more air-quotes "to give the Court jurisdiction under the Constitution to hear it. You got no standing, you also got no case or controversy that you can present to them. It's judicial mumbo-jumbo for 'we're not gonna touch this slug with a ten-foot pole.'"

The senator continued to stare out the window; the Washington Monument poked its unmistakable white dominance up in the distance through the misty rain, the red aircraft warning lights blinking... on, off... on, off... a dragon obelisk. "Sounds simple enough to me. Just tell these jerks... the birthers...to fold it up and just get outta Dodge...."

"Yeah, well that played out OK in the Ninth Circuit. But no one... I mean *no one* expected a majority of the Court would grant cert, much less set the thing for accelerated briefing and oral argument."

The senator redirected his gaze to Rossiter's reversed eyes in the mirror. "Yeah, coulda, woulda, shoulda... don't they get it? I mean, the first primaries start in, what, six months and the general is less than six months after that? Don't they realize what's at stake here?"

Rossiter thought: that's the problem, you numbskull. They probably now finally realize full well what, *exactly*, is at stake here. And even the leftists there, along with their more intelligent clerks, seem to be getting the message that if what the plaintiffs are alleging is true, or even *potentially* true, the issue is the biggest one to come down their pike since Nixon.... and maybe even since Washington. Get with the program, senator... the future of the republic, let alone the administration and a bunch of careers, could be crippled if a bad decision escapes.

"Senator, look... here's how I see it."

26

"Yes… Bob… tell me… how *do* you see it?"

He turned the wipers off altogether and killed the engine. "OK. Now where I'm going here can have no trail, … written… verbal… nothing."

The senator huffed a chuckle. "Bob, Bob… how long we known each other? Fifteen, twenty years? I belong to the most exclusive political club in this solar system… maybe the whole galaxy… and you're warning me on the importance of 'plausible deniability'? Cut me some slack…" Senator Brown leaned forward in his seat to emphasize his words. "I'm not even in this car."

"Awright, … it's just that… that…."

"That we're close to treason?" He huffed another chuckle. "So what's new, Bob? Treason's just another bromide they use to threaten us. Empty. Lame. Not gonna happen. And look, I understand that when you're at war, you can't fight fire with paper clips… you need more fire and a bigger flamethrower. Just get on with it… I got some really big Saudi donors waitin' for me down at The Willard. So spit it out…"

"OK. First, we both know that if the Supreme Court comes out with a decision finding standing… and overturning the Ninth Circuit…."

"Yeah…, shocking…."

"If that happened, there likely would be a remand. And then probably an order that formal discovery be allowed in preparation for a trial. If that happens, and we can't produce the document… or worse yet, a document gets discovered and produced that proves Locke's contention that Boalt isn't eligible to serve because he's not a natural born citizen… we're done… "

"What contention? That Boalt wasn't born in Missouri?"

"Or worse, that he was actually born in India… then the charade would be over. Done. Toast. Fork in the bird."

Rossiter could see the senator's hairline oscillating back and forth. "Not so fast. Even if he *was* born in India, that doesn't mean that he's ineligible to serve, does it? I mean, we naturalize people born from anywhere on the planet, don't we?"

Rossiter thought: good grief..... we actually elect people like this to represent us? No wonder the whole thing is getting set to capsize.

"Yeah, but that's not what the Constitution requires for a president. Worse, it's not what we've been telling people. The party line since we first got wind of Boalt's eligibility problem has been that he was born in Missouri. Just like he's always claimed. We posted an image of an abstract of a Missouri birth certificate on the Internet to prove it, but they saw through that. And the stonewalling on production of his original certificate... with baby footprints, the mother's thumbprints, birthplaces of his parents... all that stuff...has become farcical. Even to our former solid bloggers. Thankfully, the mainstream media is still behind us and we've been successful so far in characterizing the 'birthers' as descendants from the Roswell aliens." He paused. "But push was comin' to shove."

The senator took a handkerchief to his forehead, despite the outside temperature. "But I thought that was taken care of with the verifications we filed before the election."

Rossiter nodded. "So did we. That's why in the certificate of verification the former Speaker signed for Missouri, there was a specific reference to the fact that Boalt was eligible under the Constitution. That verification occurred nowhere else. We used a different form in all of the other states because Speaker Cardani was concerned over the potential for a false statement or perjury prosecution. But because Missouri election law itself requires that a political party's nominee be certified by the party brass as being eligible, it had to be done there since the Constitution requires a president to be a 'natural born citizen.' So the verification signed and filed in Missouri had to say that."

The senator frowned. "So you're telling me that a naturalized citizen ... is not a natural born citizen?"

"Not only am I telling you that, it's what even *our* lawyers are telling us."

"Based on what? A couple of Armani suits from Harvard?"

"Well, those... and a statute enacted by the first Congress back in 1790... oh yeah and a couple of Supreme Court cases... for openers."

"A statute?"

Rossiter nodded. "Technically, not a 'statute', since it never got codified. But nonetheless a law passed by the Congress."

"And it says...?"

"And it says that for persons born inside or even outside the United States.... say, in India... to be considered to be a natural born citizen, *both* parents of the person must also be citizens. And since only Boalt's mother was a citizen, and his father was born in India and never became a naturalized U.S. citizen... the fact is... Boalt was *never* a natural born citizen, nor could he have been. Not in school. Not at Yale. Not in St. Louis. Not in the Senate. Not during the campaign or at the inauguration. Not today." Rossiter paused. "And the crazy thing is... he even *jokes* about it at parties." He shook his head. "Wait until one of those camera-phone videos shows up on YouTube."

The senator stared back out the window at the blinking obelisk. "Yeah. I was at one of those inauguration ball parties after he won... I thought he was joking." He shifted his attention to Rossiter's eyes in the mirror. "Now that I recall... maybe that's why they confiscated everyone's phones after that." He paused. "And so you're tellin' me he was joking at the fact that he really *was* not eligible?"

Rossiter nodded. "More than that. I was there too. Remember the biggest laugh he got? When he called P.T. Barnum a piker? He was right. Barnum could harvest only one sucker a minute. We roped in like, close to eighty million in one day."

The senator looked again at the Washington Monument and heaved a deep exhale. "And the Supreme Court cases? The old ones, that is?"

"They just back up the conclusion of the statute. The biggest problem was *Happersett*. Dumb decision, but it backs up the public law, that is." Rossiter tilted his head. "Boalt is flat ineligible, and everyone in or with access to the inner circle in the Oval Office knows it. The only thing saving us up to now is the incompetence of the lawyers trying to prove otherwise through the courts. But if the Supremes find standing in the case up there now....in *Locke*..." he let the observation trail off. "Even a blind pig can find a truffle now and then...."

The senator shook his head slowly and kept staring out at the monument. "Not good."

Rossiter exhaled. "Not good... in a big way."

The senator looked into the rearview mirror, glanced down at his Patek, then stared back at Rossiter. "So what's the plan?"

The lobbyist shifted in his seat and craned his neck as far as he could over his right shoulder, focusing on the senator. "And you're still not in this car... right?"

"Not even close to being in the car. Right now, I'm in the bar at The Willard. Got witnesses who'll testify to it..." he grinned.

Rossiter nodded. "The plan is this. First, we saw this coming a long time ago... before the election. The hope was that it would just go away, and that trivializing it would put it to rest. But that hasn't panned out... and the stonewalling is wearing thin, even with our media friends and bloggers, who up to now have been solid in marginalizing the birthers and the hack lawyers trying to get the proof."

"The plan, Bob... the plan?" The senator jabbed an index finger at his Patek-equipped upraised left wrist.

"You know about Custom Alterations?"

The senator shook his head negatively, then hesitated. "Wait. You mean the tailoring shop over on Connecticut Avenue? Near the zoo?"

"Yeah. But we're not talking about blind-stitch cuffs on a pair of slacks."

The senator nodded. "Yeah, there were always rumors about them doing more than just tailoring. Wasn't the owner a civil servant loser a while back? Don't I remember some stories about him being on the carpet over something to do with… ahhh… what… that Indian stuff…?"

"Right. The Indian Gaming Regulatory Act. Hardin. Charlie Hardin. He was the holdover head of the Office of the Law Revision Counsel after Reagan was elected."

"Oh, yeah. Something about some misprint he made…"

Rossiter nodded. "Ahhh… wasn't a misprint."

The senator frowned. "So what's this office of what…?"

"Office of the Law Revision Counsel. OLRC."

"The what? I'm a senator, Bob. Could care less about what goes on over there. What's that?"

"The OLRC is an appendage of the House of Representatives. It's under the control of… get this… the Speaker of the House. It's supposed to 'clean up' the laws that you guys… sorry…, that the Congress enacts and that the president signs. Get the inconsistencies out, pick and choose where in the books particular sections of an act should be placed. That kind of stuff. But no matter. The point is that what Hardin and OLRC did in the House… Custom Alterations does for anyone, but outside the gub'mint. … for anyone, that is, prepared to pay the fee…"

The senator frowned slightly. "And what, exactly, does that mean?"

Rossiter grinned and adjusted the rearview mirror again. "After Hardin left the House, he set up operations as a high-end haberdashery and tailoring business. Only the best. Take your most high-end, custom tailored Gucci or Armani or whatever and turn it into something even better. Like a Benz after going to AMG…. Strictly legit."

"Spare me, Bob…." Another jab at the Patek.

Rossiter nodded. "But the real work takes place in the back… and off-site… with the computers and…. ummm… other systems. The tailoring work… great as it is… is just a cover." He then produced his combo sneer-smile that he had perfected; the one that telegraphs the treachery that can be honed only through decades of "K" Street, Wall Street and D.C. Hill lobbying. "Well, for a fee… if, say, you want a public law altered… *after* it has been passed by the Congress and signed by the president, but *before* it gets put into the books where the judges, lawyers and law review junkies get their mitts on it… you go see Hardin."

The senator dipped his chin, a thin crease of doubt cutting into his forehead. "*After* it's signed?"

Rossiter bobbed. "After. No trace, no trail. No hearings. No media questions. Just the law as passed and signed,… but 'altered' and 'tailored' to suit your needs and instructions." Rossiter grinned. "If a law says 'shall' and you want it to say 'may' … or even 'shall *not*'…. Charlie's your man…"

"But how…?"

"When you think about it, it's not so hard. I mean, when you want to know what a law says, where do you go? Statutes at Large? The Public Law itself? No. You go to the commercial publishers. West. Lawyer's Ed. Westlaw and Lexis. Thomas. Other online sources."

The senator's frown deepened. "You mean they're in on it too?"

Rossiter smiled and shook his head. "No, no. Absolutely not. That's the beauty of it. By the time the OLRC document is sent to them for publication in the books or loading it online, if it's a law that's gone through Charlie's 'special' process, it's already changed… and no one's the wiser… unless they actually go back and compare what's published with the Statutes at Large version put out by the GPO. And the likelihood of that happening is, like…, next to zero."

The senator nodded again. "And he's done this before…? Besides the Indian gaming thing?"

"He has. I don't know how many 'custom alterations' he's got under his belt, but my sources tell me it's now over two hundred successful assignments. Small changes, mind you, as they must be, but with tailored, specific impact."

"And no trace? No questions?"

Rossiter grinned again. "None. Like they say…, the perfect crime is the one that's never discovered."

The senator's frown slowly metastasized into a churlish grin, like the one a schoolyard bully would produce after he's just gotten away with shifting the blame to an innocent bystander student for a punch he had delivered elsewhere. "And…?"

"And… one of the 'special' projects we've had Hardin on just recently… after the *Locke* case got in the front door over there…not exactly an alteration… is 'the plan.' Code name is 'Saberjet Onyx.'"

"Saberjet who? Saberjet Onyx?" the senator frowned. "Enough with the tease, Bob. Haven't got the *time*…," he lifted his left wrist again, "or the patience. Give it to me short. Give it to me straight."

Rossiter turned back forward in his seat, then adjusted the rearview mirror so that the senator was centered in it. "OK. The Supreme Court may likely hand down a ruling on the standing issue in *Locke* within the next week to ten days. In the meantime, probably this coming Tuesday morning… the exact timing is still being discussed… one of our team players is going to make a big announcement. The discovery of a new essay in the series of papers, The Federalist Papers. Heard of them?"

"Wasn't born yesterday, Bob…" Then the senator's frown deepened. "But a *new* essay? How can that… what are you sayin'…?"

"I'm sayin' that this 'new' essay will be discovered in a heretofore hidden filing cabinet at the archives. Or maybe the Library of Congress... that detail still needs to be worked out too. The story will be that a graduate student doing research came across it stuffed in with a bunch of old, obscure national historical documents. The essay will be entitled 'Federalist 86'. That's why they chose 'Saberjet'."

Rossiter could see the senator's confusion growing.

"See, senator, back in the '50's, in the Korean War, the fighter aircraft that stopped the commies was the F-86 Saberjet. Get it? 'F' for Federalist... '86' for the last in the essay series." Rossiter nodded. "And 'Onyx' because the project is as black and under the radar as it gets. Six... maybe seven people know of it at all... Boalt... Ross Ellis... Hardin... Cassini... me... and now you..."

Brown stared ahead, the confused frown on his forehead building toward complete befuddlement.

"F-86... Federalist 86...," Rossiter continued, "will set out what the original framers intended... or what we *say* they meant and intended... when they used the term 'natural born citizen' in the Constitution."

The senator's eyes widened; the frown quickly turning into a contorted grin which slowly began evolving into a smile. "Are you... are you sayin'...?" he trailed the sentence off, awaiting a response.

Rossiter continued. "Right now, the original of the Federalist Papers ended at Number 85. But the Supreme Court has cited the Federalist over 200 times in its opinions to support or refute one or another interpretation it wants to engraft onto the Constitution." He paused. "But up until now, they've not had anything in the original *genuine* Federalist Papers dealing directly with the very question now pending before them in *Locke*." Rossiter smiled. "Ironic coincidence the essay should be discovered now... huh?"

The senator leaned forward, toward the rearview mirror. "You mean… they're actually going to use this fake, 'Federalist 86' to … what… try to get the Supreme Court to rule in a certain… way…? Find that Locke has no standing?"

Rossiter stared at the senator's left eye in the mirror. "Senator, the word 'fake' is so… hard. But, yeah, that is *exactly* what I am telling you… and more. Yes. And with due respect, … ahhh… … do you or any of your… colleagues… up on the Hill have a better idea… or one that can be implemented in the time-frame needed…, which is… *now*?"

Brown drew in a deep breath, then blew it out with a 'whoaaa'."

Rossiter grinned. "And it gets better. Even *if* they find standing, the text of the document is going to support the conclusion that, in fact, the Framers of the Constitution intended to define what a natural born citizen was in a way that will nail down and actually *confirm* Boalt's eligibility."

The senator's smile widened further. He looked out the fogging window toward the blinking Washington Monument and began chuckling, shaking his head back and forth slowly. "This is genius." He looked back at Rossiter's eyes in the mirror. "Pure, diabolical… never waste an opportunity genius. Who concocted this? Ellis? Boalt?" He looked back at the Washington Monument. "But… but… how can they pull it off? I mean, a brand new…"

"Uhhh… that's why Hardin has his own Gulfstream III out at Dulles, condos scattered from here to Dubai to Sydney and a yacht that would put Greg Norman's to shame."

"But a brand new essay from, when, seventeen…"

"1788. Sometime in mid-June, 1788, to be exact."

The senator sat back against the leather. "But I mean, the document itself… how are you going to…"

"The essay will be handwritten in Hamiltonian cursive onto parchment that actually carbon-dates back to 1788, the time-frame for the original Federalist papers that got published. Hardin's even recruited a bunch of Japanese-trained calligraphers who can replicate to a 'T' any particular person's handwriting, assuming an examplar can be found. Like Hamilton's. Like Jay's. Like Madison's. They say the guy who does Lincoln is unbelievable."

"So...," the senator drawled, "we're talking... forgery...?"

Rossiter smiled. "Forgery? *Fake*? Senator, that language is so... outdated. Last century. 'Replica' is the accepted term today. More accurate and... not so.... harsh... or so criminal. Hardin uses the same inks, spectro-aged and correctly evaporated. Even the same linguistic syntax and grammatical nuances found in Hamilton's original essays are being used." Rossiter smiled broadly. "I'm tellin' ya, senator... Hardin and his crew are good. I mean *really* good."

"Parchment?"

Rossiter nodded. "Yeah... the real stuff. We just took delivery on ... get this... some of the parchment that was cut from the original of the Articles of Confederation at National Archives. From 1788. Trimmed... discretely, of course..., from the margins... then micro-epoxy laser welded into a single sheet. Actually, three sheets. The original Articles will still look the same, to the untrained eye. The White House..." he cut himself off.

The senator frowned. "Yes?"

Rossiter swallowed. "Eighty-six is supposed to be around 1,900 words long, and Hamilton's cursive, drawn out over that many words, translates to two and a half pages of parchment."

The senator persisted. "The White House? They're actually behind authorizing a plan to cut pieces off the original Articles of Confederation? Look, it's one thing for Boalt to know of and allow others to do this... it's quite another for him to be the one shoving it forward."

Rossiter exhaled and adjusted the rearview mirror to again center Brown's face in the rounded rectangle. "Senator, let's just put it this way. Anyone who thought that Nixon was a crook during Watergate would be floored by what is going on in this administration. Dumbfounded. This makes Watergate and the Pentagon Papers combined look like kindergarten. No... actually, kindergarten recess."

Brown frowned. "So this doesn't stop at the chief of staff? Ross Ellis?"

Rossiter smiled. "Chief of staff? Senator... you gotta remember... water still runs downhill... not the other way around..."

"So the scheme originated... higher upstream...?

Rossiter nodded. "At the headwaters. As high upstream as it gets." He shifted in his seat to lean closer toward the politician. "And the beauty of it is... this is not the only project in motion. Not by a longshot."

"There's more?"

Rossiter exhaled. "Senator Brown... do you really want to know...?"

Brown sat back in the seat. "Not really... not really...." He returned to smiling and shaking his head in disbelief, then he squinted. "Okay, so the document surfaces. Then...?"

"Then..." Rossiter said, exhaling"... *you*... as the sitting chairman of the Senate Judiciary Committee, call for an emergency hearing to delve into the impact of the discovery on the pending case."

Brown's eyes ballooned. "*Me?*"

"You. Because if Federalist 86 can shed any light on what the Founding Fathers meant by the term 'natural born citizen,' that intent needs to be made public *before* the Supreme Court makes any decision on standing in the *Locke* case." Rossiter shifted in his seat. "*Before* the decision... not after.... so they can take the discovery into account when they issue the opinion."

The senator nodded.

Rossiter continued. "And we also have a line into one of the justice's clerks. We're certain that if this can be pulled off in the next week or so, the Court will have no choice but to hold off on a ruling and maybe even call for additional briefing to address the discovery of Federalist 86."

"Week? *Week?* The Senate's in recess... and you want a hearing next *week?*"

Rossiter nodded. "That's the plan. Gotta move quick, before a decision comes out in *Locke.*" He adjusted the mirror again. "And, with a little bit of creative media work, it shouldn't be too hard to get the 'right'" two more air-quotes "editorial spins on the discovery. Maximize the need for the Court to make the *right* decision in *Locke,* not just a quick decision." He tilted his head. "We even have one writer at the *Times* working on a biographical sketch of the grad student who will be credited with making the discovery after..." he winked in the mirror at the senator "after searching and diligently working on it for the past couple of years," another wink, "to provide cover for the timing of the discovery now."

The senator slouched back in his seat, smiling, slowly shaking his head. "Bob... never in my career in this town have I even heard of *anything* like this. Never. This is... just... brilliant. Brilliant."

"And bold?" Rossiter added. "Gimme 'bold'. And 'outside the box' too, will ya?"

"Outside the box? This is outside the warehouse where the box is stored." He leaned forward again, releasing his seat-belt. "But lemme tell you. Once this Federalist 86 thing gets done, I need to know more.... a *lot* more about Hardin's operation. And what I might be able to get... tailored... altered. I mean, do you have *any* idea of what that capability could be worth?"

Rossiter looked over his right shoulder at the senator. "Like I said, that's why Hardin's yacht puts Norman's to shame..."

"And before this hearing… you're going to brief me on all the particulars, right? No surprises… right?"

Rossiter nodded. "Absolutely. All choreographed. No surprises. In fact, Hardin's already working on the briefing book. Should be ready by tomorrow evening.

The senator nodded, smiled and looked at his watch again, then back at Rossiter. "The Saudi's can pound sand. Got time for a drink?"

Rossiter started the Benz, flipped the wipers back on, pulled the shifter to "D" and slowly pulled away, toward the Jefferson Memorial.

FIVE

Senate Hearing Room 226 was awash in quartz-white television and video camera lights. Senator Brown grasped the gnarled hickory gavel, raised it to eye level, then slapped it down on the strike plate with a 'crack' that ricocheted around the hearing room like a spent round from an M-16... followed by two quick additional rounds, for good measure.

"This hearing of the ad hoc Foundation Documents Select Subcommittee of the Judiciary Committee of the United States Senate will now come to order" he barked into his microphone.

The tide of chatter that had filled the room quickly receded, until only the rustling of papers on the table where the witnesses sat could be heard. The video cameras and directional microphones from every network imaginable – with a few exceptions – were trained on the subcommittee panel and on the witnesses, each operator straining to capture some gesture, some word... even a bead of sweat... as ammunition for an evening talking head to expound on what the gesture meant, why that word instead of some other was used or what the hidden reason for the perspiration might have been.

Brown stared around the room, trying to look important...senatorial... in control. He adjusted his microphone and cleared his throat. "Ladies and gentlemen... the events of the last few days have been, to greatly understate it..., unprecedented. Unprecedented in the history of the Congress..., unprecedented in the history of the nation. That is why Majority Leader White and I determined by telephone last night that this extraordinary development warranted an extraordinary public hearing, despite the current recess of the full Senate for the holidays. I regret that more members could not be in attendance, but the few who are here will be witnesses... trust me... to some historical revelations."

He paused and took a sip of water. Senator Beth Cantor took in a deep breath and waited for the other shoe to fall.

"As all in attendance here today know," Brown drawled, "and as all watching these proceedings on television and over the Internet know, we stand on the verge of hearing from the highest court of the land a decision bearing directly on the future of the nation and the future of the presidency." He brought the tumbler of water to his mouth again, sipped, then continued.

"The *Locke* case now pending before the Supreme Court draws into direct question the eligibility of President Boalt to serve. It is contended that he is ineligible because, according to the challengers' theories, he was not born in Missouri, but instead was born in India. And even if he was born in Missouri, since his father was a British subject and citizen of India and only his mother was a citizen of this country, the challengers say that he is ineligible under the Constitution, since they believe it requires both parents to also be citizens when the person is born. This is what they say is required for a person to be what the framers called a 'natural born citizen'... whatever that actually means..."

A quick huffing of reportorial chuckles rippled across the room. Brown grabbed the gavel and banged it down again, but said nothing. He grasped his microphone.

"Bear with me, my fellow Americans, because you're going to learn something here this morning. What, you might ask, is a natural born citizen? And what difference does it make anyway? Let me tell you. I believe in the Constitution. I believe in original intent. I think a 'living, breathing, evolving Constitution' as seen through the glasses of some law school professor or judge is a figment of his... or her... imagination, so he... or she... should lighten up and switch to decaf. The Constitution says what it says.

"So, for example, when it says that one of the eligibility requirements for someone to serve as president is that the person be 35 years old... and it does, indeed, say that ..., then someone who is only 32 is not yet eligible. Now, there are many advantages to being 32… like not being 75….” more muffled chuckles, but no gavel banging, “but eligibility to be president is not one of them. The person may be the best qualified leader the nation could ever hope for… but unless he… or she… is at least 35 years old, the candidacy is doomed until the age requirement is met. And if we want a different result, there is a way to do that. It is called the amendment process.”

Another sip of water.

“Likewise, the Constitution requires that a president must have been a resident of the United States for fourteen years immediately prior to taking office. So a forty-year old who has lived in Cairo until he was thirty, then moved here for only ten years is similarly not eligible. Don’t like that? Amend the Constitution.”

Brown leaned forward in his chair; Senator Cantor listened intently.

“Which brings us again to the natural born citizen requirement. If the person is, say, forty-eight years old, has lived here for the past, say, thirty years, but is not a natural born citizen, then that person is ineligible to the presidency. And if he or she has defrauded the nation by knowingly running for, getting elected and usurping the office of the presidency following election through false pretenses, then that is, as we say, a high crime or misdemeanor for which an impeachment could lie in his or her future.”

He leaned back in his chair; Cantor thought: surely he is not saying that Boalt needs to be impeached.

“On the other hand, if the person is, in fact, a natural born citizen and meets the other eligibility requirements, eligibility to the office will be confirmed. But the problem is that the actual term… ‘natural born citizen’… is not defined in the Constitution. So we are forced to look elsewhere. And where do we look?”

Brown held up a copy of a small paperback book: "The Federalist Papers." The electro-mechanical chatter of camera lenses and strobe flashes exploded across the room, sounding like so many startled crickets and cicadas. The flashes reflected off of Brown's glasses like so many fireworks.

"These are the Federalist Papers. And perhaps more than any document other than the Declaration of Independence and the Constitution itself, they form the basis of what the Founding Fathers, the framers of the Constitution, intended at the formation of our nation so long ago.

"As any high school sophomore can tell you.... at least when I was growing up, they could tell you... sadly, maybe not now... these papers were intended to persuade the Colonists that the new governing document for the nation... the Constitution..., was, in fact, the best way to secure the freedoms and liberties promised to the citizens of the country who at the time lived under the Articles of Confederation and the Continental Congress following the Revolutionary War.

"In a way, they constitute the nation's first organized lobbying effort, but by a group of men dedicated only to the formation of a solid backbone for the new nation rather than some well-heeled client with a desire for an exemption from a law or a special favor in a law. Or worse..."

The slap aimed at "K" Street was silent, yet palpable; a low murmur of garbled "wow, did he say that?" growled across the room and more strobe flashes sparkled over his glasses.

"The 85 original essays constituting the Federalist Papers were submitted to various newspapers in the Colonies, and mainly New York, since the battle for the support of the citizens favoring ratification of a new constitution to replace the Articles of Confederation was most hotly contested there. The essays by Alexander Hamilton, James Madison and John Jay were composed between 1787 and 1788, a time when the Constitution had been drafted, but not yet ratified by the required number of states under the Articles of Confederation. They were first published in two newspapers in New York, *The Independent Journal* and *The New York Packet* under the pseudonym *Publius*, after the Roman consul Publius Publicola, meaning a 'friend of the people.'"

Brown paused, and looked up from his notes. "And, yes, my research staff found this history for me so that I could refresh all of your memories…"

A wave of laughter swelled up through the room and, again, an explosion of strobe lights bounced off the walls.

"Well, for all of you lawyers out there… and I'm going to assume there are one or two paying attention here…. and, as one who left the practice a long time ago to run for this office, I describe myself as a recovering lawyer…" a few pseudo-polite 'yeah, never heard that one before' snickers, "I know a little bit about how attorneys think and what they do. They sometimes file what they call '*amicus curiae*' or 'friend of the court' briefs… which in reality are actually thinly-veiled advocacy briefs for one side or the other rather than anything intended to help a court reach a 'right' decision.

"Similarly, the men who were *Publius* were, as 'friends of the people,' setting down the conceptual principles and core intentions of those persons, including them, who had drafted or contributed to the drafting of the Constitution. Who better to explain what was meant by a particular phrase or word in the Constitution than they?"

He sipped some more water.

"Who better, indeed? In fact, the United States Supreme Court, which, as the highest court in the land, has the final say on what, exactly, the words of the Constitution mean, has on more than 250 occasions cited to these essays to explain, either in support or dissent, what is believed to be the intent of the Founding Fathers and thus, the meaning of the Constitution. And… here's a fact I'll bet you didn't know… one of the anonymous essayists submitting arguments as a 'friend of the people' in support of ratification of the new Constitution, John Jay, became the first Chief Justice of the Supreme Court in 1789, following the successful adoption of the Constitution."

Brown looked up again. "And, yes, my staff found that for me too." Reserved chuckles; several strobes.

"So here you have it..." he raised the small paperback in his right hand, displaying it back and forth for the photographers, "the Federalist Papers. The blueprint, as it were, not only for the ratification of the Constitution, but also for the proper interpretation of the Constitution in the future by the Congress, by the executive and, most importantly, by the Supreme Court."

Once again, he paused, placing the book on the desk just below his microphone. He removed his glasses. "Which brings us, of course, to the reason for this hearing. As you know, the original Federalist collection consisted of 85 essays written by Alexander Hamilton, James Madison and John Jay."

He paused and took another, larger drink of water; and he could feel his heart rate accelerating. He pumped the water around his mouth and felt the urge to spit it out, but swallowed it instead.

"But late last week... something... extraordinary happened. Truly extraordinary. Unprecedented in the history of the republic and warranting the calling of this special hearing. After several years of tracking down obscure letters and footnotes in historical journals, a doctoral candidate from a university in Massachusetts... yes, Harvard.... Mr. Rod Clark," he nodded to a slight, balding figure seated at the witness table before the subcommittee panel, "was going through some long-ago archived books at the Library of Congress across the street here, and found...." he reached under the desk and produced a thin wood and glass case the size of a magazine, holding it up for the cameras "this." A volley of strobes and electromechanical chatter of camera shutters – not unlike distant machinegun fire – detonated across the room. Reporters, lobbyists, staffers... everyone craned to get a glimpse of what the politician was holding up on display.

"This," he slowly pronounced into his microphone, "is what will come to be known as... Federalist 86."

That quiet "gasp" that normally accompanies significant events... news of the death of Princess Diana.... news of the second World Trade Center tower hit on 9/11... inhaled across the room.

Brown continued. "It is, as the testimony will show today, the last in the series of Federalist essays produced by *Publius*. And while additional analysis of the document continues, from all appearances and present examination, it was likely authored by Alexander Hamilton, since he is widely regarded as being the author of most of the final essays in the collection. Lying undiscovered between the pages of a diary in the basement of the Library of Congress for nearly 230 years, it now comes to light... thanks to the diligence of Mr. Clark here," another nod to the witness-to-be.

The strobes and cameras swung around and began firing away at Clark, who was clearly uncomfortable at the attention being focused upon him. He squinted at the flashes of light and tried to force a tolerant smile, his receding brow and hairline revealing the faint formation of sweat beads.

"But the significance of the discovery," the Senator droned on "lies in the topic of the essay, for it could not be more timely. Because Federalist 86... this" he held it up again, "deals with the very issue now embroiling the country: the meaning of the term 'natural born citizen' under the Constitution."

The oh-m'-gawd gasp from the audience quickly erupted to increasingly animated exchanges between and among reporters, staffers, and the omnipresent lawyers. Brown banged the gavel down three times, then coughed in his microphone "Order! *Order!* I will not allow these proceedings to become a circus!" The din began to subside as he banged the gavel down two more times. "Order!"

The cameras swung around again from the diminutive Clark back to the ringmaster.

"And so, rather than hear me paraphrase what Hamilton said in Federalist 86 regarding the meaning of the term 'natural born citizen,' I have asked Mr. Clark to come here before the subcommittee..." he paused and looked around at the battery of reporters, cameras and regime apparatchiks packing the room, then continued "and, from the looks of it, everyone else in the English-speaking world... to tell us exactly what he has found."

With that, Brown propped up the encased document on a small stand on the mahogany semicircle that was the subcommittee's desk, just to the left of his microphone. The senators and their staffers all began shifting and adjusting their torsos in their chairs in preparation for Clark's testimony. Brown asked the witness to stand, then administered the oath. Clark retook his seat.

"Good morning, Mr. Clark," Brown announced.

"Good morning, Senator Brown."

Brown smiled. "Quite a discovery you've made here, wouldn't you say?"

Clark shoved his steel-rimmed glasses farther up on his nose. "Well, that's what a number of others are saying, so maybe they're right."

The gathering chuckled in unison.

"Oh," Brown began, "I'd venture a guess that's a bit of an understatement. But that aside, I want to thank you for coming here today..." Somehow, Brown forgot to mention the subpoena that had been delivered to Clark day before yesterday, compelling his attendance. "... because it is important to know the circumstances surrounding this... this... historic discovery."

Clark nodded, but remained silent.

Brown continued. "First, tell us a little about yourself. For context."

"Well, my name you already know. Rodney Clark. I am a doctoral candidate in political science at Harvard University. I did my undergraduate work at Harvard too."

"And what is the topic of your dissertation?"

Clark cleared his throat. "The historical underpinnings of the foundation documents, from the Articles of Confederation through the Bill of Rights."

Brown nodded. "And so, can we assume that your research would have included an examination of the Federalist Papers?"

Clark nodded back. "Well... yes..."

Brown frowned slightly. "You hesitate...?"

"Only because of your terminology, senator. As originally published, the essays were simply called 'The Federalist.' The term 'Federalist Papers' wasn't used until much later."

Brown leaned back in his chair and fired a quick, scolding blink at a staffer – likely soon-to-be-ex-staffer – seated behind him.

"I see," Brown recovered. "Please continue."

"Well, I had been researching a number of old pieces of correspondence and letters that had been collected in various anthologies. Some were at the National Archives, some at Harvard... and one, in particular, was even in a private storage section of the library area at Monticello, Thomas Jefferson's home in Virginia. They were good enough to allow me access to the library there."

Brown nodded approvingly.

"As it turns out, I came across a letter a couple of months ago there... a letter dated in... May or June, 1788, I believe... from General George Washington to Thomas Jefferson. But the letter indicated that a copy was being sent as well to someone I had never heard of before. Someone named Hardesty. One Patrick Hardesty. In any event, the recipient of the copy aside, the letter had to do with the continuing debates over the ratification of the new constitution and the essays that were being published in New York City... the essays we now call the Federalist Papers."

Clark lifted a bottle of water and took a brief swallow.

"But in the letter, something else caught my eye. General Washington seemed to be suggesting to Jefferson that there was still some confusion among the people with whom he had spoken on the matter regarding a number of provisions in the new constitution. One of them related to the issue you have previously discussed here this morning. The issue of what was meant by the term 'natural born citizen' in the draft being considered."

Brown removed his glasses and peered over his microphone at the witness. "But did the letter mention anything about what was intended by the term?'

"No. Only that there was confusion and debate in some circles."

Brown produced a deep, slow nod. "Oh, if he thought there was confusion back then, he should see the lay of the land today."

Reportorial chuckles.

"In any event, the letter did mention that an aide to Mr. Hamilton of New York... this fellow named Hardesty... had suggested that some clarification might be good and that the same might be somehow communicated to those who were responsible for writing and publishing the essays in question. I believe the words used were '... someone might do well to contact Publius about these matters...' or something like that."

Brown put his glasses back on. "So you're saying that in this letter, George Washington is telling Thomas Jefferson that this Hardesty person thinks someone should talk to one of the authors of the Federalist Papers? I thought that no one knew who the authors were, at least back then."

"True, no one knew for sure. But of course everyone had their suspicions. I mean, it was not a matter of common knowledge, but many people suspected that if Hamilton was not Publius, he could have been his twin brother."

Laughter again erupted across the room, only to be quickly gaveled back into silence by Brown.

"Oh, I'm sorry... I didn't... I apologize," Clark offered.

"Not at all, not at all," Brown said. "But continue. I must tell you, not only is this historic... it is downright fascinating."

"Well, they allowed me to make a copy of the letter. I scanned it onto my laptop... the copy is in... a safe place. Then I went back to my apartment in Boston, thinking that I would try to follow up on who this Hardesty guy was." Clark paused, looked down at the desk, then back up at Brown. "Then something... curious... odd happened."

"Odd?" said the senator.

"Yeah, odd. You see, a few days later..., I got an e-mail. It first went into my spam folder... I get a lot of that, even with the filters on. I would have normally deleted it without opening it and without any further thought... except..."

"Yes?"

"Except the spam folder showed the message coming from... coming from someone named Allison Hardesty..."

Another in that same family of "o-m'-gawd" gasps heard before sucked in across the room.

"Hardesty?" Brown inquired.

"Yeah. Hardesty. And there was something else odd. The e-mail server was one I'd never heard of before either... something called," he looked down into a small black notebook he had opened on the table, "'tangello25.com.'"

"And?"

"Well, I hesitated opening it since... you know, it's probably one of those pleas from Nigeria or Kenya that you help the son of the prime minister who just died in a car crash to get a vast sum of inherited money out of the country. And that you have been vouched for to them by only the most trustworthy persons...."

"P.T. Barnum was right," Brown offered. More chuckles.

"Anyway, in the e-mail, this Allison Hardesty said she was the great-great-great.... not sure how many 'greats' were in there... but she was a distant related granddaughter of Patrick Hardesty. She apparently had tracked me down through one of the curators at Monticello... I gave them one of my cards... who knew that I was doing research on the founding documents.

"She said in the e-mail that the family tale was that Hardesty had been a close advisor to Alexander Hamilton back during the years leading up to the signing of the Declaration of Independence and later, the Constitution. But she also said that the rumor had always been that he had also helped Hamilton with several of the essays that became the Federalist, including one that addressed this question of citizenship."

Clark took another swallow of the Dasani.

"Then the e-mail went on to say that family legend was that, on Patrick Hardesty's deathbed, Hamilton himself promised him that he would consider including in one of his Publius essays.... she specifically used that name... an essay on the citizenship question. She explained that Patrick Hardesty was very interested in the issue and gave to Hamilton in his will some notes he had placed into a diary that he kept."

The Senator nodded, but glanced up at the large clock on the wall to his right, telegraphing the message to Clark that, while interesting, he needed to get to the "meat" of the testimony.

"In any event," Clark continued, "the e-mail ended by suggesting that, since Hardesty's diary had been given to Hamilton and was no longer in the family's hands, there was a chance that it might be in Hamilton's papers, some of which, she added, she believed had long ago been archived at the Library of Congress. And she ended by asking if I had ever searched there under 'Hardesty'. Well, of course not, because I had never heard of the guy until I went to Monticello."

Another sip of water.

"So over to the Library of Congress I went looking for documents under Hardesty. There was nothing on the computers, of course, but then one of the librarians – nice lady, but she had to be in her eighties – she asked if I knew how to use the old 'Dewey Decimal System,' which is how they catalogued books and documents a really long time ago. Oddly enough, I did know, so she led me back to a basement area in the library where they kept a whole collection of card catalogues and file cabinets full of documents and miscellaneous papers, mostly in big time disarray."

"Big time?" asked Brown.

"Really big time. Frankly, some of the file cabinets looked like miniature landfills and a lot of the papers in them were in sad shape, cracking and on the verge of disintegration. One of the cabinets housed the old Dewey Decimal cards, so I fished through them into the "H's"... Hadley.... Hall... Hamilton... lots of things under Hamilton... and then..."

He paused and reached again for the Dasani, and before he could raise the bottle opening to his mouth, his pause triggered the re-aiming of dozens of cameras at him, the high-pitch of battery-powered servos adjusting the compound zoom lenses to get the best image of what would next escape from his lips.

"Then there was "Hamilton/Hardesty: Diary of Patrick Hardesty, 342.1789C. I specifically remember the 342, because that's the section of the Dewey system relating to constitutional law and..." he hesitated and looked up, then around at the audience. "Sorry. Probably more information than you need."

Brown nodded. "Please continue."

"I looked at each of the file cabinets in the room... they all had the corresponding ranges of numbers from the card catalog... but I couldn't find the one for the 340 to 350 range. Until..."

More zoom lens adjustments.

"Until I found a cabinet behind a cabinet. Looked like it hadn't been opened in, literally, a hundred years. Dust, cobwebs, you name it covered the thing. It was wood... ash, I think. I moved the metal cabinet blocking it and started going through the drawers. There were newspapers, literally, from the early 1800's in one drawer. In another, what looked like letters and correspondence between people relating to the Civil War."

He paused again: strobes popped, shutters chattered.

"Then in the bottom drawer, there were a number of books of different sizes. Some were small calendars, others looked like ships logs.... and then there it was: 342.1789C." Another swig of water, this time a long one. "I gotta tell you, senator, my heart was racing like a fighter jet. So I picked it up and opened it... and at the last page where there were any entries, there it was, sandwiched between the last two pages of the diary...," he stopped in mid-sentence and pointed to the document encased on the stand next to Brown's microphone.

Once more, the strobes and shutters, along with a rising tide of animated voices from the audience inflated the room. Brown fired two more rounds of the gavel on the strike block, but said nothing either: the cracks of the gavel were enough to return a semblance of quiet to the room.

"And?" Brown asked.

"Well, I wasn't really sure what to do. I mean, I read the document right there on the floor next to the cabinet. This was like... like gold.... historical gold in my hands... I was shaking by the time I finished it. Literally shaking. Just when I was trying to figure out what next to do, the librarian came down to check on how I was doing. I... I started laughing. She didn't know why I was laughing, but she started too. And we both laughed together... me out of knowing what I had just discovered, she... just because. You know how it is, sometimes..., you just start laughing, and others join in just because of that... and it just keeps on going...?"

Brown smiled. "Well, I used to know how to laugh.... until I took this job...." More reportorial chuckles.

"Anyhow, after regaining some composure, I explained what the document appeared to be. We put it back in Hardesty's diary and went back upstairs to the head guy... the Librarian of Congress, and explained the whole thing to him." Clark looked over his left shoulder, and nodded. "Yes, Mr. Sullivan, the Librarian, is here today."

Brown bobbed his head toward Sullivan, a grey-haired portly man in a grey flannel suit seated in the gallery. "Yes. Thank you, Mr. Sullivan."

Sullivan returned the nod.

"He correctly took immediate possession of the diary, and the document I found in it, and called his security chief. We discussed briefly how to handle the news of this discovery, and I believe he... or his chief of security... contacted the Majority Leader's Office, but since he wasn't there, they referred the call... I believe... over to your office..."

"Yes," Brown confirmed, "Mr. Sullivan's security chief called and got hold of my chief of staff, who contacted me that afternoon at my home."

"Well, then, I guess you know the rest. The decision was made to make sure that the document was genuine, and not a fake or an elaborate prank by someone posing as a relative of someone who asked Alexander Hamilton to write an essay on citizenship for him. I mean, with all of the goofy things going on and the things you can see posted on the Internet, the last thing anyone wanted was to go public with the discovery and find out later they'd been the victim of a practical joke."

Brown nodded slowly. "Son... you got that right. You got that soooo right..."

"Well, the first thing that Mr. Sullivan's security chief suggested..."

"Charlie Tipton," Brown interrupted. "Charlie Tipton is the security chief we're talking about. USMC, retired. Semper Fi."

Clark nodded. "Yeah, Mr. Tipton... I remember now. He suggested that the first thing to do would be to do a full forensic examination of the document."

"Yes," Brown added, "we'll have testimony on that later."

"The examination, he said, would likely include not only handwriting analysis... comparing it to known exemplars of Alexander Hamilton, John Jay or James Madison."

"And do you know if that was done?" Brown asked.

"Yes, I do. And it was. Yesterday, I received confirmation that there was over a 98.8 percent likelihood that the handwriting was that of Alexander Hamilton."

"And who did the examination?"

"Two agencies. The FBI and the CIA... at least that's what I was told."

"Go on."

"The next step was an analysis of the ink that was used. I think they said it was an inferential scan or gamma ray scattering analysis... some new computer process..., because they didn't want to scrape any of the actual ink off the document for a spectral analysis or carbon-14 dating sample."

"And?"

"Same conclusion: the ink was 95.6 percent likely to have originated between 1785 and 1788."

More strobes, more whistling zoom lens adjustments.

"And the same agencies did the testing?"

"Yes. The FBI downtown here and the CIA out at Langley."

"What else?"

"The final analysis was of the paper itself."

"Yes?"

"The paper... actually a type of parchment... was similarly subjected to the inferential computer analysis... gamma ray scattering technique ...that was used for the ink. Again, both the

FBI and the CIA did the analysis… and also independently, so as not to influence each agency's conclusions."

"And the result?"

Clark bobbed his head and took another sip. "Same. The parchment dated to sometime between 1780 and 1789. They even compared it to the same type of digital 'fingerprinting' analysis the National Archives did many years ago on the Articles of Confederation, which dates to 1781, and the Constitution itself, which was signed in 1789."

"And their conclusion?"

"Their conclusion was … 100 percent…that the paper…. the parchment… originated between 1780 and 1789."

Brown looked down over his glasses at the witness. "One hundred percent?"

Clark nodded. "One hundred percent."

Once more, the chatter of shutters, strobe explosions and undifferentiated expressions of excitement and anticipation over Clark's testimony swelled up in the room. But this time, Brown simply held the gavel in his hand, making no attempt to silence the growing noise of the crowd. He smiled at Clark. "Thank you for coming this morning, Mr. Clark. I'd like to invite you back here to finish up your testimony after the lunch break. Could you do that?"

"I'd be happy to do that, senator."

Brown banged the gavel once. "This hearing will recess for the lunch hour. We will reconvene at 1:00." He banged the gavel again, then stood, grabbed the encased document and disappeared through a door behind the dais.

SIX

Senator Brown entered the room from the same door through which he exited before lunch, sat down and removed his glasses again. One quick bang of the gavel, and the hearing was under way again.

"Mr. Clark, thank you again for coming back," again, no mention of the subpoena. "I'll remind you that you're still under oath."

"Thank you, senator. I'm pleased to return."

Brown nodded.

"Mr. Clark, I know you're not a judge or a lawyer.... are you?"

"No, senator, I am not. And I have no such desire either."

"Good... too many lawyers in this town anyway.... Shakespeare was right. My point is, as a researcher and grad student, you can read English, can you not?"

"I can."

"So what does this document... this Federalist 86 have to say about who is and who is not a 'natural born citizen'?"

Clark shoved his glasses higher on the bridge of his nose. "Well, I will leave it to the judges and lawyers to argue what the words mean, but I can summarize for you what the English words say."

"Please do."

"The main conclusion of the essay.... Federalist 86, if I may.... after a lengthy discussion of the proposed constitutional eligibility requirements of age and residency... is found in the last sentence." Clark opened a folder he now had in front of him, not present in the morning session, and lifted a piece of paper up to his eyes. "And I quote: 'Accordingly, in all debatable questions relating to the eligibility of the Magistrate'..." Clark looked up at Brown, "...that means the president...," he returned to the copy

57

"'to become a candidate as well as to thereafter serve, if having been first elected, but in particular with respect to questions relating to the person's loyalties and allegiance to the republic as implicated by the third criteria, *viz.*, that of being a natural born Citizen, it is seen that these are matters properly reposed in the People alone, and nowhere else.'"

Brown nodded. "The people alone?"

"Yes. The people alone. Not only that… to underscore it, it adds 'and nowhere else.' That's pretty strong language, if you ask me…"

"Strong indeed. What else?"

"Well, before that, the essay seems clearly to make the point that, by placing the final authority for the determination of natural born citizenship in the hands of the voters, the mere fact of the candidate's election, without more, would serve to self-authenticate the natural born citizen status or, at minimum, render it moot. The essay even uses a Latin legal term from Blackstone's legal dictionary – *res ipsa loquitur* – meaning 'the thing speaks for itself' to analogize the election by the people of an individual to the ratification of that individual's status. As a 'natural born citizen'."

"The thing speaks for itself?"

"Yes. It generally means that no other proof of the thing's existence is required, as the fact alone self-authenticates itself. And under such an approach, the essay notes that several problems will be averted."

"Such as?"

"Well, the essay notes that one school of thought held that for someone to be a 'natural born citizen,' both parents needed to be themselves citizens. Like you said this morning. One problem that would be eliminated under the essay is, what if at the time of conception, both parents were, in fact, natural born citizens, but thereafter, the father dies?

"When the child is actually born to the natural born citizen mother, she will be at that time either a widow or may have remarried someone who is not a natural born citizen. Does that mean that the child, born only to a living natural born citizen mother, is disqualified? Who knows? The essay suggests that by putting the ultimate question to the voters, that problem is solved... or at least averted."

Brown frowned. "But what if the people are wrong? What if the person elected is in reality actually not, under these criteria, a natural born citizen?"

Clark shrugged his shoulders slightly. "That's a legal question, senator. I just don't know. But I suspect there are some lawyers and judges around who would be more than eager to offer you an opinion."

Brown grinned. "I'd bet the farm on it, Mr. Clark."

"But the words of the essay... if I may, Federalist 86... the words seem pretty clearly to state that all of these issues will be rendered academic... moot... once the person is actually elected."

Brown nodded and removed his glasses. "Mr. Clark, thank you. Thank you for coming today to share with us these...these momentous facts. You..."

"Mr. Chairman," a voice from Brown's right cut over the room's speaker system. Brown jerked his attention to the source, Senator Bethany Cantor, a middle-aged woman with long, dark brown hair. Again, the chatter of shutters and the sparkle of strobes filled the room.

Brown replaced his glasses on his nose. "Yes, Senator Cantor?"

"Mr. Chairman, I'd like to know, will the other Senators on the subcommittee be permitted to ask questions of Mr. Clark?"

Brown nodded. "In due course, Senator... in due course..."

Cantor frowned. "Does that mean later, rather than now... before the witness is excused?"

Brown, clearly irritated, grabbed his microphone. "It means when I deem it appropriate, Senator."

Cantor allowed a grin to curve across her mouth, having made the point that what had been advertised as a "hearing" was, instead, not much more than a one-sided dog and pony show. She sat back in her chair and smiled for the cameras.

Brown looked back at Clark. "Mr. Clark, there are other witnesses here whose testimony bears particular relevance to current events. But since they have extremely tight schedules and must attend to other compelling national affairs, I intend to hear from them next, but only if I can persuade you to either stay here for follow-up questions from the subcommittee members," he tossed a glance at Cantor, "after the other witnesses have finished with their testimony today or come back tomorrow. Can you accommodate that request?"

Clark leaned into his microphone. "Yes, Senator, I can. I will stay today and if needed, come back tomorrow too."

"Thank you," Brown replied, firing a thinly-disguised dart of contempt toward Senator Cantor, who responded to the zing with another smile.

Clark rose from his chair, nodded to the subcommittee, and took a seat in the front row of the audience sitting behind the witness table. At the same time, a tall, slender female rose from her chair in the audience and made her way to the witness table. She was, as they say, a "suit from the DOJ" and she exuded a professional, no-nonsense demeanor, her dark hair pulled back into the tightest of French twist buns. Merely watching her hairline was painful. She placed a black document case on the table and took her seat as another volley of strobes detonated. The shutter chatter gradually died away.

Senator Brown fondled his microphone. "Please, if I may, would you state your name for the record?"

She leaned toward the microphone. "My name is Antesar O'Hara."

Brown administered the oath and removed his glasses. "Ms. O'Hara, what is your occupation?"

"I am an attorney at law."

"And where did you take your degree?"

"I graduated from Columbia with a degree in political science and I earned my J.D. at Harvard Law."

"And are you presently employed?"

"I am. I am Senior Litigation Supervising Counsel in the Constitutional Law section of the Civil Division of the U.S. Department of Justice here in Washington. And, if I may, Senator, I'd like to express my appreciation... as well as the appreciation of the Attorney General, for your accommodating my schedule here today. I must be at the Supreme Court ...," she glanced at her watch, "... in less than two hours."

Brown smiled. "Not at all. You are quite welcome. This is, after all, an important hearing."

Senator Cantor looked down at the desk in front of her in a half-hearted attempt to camouflage a deep roll of her eyes.

Brown nodded. "And how long have you been employed at the Justice Department?"

"Four years. I started as a trial litigator and was promoted to section chief two years ago. I assumed the position of senior litigation supervising counsel three months ago when my predecessor moved on."

"Moved on?"

O'Hara nodded and adjusted her own glasses. "To a new position within the administration. He now works as Deputy Chief Counsel in the White House."

"Ah. So he is no longer with the Justice Department?"

"Correct, he is not."

"So that would be Craig Cleveland?"

She nodded. "It would."

Brown reached over to the encased document of the moment. "Now Ms. O'Hara, you've listened to the testimony of Mr. Clark this morning, haven't you?"

She nodded again. "I have indeed. Incredible."

Brown stared at the document. "Incredible, indeed. Now you heard Mr. Clark confirm that he is not a lawyer, did you not?"

"I did. Yes."

"And I believe you were here when I mentioned that the 'Federalist Papers'… that is, the 'Federalist' is a series of essays upon which the Supreme Court has frequently relied in reaching its decisions, weren't you?"

"Well, yes, but to be technically correct, the better way of characterizing the Court's reliance on the Federalist would be to note that, if it found an ambiguity in the Constitution or if it found that two, equally plausible interpretations could be drawn from the words of the Constitution, then it would look to documents like the Federalist to provide a backdrop or matrix, if you will, for reaching a constitutional conclusion that would be consistent with, rather than antagonistic to, the Constitution itself.

"Since the object of any effort to interpret the Constitution is to determine the intent of those who authored it and ratified it, who better to look to than those who had an actual hand in the drafting and processes which ultimately produced the Constitution, Alexander Hamilton, James Madison and John Jay?"

Brown nodded in feigned understanding of what the attorney had just said. "Please go on."

"You mentioned in your opening remarks that the Supreme Court had cited to the Federalist in seeking the likely intent of the founders over two hundred fifty times. Actually, at last count, the Federalist had been cited over three hundred times in support of one or another principle of constitutional law. Three hundred seventeen, to be precise."

Brown allowed a small smile-frown to crease over his forehead. "And how do you know that... have you counted them?"

O'Hara smiled. "As a matter of fact... yes. Numbers 305 and 306 were mine.... I mean, actually, ones I had included in a discussion draft I did... when I was a clerk there."

Brown's eyebrows peaked. "You clerked at the Supreme Court too?"

"Yes. Before I was hired at Justice."

"For whom did you... never mind. The fact that you were a clerk alone speaks volumes. Please continue."

O'Hara took a sip of water. "The Federalist, therefore, represents one of the core documents upon which the nation... and the nation's highest court... has relied over the years in determining the intent of the Founding Fathers. In my view, it ranks behind only the Constitution itself... and even ahead of the Declaration of Independence... as being the compass for the ship of state."

Senator Cantor closed her eyes.

Brown held up the encased document of the day. "And this?"

O'Hara nodded. "Well, Senator, I have to tell you that this discovery will likely be the subject of hundreds of law review articles over the next few years. It is truly... truly... an amazing and extraordinary discovery."

Brown took a sip of water himself. "Have you had a chance to review it?"

O'Hara nodded. "Yes. Your chief of staff supplied the Attorney General with a copy of it day before yesterday, after you requested Justice Department attendance here."

"And your opinion?"

"Well, Senator, to be honest, until I heard Mr. Clark's testimony this morning, I had some doubts about its authenticity. I mean, a document of this nature being 'lost' for over 220 years and with no suggestion that I'm aware of that any more than the original 85 essays of the Federalist were ever written raised some concerns in my mind."

Brown nodded. "And what of those concerns now?"

O'Hara removed her glasses and stared at Brown. "Gone. After hearing Mr. Clark's explanation of the carbon-14…, no, not that… umm… the gamma ray spectral analysis of the ink and dating of the parchment by the CIA… and the handwriting analysis, I'm satisfied that the document is genuine."

"Genuine?"

"Yes… genuine. Authentic."

"And how satisfied are you?"

O'Hara placed her glasses back on her nose. "Senator, as a lawyer, I deal with varying degrees of proof. There's proof by a 'preponderance of the evidence,' there's proof by a higher standard, 'clear and convincing,' and then there's the highest standard of proof, the one we use in criminal proceedings. 'Beyond a reasonable doubt.'

"The last one doesn't mean 'beyond any and all doubt,' but rather means beyond a doubt which is founded upon a rational and reasonable basis." She held her microphone between her thumb and index finger. "And I believe that the document is, beyond a reasonable doubt, the 86th essay in the series our founders called 'The Federalist.' And based on my experience, I have reason to believe that others would concur in that conclusion."

Yet another flurry of strobe flashes – do those batteries never die? – and electromechanical shutter noise filled the room.

Brown nodded approvingly. "Then let me ask you some questions about the content of the document itself… if I may…?"

"Of course."

"Thank you. First, do you have any particular familiarity with the essays themselves…. The Federalist?"

"You mean other than with this one… Federalist 86?"

"Yes."

"Well, yes, as a matter of fact I do. My review article traced the historical underpinnings of the essays and attempted to extrapolate them to early Twenty-first Century events. And, as I said before, I had several occasions when I was clerking at the Court..."

"The Supreme Court?" Brown interrupted.

She smiled. "Yes... usually when former clerks mention a 'court' without naming it fully, they are referring to the U.S. Supreme Court."

"I see."

"I had several issues presented to me for draft sections of discussion opinions where The Federalist played an important role in either framing the issue or supporting the point being advanced."

"Please. Continue..."

"Well, as you correctly noted in your opening remarks today, and as Mr. Clark corroborated, The Federalist is now recognized... at least by the Court... the U.S. Supreme Court... as being one of the primary 'backup instruments'" she twitched two air quotes "against which the actual language and the underlying intent of the words of the Constitution itself are properly analyzed. There are, of course, differences of opinion as to how much weight is properly given to the essays in any particular situation, but the propriety of referencing them as part of the analysis is, I think, pretty much settled."

"Pretty much?"

"Well... settled. After all, if the Court has cited the essays over three hundred times since 1798, I think a persuasive argument can be made that, as far as the Justices on the Court are concerned, the propriety of citing the essays as part of the analysis of the intent of the Founding Fathers... is settled."

Brown nodded again. "All right, Ms. O'Hara, let me ask you about the content of this... this... Federalist 86. You've had a chance to review it, at least briefly, have you not?"

"Yes. As I said, your chief of staff hand-delivered a copy of it to Attorney General Fitzpatrick day before yesterday as it was assigned by him directly to me for review and preparation for the testimony to be offered here today."

"OK. After that review, can you offer us any opinion as to its significance?"

She nodded her head vigorously. "Oh, I certainly can."

To his left, Senator Cantor slowly lowered her head into her hands and stared at the witness.

"To begin with," O'Hara said, "this essay seems clearly to supply one additional brick in the foundation of the nation, at least insofar as what the drafters intended when they set the qualifications for a person to be eligible to the presidency. The 'natural born citizen' term used in the Constitution is not defined, and, until now, the lower courts have been forced to look to secondary sources for guidance in determining just what the founders meant when they used that term."

"Secondary sources?"

"Yes. Scholarly legal writings of the late Sixteenth Century. Mainly an English scholar, William Blackstone. His work "Blackstone's Commentaries" is generally recognized as having played a significant role in the framing of the Constitution and the development of the so-called common law in this country."

"Any others?" Brown asked.

O'Hara squinted slightly, as if the inquiry came from left field. "Ahhh... yes, well, there is also some evidence that... that the work of another legal scholar was also examined by the framers. There was at the time a Swiss-German writer and philosopher named Emmerich de Vattel. His main contribution was a work entitled 'The Law of Nations' and which, some argue, discusses what it takes to be considered a 'natural born citizen.'"

"Yes?" asked Brown.

O'Hara squinted slightly. "Blackstone noted..."

"No no," Brown interrupted. "That other fellow. De… umm… de Vattel?"

"Yes," Brown nodded. "What did he have to say about all of this? This 'natural born Citizen' issue?"

O'Hara's prior squint furrowed into a puzzled frown.

"May I have a moment, Senator?"

Brown dipped his chin slightly. "Sure…"

O'Hara turned to an assistant sitting behind her and muttered something to her. The aide tilted her head and produced a slight, but unmistakable shrug, then mouthed something into O'Hara's ear. The witness then turned back to her microphone.

"Well, Senator Brown… de Vattel argues in his writings that the natives of a country, which he calls 'natural-born citizens,' are those persons born there whose… ahh… whose parents are also themselves citizens of that country. All others, whether born to parents only one of whom is a citizen or who are born to parents outside of the country, are not.. and by definition… de Vattel's definition, that is… cannot be 'natural born citizens.' That was his contention."

"All right, but if they aren't natural born citizens, then what are they?"

"They may be what he called 'native-born citizens' or even, if procedures are followed, 'naturalized citizens.' But they are not 'natural-born citizens' and, at least under de Vattel's theory, they would thus not otherwise be eligible to be president under the Constitution." She paused. "On the other hand…"

Brown nodded and interrupted. "But this new discovery… this new essay in the Federalist series changes that?"

O'Hara bobbed her head. "Dramatically. Yes, dramatically. But there are other decisions of the Court… the Supreme Court, Senator …, which seem to be more in line with the new essay's conclusion than with de Vattel's theories."

Brown nodded. "Please. Continue."

"Well," she complied, "although there are a few older cases which suggest, in dictum, that the...."

"Dict-what?..." Brown blurted.

"Oh," O'Hara replied, "sorry... dictum. It's a legal term meaning, like, a side comment. Language in an opinion which, while illuminating on a point, may not be directly material or relevant to the issue before the court and certainly not part of the direct ruling or holding in the decision."

"Thank you," Brown replied.

O'Hara nodded and re-positioned her microphone. "In any event, while the older cases acknowledged de Vattel and his writings, the more recent rulings tend more to rely on Blackstone for a backdrop against which to try and determine what the Founding Fathers intended when they used the term 'natural born Citizen' in the Constitution."

Brown fondled his microphone. "Well," he began, "are you saying that the Supreme Court has changed its opinion of what that phrase means... from the time of the writing of the Constitution... when de Vattel's writings may have swayed the Founders... and today?"

O'Hara tilted her head to the left slightly. "Unnnn..., no, Senator. Not exactly. What I'm saying is that the Supreme Court has never directly addressed this issue in a live case or controversy... at least not until recently. What I'm saying is that, as the times have evolved since the drafting of the Constitution, the Supreme Court's interpretations of the document have, yes, also evolved." She leaned forward. "That is one of the reasons, of course, that from time to time, a case once decided in a particular way is subsequently overruled... perhaps decades later... as now being seen to be inconsistent with the Constitution."

Brown nodded. "So the current Justices reverse the decisions of prior Justices?"

O'Hara shook her head. "No. The Supreme Court reverses lower or inferior court rulings, like federal circuit court decisions.

But as for prior decisions of its own, the process is to overrule it, not merely reverse it."

Brown nodded. "So the effect is the same. It goes away."

O'Hara tilted her head instead of generating another negative movement. "Actually, while the binding precedent of the overruled case goes away, the case itself remains on the books forever. The volumes are full of cases which were once deemed to be 'the law' under the Constitution, only to be later decreed... by a different set of judges... to be *not* the law."

Brown leaned back in his chair. "So how does all of this play into what we now seem to have discovered as a new interpretation of what it means to be a 'natural born citizen'?"

O'Hara nudged her glasses up slightly on her nose. "Well, with due respect to de Vattel's work and his theory and to the older Supreme Court decisions seeming to adopt his definition, the more recent cases, as I said, tend more to interpret the phrase under the common law theories of other legal scholars."

Brown nodded. "Such as Blackstone?"

"Yes. Including Blackstone."

Brown tilted his head to the left. "And so what has the Supreme Court had to say on the matter? Blackstone versus de Vattel?"

O'Hara nodded. "Not much. And, up to this point, mostly only by way of dictum."

"That 'dictum' thing again?"

"Yes."

"Ah. Please go on."

"There are four cases generally seen as having established, at least in dictum, that de Vattel's definition was most likely what the framers of the Constitution had in mind when they drafted the phrase 'natural born citizen' into the document. The oldest one, the one decided closest to 1789, when the Constitution was finally ratified, is called '*The Venus*,' where the Court for the first time since the nation was established favorably quotes de Vattel on the point in the process of reaching its decision. The case involved a question of maritime law. But the important thing, at least as far as the present issue…Federalist 86… is that the Court cited with approval de Vattel's work regarding the definition of what, exactly, constituted a 'natural-born citizen.'"

"And the other cases?"

"They say much the same thing. *Minor v. Happersett* is one, but it's been highly criticized on other grounds. Two others, in particular, called *Wong Kim Ark* and *Perkins v. Elg*, go into an extensive discussion the history of the decisions addressing these types of citizenship issues. In fact, a while back, as I recall, there was a report issued by your research arm here… the Senate… umm…"

Brown leaned forward. "You mean the Congressional Research Service?"

"Yes, that's it. The Congressional Research Service. A report was prepared and issued directly addressing these issues, including the issue of whether under the decision in the *Perkins* case a person born here could be considered a 'natural born citizen' under the Constitution. It concluded in the affirmative, but since it was just a congressional report and not a Supreme Court decision, it carried no judicial or precedential force. Do you want me to elaborate?"

"No, I don't think that's necessary. But tell me this. If these cases are out there, *Venus, Perkins*, whatever and have not been reversed… excuse me, overruled…, what difference would this discovery… Federalist 86" he glanced at the encased document on its stand "… what impact would it have on the question?"

O'Hara's head started bobbing. "Oh, Senator, the impact would be… I don't want to overstate this… or infringe on what the Court might do…. but I think the impact would be immense."

"Why?"

"Well, to begin with, unlike the work of Mr. de Vattel, who was a Swiss-German citizen, this document... Federalist 86 is... or certainly appears to be, the direct work of Alexander Hamilton. Hamilton is indisputably one of the nation's Founding Fathers... and he knew full about the existence of the term 'natural born citizen,'... because he was not one."

The muffled inhalation of surprise for the audience caused her to pause.

"Hamilton," she continued, "was born to parents of French and Scottish heritage in the British West Indies, and reportedly out of wedlock. So those circumstances certainly could be among the reasons why he never considered running for president." She took a sip of water. "On the other hand, if, in fact, Federalist 86 represents not only his views, but the views of his contemporaries, especially John Jay... the first Chief Justice of the Supreme Court ... then the document could also be interpreted as an attempt by Hamilton to directly address the issue, if not for himself, then for future aspirants to the office. After all, since he was likely quite familiar with de Vattel's work, his sentiments as to de Vattel's conclusions, which would have disqualified him from seeking the presidency himself, are likely set forth in Federalist 86."

Brown nodded and took a sip of water himself. "Well, then," he said, "what conclusions can we draw from these facts?"

Senator Cantor grabbed her microphone. "Mr. Chairman?"

Brown jerked his attention to Cantor as the strobes and shutters sprang back into action. "Excuse me? What did you say?"

"Point of order, Mr. Chairman. When you say 'what conclusions can *we* draw from these facts, just who is the 'we' you are referring to? I certainly hope it isn't me."

The audience erupted in a murmur of 'wow-did-she-say-that's?' and the cameras zoomed in on her. Brown discharged three rounds from his gavel in an effort to quiet the crowd. "Order!" he barked. "Order!" and he stared at Cantor. "It was a generic thing, senator. If there are two people in this room who think this is a significant discovery and one worthy of explanation from the witness, that is enough of a 'we' for the chair's purposes. But if you wish to be excluded from that group, fine, let the record so reflect."

Cantor shook her head is disgust and pushed her microphone away.

Brown turned his attention back to the witness. "Let me ask you this, Ms. O'Hara. What conclusions do *you* draw from these facts?" He shot a quick, rebuking glance down and toward, but not at, Senator Cantor.

O'Hara adjusted her glasses again. "Well, first, I believe that, at minimum, there is now reason to believe that the 'natural-born citizen' scholarship and writings of de Vattel, and the older Supreme Court decisions based on those writings, may be in error or perhaps simply inapplicable, at least insofar as some might argue that they have relevance to the issue under Article Two, Section One, Clause Five of the Constitution, the 'natural born citizen' clause.

"However, Mr. Chairman, please understand, I'm not saying that Federalist 86 is conclusive on the point. All I am saying is that it seems strongly to suggest that the issue needs to be revisited in light of the specific language used in Federalist 86 regarding the primacy of the vote of the people over the opinions of a Swiss-German philosopher who died over 200 years ago.

"Second, I strongly believe that these facts should be brought to the attention of the Supreme Court, and the sooner the better. As you know, and as you referenced in your opening remarks, the issue of President Boalt's eligibility under the 'natural-born citizen' clause of the Constitution is presently pending there in the *Locke* appeal. This essay needs to be brought to the Court's attention, at minimum, in an emergency supplemental brief from the Office of the Solicitor General."

She removed her glasses and positioned the microphone directly in front of her mouth. "And I am authorized to tell you that, by this afternoon, just such a brief will have been prepared and filed with the Court by the Solicitor General."

Brown nodded approvingly. "And this supplemental brief from the Solicitor General... may I assume that you were one of the authors?

O'Hara smiled. "That would be a safe assumption, Senator Brown."

Brown smiled back. "Well, then, speaking of assumptions, it would seem then that the assumptions regarding the president's eligibility to serve in the office he holds might well be now confirmed. Would you agree?"

"Could be," O'Hara replied. "I assume he will address that issue in the press conference he's called for later this afternoon."

Brown turned his attention back to the witness. "That's right... I almost forgot the conference," he lied. "Thank you for your testimony, Ms. O'Hara. Given the hour," it was 2:45, "this hearing is adjourned until 10:00 AM tomorrow, when the witnesses.... Mr. Clark... Ms. O'Hara... are requested to return for questions from other members of the subcommittee."

Senator Cantor raised her hand and looked at the chairman; he ignored her, fired off a single round of his gavel as he stood, then grabbed the encased document and disappeared through the back door. The muffled discussions of the audience from the prior hours erupted into a wave of noise, shutter chatter and strobe flashes. The clock read 2:46 PM.

SEVEN

President Boalt stood at the podium, his ebony suit cutting into the red-carpeted hallway that spilled off behind him. A glance to the left, a glance to the right to ensure the teleprompter screens were still correctly positioned.

"And so my fellow Americans, while I cannot guarantee to you that the negotiations that have been taking place in Tehran and Riyadh this week will bear fruit, I *can* tell you that the work of Secretary Tate, coupled with the efforts of Ambassador Watkins, has been critical... absolutely critical... in bringing us back from the brink of the unspeakable. The nation, as well as this president, owes them a debt of immeasurable gratitude. And as soon as the Congress returns from its recess next month, I intend to make sure that both the Majority Leader and the Speaker make these treaty negotiations one of their top priorities. And when we have any more news on the situation, we will report it to you. Now, if you have any questions... yes, Jim..."

Jim Brock stood. "Mr. President, Jim Brock with PCI. You mentioned that the Senate is in recess, but can you tell us if the Majority Leader, Senator White, has been kept apprised of the meetings with Secretary of State Tate and Ambassador Watkins over there?"

Boalt nodded. "I can assure you that Senator White is constantly kept up to date on all relevant developments. The Senate may be in recess, but there is no recess for the Senate leadership... never has been."

Brock continued. "As a follow-up, Mr. President, there is no question the situation in the Middle East is critical, and everyone here agrees, I'm sure, with your remarks about the negotiations being pursued by Secretary Tate and Ambassador Watkins. But the real 'buzz' today... and one seeming to bear directly on you and your administration... is the announcement coming out of Senator Brown's Judiciary subcommittee relating to what seems to be a new essay in the series of our foundation documents, the Federalist Papers. Quite a buzz."

"Yes," Boalt interjected, "so I've heard…"

More audience chuckles.

Brock continued. "Well, as we all here know as well, and with due respect, there have been a lot of questions raised in the past about your eligibility to serve as president. There are those who contend that you have not been forthcoming with respect to demonstrating that you are constitutionally eligible to serve because, as they claim, you have not shown yourself to be a citizen under the Constitution."

Boalt smiled. "Oddly enough… heard about that too. And it's 'natural born citizen' under the Constitution, Jim, not just 'citizen.' *Big* difference." He produced a bug-eyed expression of feigned astonishment over the word "big."

A simultaneous blast of laughter detonated through the room.

Brock suppressed a laugh too, then went on. "Well, the discovery day before yesterday of what seems to be this new essay in the Federalist Papers, Federalist No. 86, they say could have a significant impact on you and your administration."

"Jim… is there a question lurking somewhere there in your remarks…?" a shallow tint of false irritation coloring Boalt's inquiry.

"There is… there is indeed. What do you make of this discovery and, as a follow-up, do you believe this will drive a stake through the hearts of those who think you are not an American? Not constitutionally eligible to be president?"

Boalt raised his eyebrows and tilted his head to the left. "Okay, look, one thing I need to make clear here, Jim, before I get too far down the road to answering your question. Uhhh…, ultimately, the impact of this new essay… or I suppose I should say 'newly-discovered old essay'… is up to the courts. And specifically, the Supreme Court. As you know, there is presently pending over there," he looked over at a wall in the direction of Capitol Hill and the Supreme Court building, "a case where this precise issue is being considered. So it will be up to the Justices, not me... let me emphasize that... '*them*' not 'me'... to make the call. And I continue to believe that they will make the right call." He took a sip of water from a glass in the rear of the podium, then put it back.

"That said, let me say this. Look, it's no secret that these folks... some call them 'birthers', some call them other, less polite things..." he let the suggestion drift for a moment, "they believe that I have not been forthcoming. They think I've been hiding the ball, skulking around town like the Manchurian candidate they want to believe I am. And that I'm not eligible to serve under the Constitution.

"With respect, I disagree. And apparently, so do, like, eighty million other Americans who voted for me. Those who have questioned... and still question... my eligibility are entitled to their opinions. But with respect, I think they're wrong. Dead wrong. But, hey, it's a free country where you are still entitled to your beliefs, even *if* they're wrong. But don't try to impose your wrong beliefs on everyone else.

"I was born in Missouri. My birth certificate proves that. Frankly, I have been baffled over the issue since it first surfaced before I was even nominated, because the documentation shows that my birthplace was St. Louis. And the last time I Google-earthed that town, it was still in Missouri."

Muffled chuckles.

"So I don't get it. I even posted my birth certificate on the Internet..." he paused "thanks to the work of that Nobel Peace prize winner who invented it ...," additional snickers, "so that anyone and everyone who wanted to check it out could do so. Plain and simple. But the fact is that, even if I had *not* done that... which, by the way, no other candidate or president in history has done... it now turns out that this Federalist 86 seems to prove that it wouldn't matter *anyway*."

Brock cocked his head slightly, like a terrier who has heard something he doesn't quite understand and seeks more explanation. "So you've read it?"

"Of *course* I've read it, Jim. I'm the president. When something this big comes down the pike, that's what I'm *supposed* to do. I've read it several times... it's not that long. As recently as this morning, in fact. Federalist 86... written, it seems, in 1788 by none other than Alexander Hamilton... goes through a lot of explaining as to what the founders thought was meant by the term 'natural-born citizen' in the draft of the Constitution before it was ratified.

"Now I've heard that Senator Brown had the fellow who made the discovery appear before his sub-committee earlier today. I've not been fully briefed on what he testified to, but I'm relatively sure that he told Senator Brown and the subcommittee members that the document concludes that the final 'jury' if you will," two air-quotes, "as to whether a person is or is not a 'natural born citizen' under the Constitution is the body of the electorate rather than the legislative branch or the judicial branch."

Boalt looked at the reporter. "Is that right?"

Brock nodded. "Well, yes, that's what the document says... or sure seems to say."

Boalt nodded. "So, yes, Jim, I think that this essay... Federalist 86... can teach us a lot about not only what the Founding Fathers believed their new Constitution meant, but it is also instructive with regard to those folks out there.... mistaken as they might have been... and are... who question or doubt my eligibility.

"I don't know what really motivates them, but, sure, I hope this document will put an end to their efforts, foolish and misguided as they have been and are. I mean, there are a lot more important things on the national plate than this. And I hope that the Supreme Court will take the document into consideration when it hands down its ruling in the *Locke* case. I mean..., enough already."

Brock nodded.

Boalt acknowledged another question. "Yes, Frank?"

Frank Potter stood. "Yes, I'd like to... excuse me, Frank Potter from ABS... I'd like to follow-up on something Jim said in his question. He asked if this discovery would 'drive a stake' into the hearts of your opponents... these 'birthers'... and I'm not sure we got a complete answer. I mean, you said they're entitled to their opinions, even if they're wrong..."

"I did say that," Boalt interjected.

"But that still doesn't answer the question of whether you think this will be enough to stop them. After all, the Fourteenth Amendment and the Civil Rights Act haven't stopped racism in this country. Are we to believe... do you believe that Federalist 86 will finally put an end to this nonsense?"

Boalt smiled. "Frank, all I can tell you is that once upon a time, everyone thought the world was flat. Then along came two fellows, Copernicus and Christopher Columbus, separated by a couple of centuries. The first dared to claim that the Earth was not at the center of the universe and that, in fact, it orbited the sun. The second demonstrated that if you sailed a boat far enough west, you wouldn't fall off the edge into some huge dragon's mouth..., but you might discover something new.

"And yet, even today, we still have folks who think the Earth... or at least their part of the Earth... lies at the center of the universe... and yes, that it is flat. And there are still folks out there who think something weird happened at Roswell and who think the landing on the moon was staged from a movie set or hangar at Area 51." He shook his head slowly. "Frankly, they're entitled to their opinions. But unless they are willing to face facts, a lot of other folks think they need to move into the Virginia home for the bewildered."

The crowd of reporters laughed heartily; Boalt basked in the noise.

"So the answer to your question is, I will let the Supreme Court rule on the issue and abide by the result. But I'll leave it to you to decide whether Federalist 86 will be enough to convince folks out there that the Manchurian candidate... I ain't. But I wouldn't bet the farm on it."

Boalt looked back to his right and pointed at a slim brunette. "Yes, Catherine?"

Catherine Fisher rose. "Yes, Catherine Fisher with the BBC. To the point that Jim made regarding Federalist 86... that it 'seems' to say something about your eligibility..."

"Whoa," Boalt interrupted, "let's make sure we're on the same page, Catherine. Federalist 86 says nothing about *me* personally... obviously... wasn't even born in 1788, although this last year in office sure makes it seem a lot longer..." added chuckles, "But what it has to say about *all* presidents, before me and after me, is what matters here. Look, as time goes on and the world becomes an even more complex place, there may be a lot of people out there who, even though not born on U.S. soil of American parents, would nonetheless be great leaders of this nation. And that is what the spirit, if you will, of Federalist 86 seems to be saying."

Fisher nodded. "Of course. But what I meant was, since most of us have not yet seen the document or read its text, I'm wondering whether you agree that it only 'seems' to declare the electorate to be the final determinant. Do you?"

"Well, as I said at the beginning, I am not here to second-guess what the Supreme Court may have to say. To quote one of my predecessors: 'Wouldn't be prudent.'" He shoved his two opposing palms back and forth over the podium, producing hearty media laughter. "The Constitution says a lot of things, but one of the things it is a bit vague about is exactly what the framers... by the way, who included among their members Alexander

Hamilton… meant by the term 'natural born citizen.' And that is why, among other reasons, we have a Supreme Court. What some law professor thinks is one thing, but what a Supreme Court Justice decides is quite another."

He paused and took a sip of water. "And to that point, speaking of the Supreme Court, I want to again offer my deep condolences to Justice Montgomery's family following his stroke. I know everyone in this room will join me in prayers for his swift and full recovery."

Fisher raised her hand. "Mr. president, on that point, we've heard that, given the massive damage likely to have occurred to Justice Montgomery,… well, there's a story now circulating that he will be resigning from the Court in the next few days, creating a vacancy that…"

Boalt held his hand up like a traffic cop. "Please… please. That question is far too premature and speculative to merit an answer. So, please, I apologize for bringing the Supreme Court issue up in the first place. Please… what was your question about the Federalist essay?"

Fisher nodded. "Forgive me, but I'm still a little confused. Jet-lag perhaps. My question was whether you agree with the essay… Federalist 86… that the electorate has the final say, and that neither the courts nor the Congress should… or even *could* override that decision?"

"Well," he hesitated for a moment, "I think the best answer I can give to you today is, one…" he raised his left-hand index finger, "Federalist 86, which is only the opinion of one man, Alexander Hamilton, strongly suggests that in cases of doubt or challenge, the issue of presidential eligibility should ultimately be left up to the electorate, not the courts or the Congress. And two," he paired his index finger with his middle finger, "if a majority the Supreme Court decides that is a correct principle underlying the words of the Constitution and engrafts that interpretation onto the Constitution… I'm not gonna lie to you…, yeah, that would not upset me." Boalt flashed a toothy grin. "But three..." he completed the Boy Scout's gesture with his ring finger, "if the Court decides otherwise, well, that's OK too, because as I've said from the start: my birth certificate says I was born in St. Louis. And, like I said before, last time I checked, that city is still in Missouri."

The sea of reporters nodded in unison, not unlike the gentle undulations of small boats on a body of water.

***

Senator Cantor sat at her desk in her office on the fourth floor of the Senate Hart Office building and stared at Boalt's live image on the Sony 40-inch LED in the bookcase. She lifted a cup of coffee from a circular cork coaster, then muttered to herself: "Missouri, huh?" She sipped the coffee then leaned forward on her desk toward the Sony. "Missouri. OK... show me."

EIGHT

Senator Cantor tapped the intercom button on her desk phone. "Annie?"

"Yes, Senator?" Annie Sutter's voice came back.

"Could you and Steve come in here? Please?"

"On the way."

Shortly, a petite blonde and a 220-pound Black – with the body mass index of a Super Bowl halfback – entered the office. Cantor motioned both of them to the chairs at the side of her desk, then gestured for them to look at the television: Boalt was smiling and shaking hands with several of the reporters as the press conference was breaking up.

"In a minute," she began, "the talking heads will be all over the airwaves and cable channels, yapping themselves silly over how this lays to rest all questions of Boalt's eligibility. How the 'birthers' are the newest, right wing-nut version of the flat Earth academy. It makes me sick. Sick."

Annie leaned forward in her chair. "But Senator, remember... the Court seems prepared to rule that Professor Locke has standing in his case. I was there... I listened to the questions. And since it's a *quo warranto* case, the odds are..."

"Quo warranto, schmo warranto, Annie..." Cantor snapped, "with this Federalist 86 revelation and the media blitz it will produce, we're toast. I mean, we... are... done..." She muted the television with the remote. "And I could really care less about this 'birther' movement. The important thing here is what's being done to the Constitution. It's being shredded. Worse. It's being turned into toilet paper. Used toilet paper, at that." She paused. "I need a barf bag."

They all looked around at each other, Cantor at Annie and Steve, Annie at Cantor, Annie at Steve; Steve at Cantor, Steve at

82

Annie. After several silent, seemingly minute-long seconds, Steve raised his hand.

"You want that bag half-empty or half- ...?"

Steve always had a way of taking the edge off of things. First Cantor grinned, then allowed a laugh, quickly followed by Annie's high-pitched, unmistakable squeal and Steve's low, growling guffaw.

"OOoooo...," Cantor exhaled, "that was... that was... disgusting, Steve. Thank you."

Steve smiled. "You're welcome, Senator. Ahhh... so, if we're done, does that mean ... I can go home early...?"

Cantor grinned, but shook her head. "No, Steve, it does not." She cut the power to the TV. "First, when I said we're done, I lied. A senator's prerogative, yes?"

Annie and Steve smiled and nodded in unison.

"Thank you. Second, it is now, what..." she looked at her watch, "4:20. That means the three of us have... sorry, it means every person on my staff has approximately seventeen hours to do everything possible to get me prepared for the questioning I intend to let loose on O'Hara and Clark tomorrow. And I mean everything. This 'discovery'" another pair of air-quotes, "seems just all too convenient... *way* too convenient. I want to know all I can about both Clark and O'Hara and why they were tapped by Brown to be the witnesses at the hearing..."

Steve raised his hand again; Cantor nodded. "Maybe because Clark made the discovery?"

Cantor nodded. "Yeah... but who, exactly is this Clark? What's his bio? Is he legit? And what is up with that e-mail he said he got from some distant relative of a friend of a friend of a friend of George Washington? Huh?"

Annie began quickly scrolling through her iPhone, mixing upward finger sweeps and taps, down sweeps, more taps... "Allison Hardesty?"

Cantor generated a combination curiosity-frown. "Yes. How did you get that so fast?"

Annie held up the iPhone. "Most of what took place at the hearing is already posted on the Internet."

Cantor's frown deepened. "You're kidding."

"Nope. Check it out." She handed the device to Cantor, who stared at the information displayed on the screen. "Sheesh..." she muttered, handing it back.

"OK," the politician began, "if the hearing information is already posted worldwide, then these guys are either really, really fast... or..."

They looked at one another again. Steve tilted his head slightly, "Or... someone got a head's up...?"

Cantor allowed a small grin. "Stranger things have happened in this village...."

Now Annie frowned. "Ummm... not sure what you're suggesting. Are you saying that some Internet site or blogger...."

"Annie," Cantor raised an index finger, "I'm not sure exactly what I'm saying right now. But that's why I pay you two the big bucks..." she winked; both Annie and Steve smiled, with Steve rolling his eyes, "... to find out what it is that I *am* saying and then inform me so... I don't look like an idiot."

Annie looked again at the iPhone. "So maybe we try to find out a little more about this Clark. And Allison Hardesty?"

Steve motioned for the iPhone, which Annie handed to him. He did a few taps and finger sweeps as well. Then he frowned slightly and looked up at them. "And the server that Clark said Hardesty's e-mail came from? Tangello25 dot com?" He held the device up, screen toward Cantor. "No such animal or URL."

Cantor looked at Steve, then at Annie, then back at Steve. "Meaning?"

Steve turned the device to his face. "Meaning that either Clark was mistaken… or that the URL for that server was masked or camouflaged."

Annie looked at him "ummm … or has since been…" she paused and looked back at Cantor, "… removed from the web."

That uneasy pause that seeps up when something unexpected or out of the ordinary and odd intrudes into a conversation began inflating the room. They exchanged glances again: Cantor to Annie to Steve; Annie to Cantor to Steve; Steve to Cantor to Annie.

"OK, look," Cantor began. "No jumping to conclusions. There's no time for that. This is waaay to serious for mistakes. Understood?"

Annie and Steve nodded.

"You say the site from which Clark said the Hardesty e-mail came… isn't there?"

Steve shrugged. "Looks like."

Cantor looked at Annie. "When did Clark say the e-mail came?"

Annie brushed and jabbed at the iPhone, her eyes darting over the screen. "Didn't say exactly. Just that it was a few days after he got back to Boston after copying the letter at Monticello."

Cantor flipped through a small desk calendar next to her phone. "So that would have been, what, sometime last month?"

Annie tapped the iPhone again. "Looks like," she confirmed.

"Steve?" Cantor asked, still looking at Annie.

He looked up from his own device: a Droid. "Yeah?"

"Do you know anyone who can find out who set up that website? And when?"

Steve frowned. "You mean the one with the nonexistent URL? That one?"

Cantor looked at him. "Yeah. That one."

He drew in a deep breath, then blew it out. "I'll see. No guarantees... but I'll see... I got a bud... Mike Tippett... used to work at Microsoft after we got out and he's pretty savvy..."

Cantor frowned slightly. "Savvy is good,... but...is he discrete? Trustworthy?"

"Mike? Both."

Cantor tipped her head, signaling that "oh-really?" look of doubt.

"Trust me," Steve said. "Semper fi. We did a tour together outside Kandahar. He took an IED to his leg for this place," a general sweep of his eyes around the room, "and they Purple Hearted him, shipped him back here. He'd prefer to have his leg back... but he's got the medal framed and sitting next to his computer." Steve nodded. "Ooo-rah."

Cantor's doubt evaporated. "Where does he work now?"

"Out of his condo in Crystal City. He's a free-lancer. His own boss. Does *really* well for himself."

Cantor nodded. "Good. So there's the deal," she looked at her watch. "First, I hope you both went to bed early yesterday, because both of you are on task for an all-nighter. It is now 4:35. By midnight, I need all of the information you can gather for me on all of these issues, and then be prepared for follow-up. Is Clark for real? Is Allison Hardesty for real? What about this URL thing?" She looked at Steve. "Is your Crystal City pal in town?"

"Mike?" Steve interrupted her with a nod. "Yeah, we're supposed to tip a few this weekend at his place. He's a phone call away."

Cantor raised her index finger again. "Be discrete, please. All of this may lead nowhere. And the last thing I need is for my poking around to backfire. Yes?" She leaned forward slightly. "But if there is something out there... something tangible and smoking... I need to know what it is. And soon."

Steve nodded. "Message received, Senator.

"Annie, I need you to start drafting a series of questions for me to pose tomorrow. What is this O'Hara's background? Can you find out which Justice on the Court she clerked for? And what, exactly, is her expertise in the history of The Federalist Papers? Is she really qualified to give an opinion on what this new one is really supposed to mean? I mean, why didn't Brown get some con-law professor to testify today? What's up with that?"

Annie nodded. "Already on it," she held up her iPhone again.

Cantor rolled her eyes. "Is there anything that creepy machine can't do?"

Annie smiled. "Well... so far, not much. Except it hasn't predicted the next winning numbers for the lottery."

Cantor grinned. "Then what good is it?" She held up her hand instead of her index finger. "And what I said about mobilizing the staff? Forget it. Let them go home, business as usual. If there's anything to these... ummm... irregularities that we've... *not* discussed here.... you with me...?"

They both nodded understanding.

"Right. For now, let's just keep this among the three of us. If it blows up, I want the blame without splattering the staff... other than you two." Another wink. "I've got to go to a fund-raiser this evening, but I'll be back here by 10:00. If you need me for anything before then, shoot me a text. I will respond."

Steve raised his hand. "Senator?"

"Yes?"

"You still want that barf bag?"

She thought for a moment. "Ask me tomorrow morning."

NINE

Annie sat at a booth near the back of the McDonald's, away from the constantly opening/closing door and the rush of traffic noise, loud even at this hour. She dipped a French fry into a container of ranch dressing – she was the only one of her friends who use ranch instead of ketchup on a French fry – and bit into it, then took a sip of Diet Coke. The two major food groups, fries and soda pop. McDonald's fries, she thought: they're the best, at least right out of the boiling oil.

She kept an eye on the door as two patrons would enter, one leave… a group of four would enter, a couple would leave… then a tall male in Levis and a grey "Georgetown Law" sweatshirt entered, looked around, spotted her, then began moving in her direction. He carried a laptop and had two earbuds imbedded in his head. As he moved, he popped the earbuds out and shoved them into his pocket.

"Hey, sissy," he said as he arrived and sat down across from her.

"Hey," she responded. "Thanks for comin'."

He nodded and pointed at a second cup on the table, a straw poking up from the cap. "That mine?"

She nodded. "Dr. Pepper, fully-leaded."

He smiled. "You still putting that diet stuff into your bod?"

She nodded again. "Sure. It offsets the fries."

He smiled more widely while shaking his head. "Hey, for a chick with so much grey stuff between your ears, you still can make some pretty odd health decisions… know what I mean?"

She smiled. "Look who's talking."

He nodded and took one of her French fries. "May I?"

"Sure."

He took a deep sip of the sugar-loaded Doctor, looked left, looked right, then back at Annie. "Soooo,… what's with the cloak and dagger message on my machine? You're lucky I listened to it before deciding to leave town."

She reached out and patted her brother's hand. "Thanks for coming. Umm... Jack... I'm not even sure I know what is going on, but I needed to ask you some things."

"'Bout what?"

Now she glanced around, then looked back at him. "You watch Boalt's press conference today?"

Jack took another fry, dipped it in the ranch, then bit off the tip. "Nope." He took another swallow of pop. "I try to avoid anything that guy has to say. And if you were smart, you would too."

She took a fry, did the dip and bite, and sipped her drink. "Well, given that I work for someone who makes it her job to watch and listen to everything he *does* say... and thus makes it my job too..." she stared at his right eye, "... let's just say some days are easier than others."

Jack nodded. "I know, I know. And, look, I didn't mean you weren't supposed to do what you do. I get it. I get it. I just meant that I have no respect for this guy. Zero. Zip. Zilch. So whatever he might have to say at a media grope... 'scuse me, a press conference, I don't care."

She leaned toward him. "But you should. This time, you really should."

He darted his attention between her eyes and nodded. "OK, I'll bite," he assaulted another fry, "why?"

She leaned back in the booth. "Because he's on the verge of being able to deep-six, once and for all, those who would challenge his eligibility to be president."

Jack frowned. "On the verge? Sissy, with the press now functioning as his personal propaganda machine...," he deepened his frown, "you *gotta* be kidding. He's *already* buried them."

She tilted her head toward him. "Not so fast. That *Locke* case is still pending in the Supreme Court, and from what I saw at the arguments last week, they may just be prepared to finally hear a case where his eligibility will be heard… on the merits."

Jack took another fry to his mouth. "Don't count on it. Just because they find standing to let Locke in the front door does not mean… and in a *big* way … does *not* mean they will get to the merits of Boalt's eligibility…, which the briefs don't even touch."

Annie smiled. "Ah… gotcha…"

Jack tilted his head. "Yeah? How so?"

"You've read all the briefs, right?"

"Yeah."

"And?"

"Well, Locke's brief is OK, but it doesn't focus on the right issue. All it does is rail on about why *quo warranto* is the right procedure and why Locke has standing to raise the issue."

Annie scowled. "Quo… what…?"

"Quo warranto. Latin. Means 'by what authority' does a public officer claim to legitimately hold office."

"Ah."

"But Locke's brief doesn't really hone in on the essential point." He paused. "And, by the way, what difference does it make? We've had this discussion before, sissy."

Annie nodded. "But it's different now…"

Jack squinted. "How so? Look, I know you're embarrassed to have a 'birther' for a brother, and believe me, I take a *lot* of gas over it from the few friends I have left at school with whom I've even shared that 'dark secret'" air quote emphasized. "If everyone else wants to do the lemming cliff-leap with Boalt, let 'em. But count me out."

Annie looked at him. "So you're saying I'm a lemming?"

Jack frowned deeply. "Absolutely not… bite your tongue." He looked over at the door as two elderly women exited. "But hanging your hat… or Senator Cantor's hat on the Supreme Court doing the right thing in Ed Locke's case is…. uhhhm… a bit foolish… if you ask me."

"Ah, once again, you've fallen into my trap…"

Jack's frown quickly evolved into a grin. "You keep talkin' about your trap. What trap?"

Annie glanced at the door as two students entered just at the two women exited. "Here's the situation. I need a crash course on what, exactly, the core issue is relating to Boalt's eligibility. And by 'crash course,' I mean in the next thirty minutes. You, my only bro, are a self-professed 'birther'…albeit a closet birther… and I need to know what the central point in that debate is." She smiled, then whispered "Don't worry… you're secret's safe…," then tilted her head "… that is… if you co-operate…."

Jack smiled, then frowned again. "OOooo…. down to threats, now, are we? Huh? And don't call me a birther. The clinical, more accurate term is 'constitutionalist.' Less pejorative. And not as stupid. And, by the way, you don't have staffers on the Hill who can do that?"

Annie frowned and shook her head. "The issue is radioactive up there… I mean, it's enriched plutonium. And Cantor won't touch it, at least publicly, for fear of huge blowback. She will likely have a strong challenger… a primary election challenge from her own party, no less…for her seat next year." Annie shook her head. "Nope… you're it, at least on the timetable I have…"

Jack nodded. "OK… but you realize, of course…?"

Annie waited for a completed sentence… it did not come.

"Realize what?"

Jack stood and whispered to her, "…it'll take more than a couple of French fries to bribe me." With that, he winked, and headed over to the ordering counter. In a few minutes, he returned with an Angus Swiss-Mushroom burger, large fries, a refilled Dr. Pepper, countless Heinz ketchup packets and a fistful of tan napkins. He took a chunk out of the burger and started in, his words only slightly impeded by the food being delivered into his throat.

"First off," he took a swig of the Doctor, "you think you're up for this? There's a lot, so are ya up for the crash course? Emmerich de Vattel? The decisions in *The Venus* and *Happersett* and *Elg*? Article Eight? Are ya? Huh? Are ya?"

Annie pouted her mouth. "Try me."

"OK. First, despite all of the smoke and mirrors from Boalt and his supporters and all of the so-called 'proof' that he is constitutionally eligible... the question is still up for grabs. Boalt's supporters point to a number of Supreme Court cases which state, in dictum... the stuff that's not directly related to or controlling in a particular decision... that if a person is born here, regardless of the citizenship of his or her parents, the kid is a 'natural born citizen' based on English common law principles."

Annie nodded her understanding.

"His detractors point out... correctly... that dictum in some old Supreme Court decisions cannot properly overcome the actual words of the Constitution and the understandings of the people who wrote it based on, among other things, a recognized treatise on the issue which was in existence when the Constitution was drafted. It was written and compiled by a Swiss legal philosopher named de Vattel and called "The Law of Nations. And there's ample evidence... assuming anyone wanted to look... that the drafters were well aware of the criteria de Vattel identified as constituting one a natural born citizen.

"But, as yet, neither side has produced the 'smoking gun' which would prove, or disprove, Boalt's eligibility as a 'natural born citizen' under the Constitution. But my money is on those who say he's ineligible, and not simply because of the mounting evidence that he was born in India, not Missouri."

Annie dipped her chin. "Like?"

"OK. You need to realize... and accept... that people have forgotten ... and this operates to Boalt's advantage... that it is not solely the *place* of birth, whether within the United States or beyond its borders but within lands over which the United States has jurisdiction... like an embassy or military base... that matters." He nodded. "de Vattel confirms that It takes three things to make someone a 'natural born citizen.' Not one... or two." He paused, dipping his chin and staring into her right eye. "*Three*. And all at the time of birth... not sometime thereafter. That's straight out of *The Law of Nations*. Not that anyone cares..."

Annie nodded. "I'm all ears."

He continued. "What also matters in addition to geography is that the person's parents... his or her mother *and* father... must *both* be citizens of the United States. And there's even good reason to believe that even if the mother is a citizen when the kid is born, if the father is not at that moment also a citizen... then the kid cannot, by definition, be a 'natural born Citizen' under the controlling section of the Constitution and according to de Vattel. That's what the Supreme Court said in *Happersett*... again, not that anyone cares.

She nodded. "I'm with you... so far."

Jack continued. "When those three things... not just one or two, but all *three* combine... and at the time of the child's birth, not later..., then status as a natural born citizen attaches." He shook his head. "And an abstracted or short form 'birth certificate'" he gestured with his fingers "that shows a live birth in Missouri... or for that matter, anywhere else... Alaska, Maine, Egypt... without *also* showing the places of birth or citizenship of the kid's parents..., and at the time of birth... does nothing... repeat, *nothing*... to prove that the child is a natural born citizen."

"So you gotta have all three?"

"Well, if de Vattel and *The Law of Nations* applies... yes. All three... and all three at the moment of birth... and particularly the one regarding the father's citizenship. Not ten, twenty or more years later or with secondary documentation like a newspaper birth announcement or image of a birth certificate sent to the Internet." He shook his head. "Gimme a break."

Annie nodded and took a sip of her own drink. "Go on."

Jack swallowed and took another bite of the hamburger. "Got a story for ya to prove the point. And like Kissinger said, it has the added virtue of being true."

Annie grinned. "I'm all ears."

"Couple of weeks ago, I was jousting with my constitutional law professor after class on this very point. Professor Cohen's a Boalt supporter... duh, a con law professor supporting another con law professor... who woulda thunk?... and he considers people like me to be nuts. Oh, the school he teaches at is willing to take my tuition, of course. But they still think I'm nuts."

Annie nodded. "OK. And....?"

"He deems the eligibility argument settled because Boalt's minions – not Boalt himself, you understand – disclosed an image of what they contended was his Missouri birth certificate on the Internet for all to see. Not just the voters here. Anyone in the world with a computer. So how, he asks me, could anyone seriously debate that he has not made full disclosure of his birth certificate?"

Annie kept nodding, then started that circular index finger motion to "move along."

Jack swigged some Doctor, then muffled a quick belch. "In his office at school, he's got a picture hanging on the wall among his diplomas, certificates and ego-portraits of him with judges and politicians. Anyway, the picture... actually, a print of a painting... was originally created by an artist named Magritte. René Magritte. Ever heard of him?"

Annie shook her head. "Nope. Gonna bet he was French, though."

Jack feigned surprise. "Nothin' much gets past you, does it...?"

She repeated the index finger roll.

Jack bit into the hamburger again. "The picture hanging on his wall depicts just a brown pipe with an ebony stem against a tan background. Below it, Magritte wrote: 'This is not a pipe.'"

Annie frowned. "Ummm... you just said it was a pipe." She dipped and bit a fry. "If it's *not* a pipe, then what is it?"

Jack grinned. "It's a picture of a pipe."

Annie frowned more deeply... then, slowly, it dawned on her. "Ahhh... and so... a picture of a birth certificate is not... a birth certificate."

"Precisely. And a picture of a forgery is not the actual forgery either. And when I pointed that out to Cohen, he 'bout choked on his coffee and asked if I was actually saying the posted image was a forgery. I said, truthfully, that I didn't know, because as my evidence professor had taught me, the best evidence of a document is the document itself, not a picture or a copy of it. Cohen just turned red and 'remembered' he was late for another meeting and excused me out into the hallway." Jack put the remainder of the hamburger down. "And this, mind you, is what passes for academic excellence in America today."

Jack swallowed and took another bite of the hamburger. "And the argument that an image of such a document posted on the Internet... without the opportunity for examination of the *actual* document... supposedly proves more than that which the actual document does... is absurd. I mean, c'mon, that's *insanity*. A fourth-grader could see through that. Nah... take it back... a kindergartner could see that. And yet, that is exactly what this administration is peddling as the 'fact' purportedly demonstrating not only Boalt's status as a 'natural born citizen'" he jerked more finger gesticulations, "but that the matter is settled. No more questions from the masses. Shut yer pie holes."

Annie frowned. "But the newspaper announcement must prove something, yes?"

Jack nodded and bit into a ketchup-dipped fry. "Sure. It proves that someone prepared an announcement in a newspaper of general circulation in St. Louis, and paid for it. Like a classified ad. And when the publisher got paid, it appeared in print. Boom. Done." He chuckled. "You know, last week I got a kick out of asking my evidence professor what I thought was a really simple question. Why it was that a birth announcement in yesterday's newspaper is inadmissible in evidence because it's hearsay, while a newspaper birth announcement from thirty years ago comes in under the 'ancient document' exception to the hearsay exclusion rule."

"And?"

"And after fumbling around for a while, the best he could do was 'just because that's what the guys who wrote the rules of evidence wanted.'"

Annie frowned slightly. "That's lame."

Jack smiled. "And disingenuous... don't forget disingenuous. Ah.... academic excellence." He bit the burger again. "Sissy," he mumbled through the food, "you'd be amazed... no..., *frightened*... at some of the creepy nooks and crannies scattered throughout the law and in the recesses of law schools. Seriously."

Annie shook her head. "But how could the person who placed the ad have known that at some future date, the child might have to prove natural born citizenship as a condition of running for president? That's impossible."

Jack shook his head and bit into another fry. "Sissy... sissy... *please*. There are approximately 356 good and sufficient reasons for wanting your child to have United States citizenship instead of Indian citizenship... or Albanian citizenship... or Sudanese citizenship... which are *completely* independent of and unrelated to running for president." He shook his head. "Duh."

Annie nodded. "OK."

Jack smiled. "So back to the natural born citizen stuff... "
He applied one of the napkins to some errant Heinz smearing his
chin. "The facts are out there, for anyone willing to objectively
examine them. Trouble is, the media has so poisoned and
corrupted the process that any objective analysis that once might
have existed has been killed off and buried. Now all they're doing
is resisting the effort to exhume the body."

Annie shook her head. "The Justice Department witness
today... O'Hara.... mentioned that a while back, a report... what, a
Congressional Research Service memorandum that was issued to
all the members of Congress and that it concluded ...."

Jack snorted thin twin jets of Dr. Pepper out of his nose as
he tried, unsuccessfully, to muffle his laugh. "Wow. Are you
kidding? She referenced *that*?"

Annie squinted and handed him some napkins. "Yeah.
What's so funny?"

"The one that concludes you can be a natural born citizen
merely by being born here? In the United States?"

"Yes, Jack... that very same report."

"And the one that uses *Perkins v. Elg* to get there?"

"Yeah... she mentioned *Perkins*... or *Elg*... one of those...
why?"

Jack smiled and took another smaller chunk of Angus
burger into his mouth. "Well, sissy..." he took a napkin to his
nose again, "... let's just say that report would have been a lot
more persuasive and defensible... not to mention principled and
lawful... if it had quoted what the *Perkins* case *actually* held rather
than what the report ended up *claiming* it held." He put the
hamburger down. "Y'know, you can pull some pretty insidious
tricks out of a hat with ellipsis omissions of words and bracketed
additional concocted language. And if nobody calls you on it... or
if nobody *cares*... you get away with it. Unbelievable. Just un-
flaming believable."

Annie frowned deeply. "What on Earth are you talking about?"

"The only way that the CRS memo could arrive at the pre-determined result it sought was to alter the meaning of the *Perkins* decision. Not by actually changing or adding to the language of the opinion, you understand..." he feigned two suspicious looks, right, then left, "...that would leave too many trails. But by omitting relevant language and inserting bracketed 'interpretive' language of the report author..., *voilà*... if you are born 'in' the United States, you are eligible to be President." He looked up at her. "Game over. Side out. Un... flaming... believable...."

Annie darted her attention between his eyes. "You mean... are you saying the report... the report was intentionally deceptive?"

Jack sipped on his straw. "Go take a look at the report, then go take a look at the official version of *Perkins*... then ask me that question. If you take the report at face value... like 99 percent of every member of Congress who even *read* the report or had a staffer summarize it... it peddles the conclusion that a pregnant, non-citizen illegal alien who comes across the border on a Monday and on Tuesday gives birth to her child in Texas... or Montana... or California... renders the child eligible to be president of this nation as a 'natural born citizen.'"

Annie frowned. "Are you serious?"

"Serious as the proverbial heart attack."

She shook her head slowly. "Sad. Way sad."

Jack nodded. "'Sad' don't even come close, sissy. Lemme tell ya, that report on presidential eligibility is beyond deceptive. It is a contempt of Congress. It doesn't provide anything *close* to a principled analysis or answer; all it provides is convenient cover for people willing to be duped. And they claim it doesn't matter because de Vattel doesn't matter. The Founders are spinning in their graves."

He shook his head. "The term 'felony' comes to mind. And, what's worse, the mainstream media today only regurgitates the party line that the 'debate is over' and then paints all those who would dare to suggest that the CRS report is fudged... or that emperor has no clothes... or no papers... as loons or nut-cases. They are a pitiful collection of misguided souls who give true conspiracy theorists a bad name." He shook his head more slowly, then took yet another large chunk out of the sandwich and looked at it. "Y'know, these ain't all that bad...."

Annie did the two-fingers-to-her-eyes-then-pointed-index-finger-at-Jack thing a few times, then blurted: "Focus, bro'... I need you here."

Jack nodded. "OK, OK. Here's the long and short of it. Getting back to the 'proof' of eligibility Boalt's handlers have offered, the placement of an image of a forged document... or even a real one... on the Internet does nothing to morph it into the genuine article. *Nothing.* All it does is provide cover.

"And with a comatose media that's AWOL on the topic, because of Missouri confidentiality statutes, unless Boalt says it's OK to release the originals..., which he refuses to do, without challenge..., they stay hidden. And the only evidence available then becomes: the image on the Internet. And they say that's proof? No. That's crazy."

He sucked more Dr. Pepper up through his straw. "Like I said, the publishing of an ad or posting of an image of a birth certificate on the Internet no more 'ends the debate' over this guy's eligibility for a constitutionalist than would the posting on the Internet of a photo of a blizzard end the debate over global warming for Al Gore."

Another bite out of the Angus burger. "Despite the efforts of Boalt and his supporters to obscure and manipulate the facts, only where the three criteria of birth within lands over which sovereignty or jurisdiction of the United States combine... at the moment of birth... with confirmed citizenship status of the child's mother and *particularly* the father, can a conclusion be made that the child is a 'natural born citizen.'" He paused between bites of the burger. "You know what 'POTUS' stands for these days among us loons?"

Annie did the "I'm-gonna-guess-something-other-than-what-I-think" shrug.

"Poseur of the United States. Look, the Constitution requires that a president be a natural born citizen, which would seem clearly to exclude natural born ingénues. And yet, that's what we have now." He shook his head. "Is this a great country, or what?"

Annie grinned. "So how do you come to know this stuff?" And what about the dictum in the cases Boalt relies on?"

He shrugged. "Just read up on it. It's all out there, available for anyone. It just torqued me *big* time that no one was following up on why... *why* this guy was getting a free pass on an issue as important as this. So you go to the books, the libraries."

Annie held up her index finger. "The Internet?"

He nodded. "Yeah, that too... but *only* for direction and *never* without non-Internet source corroboration." He winked at her. "Lots of bogus stuff posted on the Internet, I'm told. *Lots.*" He grinned at her. "Shocking... I know... I know...."

"So where did the 'natural born citizen' stuff originally come from?"

He raised the remaining Angus burger to his mouth again. "Well, first off, after you dig around a bit, you come across the teachings of the guy I mentioned... de Vattel... the Swiss legal scholar. Back in the 1700's, contemporaneous with the guys who drafted the Constitution... Jefferson, Hamilton... those guys. They knew of de Vattel."

Annie frowned again. "Yeah... the Justice Department lawyer mentioned his name this morning."

Jack frowned. "She did ? Wow."

Annie nodded. "I've heard of Jefferson and Hamilton. Who was de Vattel?"

Jack took in some more Dr. Pepper. "A philosopher and legal writer. Like I said before, his main work was called *The Law of Nations*... and it gets into what does... and what does *not*... constitute a person as being a 'natural born citizen' of a country. And it's really pretty simple. Like I said, to be one, *both* of your parents must be citizens of the country where you are born.

"Even Thomas Jefferson... you've heard of him, yes?... relied on de Vattel and *The Law of Nations* in drafting the Declaration of Independence and some argue likely even parts of the Constitution. But you'd not know that from today's mainstream media screeds on eligibility. And, by the way, de Vattel was not the only one who wrote about what it took to qualify someone as a 'natural born citizen' as opposed to a 'native born citizen.'"

"Oh?"

"Turns out there were a number of Americans who confirmed the same thing. Including a guy named Ramsay... Donald... no... David Ramsay, who just happened to be a contemporary of Washington, Hamilton, Madison, Jefferson.... all of them. He wrote about it in his histories of the American Revolution. They would all have been dumbfounded at the debate going on today because it was so clear back then as to who was... and who *was not*..., a 'natural born citizen,' it wasn't even a topic of discussion.

"*All* of them recognized that a 'natural born citizen' was not only a person born here, but had to be one born to parents who *both* were citizens themselves or, at minimum, whose father was a citizen. If one or the other was not such a citizen, then you may have been a 'native born citizen' of the country... but you were not a 'natural born citizen.' I mean, the Fourteenth Amendment says a lot about 'native born citizens,' but it has nothing to do with who is... and who is *not*... a 'natural born citizen.'

"Being a 'native born citizen' under the Fourteenth Amendment... which, by the way, was not even part of the Constitution until after the Civil War... did nothing to alter the original meaning of 'natural born citizen' adopted by the Founding Fathers when the Constitution was signed, which was the one described by de Vattel and Ramsay."

Annie nodded. "Keep going."

Jack nodded. "Yeah, and guess what? The concept seemed pretty straightforward to the very first Congress too, because... wait for it... wait for it.... they enacted a law stating just that."

Annie's forehead rippled up. "Really? When?"

"Back in the first session of Congress... so, that would be, what..., 1790?"

"You got a Public Law citation?"

Jack cocked his head left. "Not off the top of my head... but trust me... it's there. Pull it up on Westlaw or Thomas. It was later repealed and replaced for different unrelated reasons, but the original 'natural born citizen' intent taken from de Vattel and set out in the second statute Congress enacted... the part about both parents needing to be citizens...was always reenacted without change. And it's still the best evidence of what was originally intended when the concept was incorporated into the Constitution.

"The issue was simple enough until Boalt came along. See, no one wants to be part of a stupendous mistake. No one wants to admit that, in electing Boalt, people believed what they *wanted* to believe, not necessarily what was the truth. So when Boalt responded to questions about his eligibility with the Internet image of an abstract, yet, of a birth certificate he claims is authentic, all of his supporters lined up in lockstep like a bunch of Tibetan monks and started chanting the party line. Ohmmm.... Ohmmm."

He lifted another fry to his mouth. "But guess what. It gets even better. The Supreme Court has actually cited and relied upon de Vattel's definition of what constitutes a 'natural born citizen.' As far as I know, the Supreme Court has never cited that 1790 law, but de Vattel's teachings on 'natural born citizens' *has* been cited with approval by the Court on more than one occasion."

"Really?"

"Yeah, really." He bit into another Heinz-coated fry. "The first one to discuss the issue was called *The Venus*. Back in... what?... the early-1800's..."

Annie frowned slightly. "The Venus? That's the case mentioned by the Justice Department lawyer.... O'Hara... at the hearing today."

Jack sipped his drink. "Yeah. It was a case involving a merchant ship called *The Venus*. The issue was whether its cargo, which was owned by an American citizen and being transported from British lands to the United States during the War of 1812, could lawfully be seized and captured as a prize by an American privateer. But the critical thing about the case is what the Court... a unanimous Court, no less... said about citizenship and what constituted a 'natural born citizen.'"

"And?" she asked, sipping on her own drink.

"The Court quoted... verbatim, as I recall... the definition from de Vattel's 'Law of Nations,' which at the time was considered to be the most authoritative statement of international law and its related doctrines... including citizenship... on the planet.

"Oh, and did I mention, consistent with Ramsay's writings on the issue too? And the Court, adopting de Vattel's treatise language, said that natural born citizens were those persons... and *only* those persons... who were born in the country or in a place over which their own country had jurisdiction, *and* where their parents were themselves citizens. Same thing Congress said in 1790... but without mentioning that law... Court probably didn't even know it was on the books.

He shook his head, picked up a fry and jabbed it into the air toward Annie's nose. "Why is this stuff so hard to understand? The inconvenient truth here... for Boalt and his enablers... is that the president... excuse me, I now just call him 'Mr. Boalt', since he has never deserved the label of the office he usurps... he is, based on that which he has offered and relied upon for proof of his eligibility... plainly ineligible under the Constitution. And he knows it, too."

Annie shook her head, then looked at her Seiko. "What else?"

Jack nodded. "Saving the best for last." Yet another French fry neared his mouth. "Truth is," he bit off the top of the fry, "the argument can be made... and maybe even compellingly... that de Vattel's writings are even referenced and, again, some would argue persuasively... actually incorporated into the Constitution itself, let alone cited and relied upon by the Supreme Court."

Annie raised her eyebrows. "Oh?"

"Yeah. In many different places in the Constitution, the founders referenced and used the word 'laws' as well as the word 'nations.' But in only one place... Article One, Section Eight, dealing with piracies, felonies and other offenses, does the Constitution make specific reference to...." he let the sentence trail off as he sucked more Doctor through his straw and squinted slightly at his sister.

"Let me guess," she took the hint. "*The Law of Nations*."

Jack grinned. "Mom always said there was hope for you..."

She squinted. "So you're telling me the Founding Fathers meant that..."

He held up a finger. "Ah ah... no. Not telling you anything other than what the ink on the Constitution says. Umm... it never changes, ya know..." He winked. "What Jefferson, Madison and all the others 'meant'" more air quotes "is for someone else to decide. Like maybe the Supreme Court. Maybe all they meant was to reference de Vattel's work in connection with piracies on the high seas and other offenses against the

104

republic. Then again, maybe not. Boalt's minions would tell you it was just a generic reference having nothin' to do with de Vattel's work of the same name." He munched another fry. "Then again… all I'm telling you is that the words say what they say."

He paused, then added, "But remember… sissy… when someone who is not eligible to the presidency nonetheless knowingly usurps the office, some would argue that this would be as much an act of piracy… not to mention a felony and an offense against both the nation and the laws of the nation… as would be the boarding and plundering of a ship at sea." He leaned toward her, pointing a ketchup-dipped French fry at her nose. "Arrrrghh, sissy…. not all piracies be limited to the theft of gold doubloons, ya know…" Then he bit the fry.

She let the words sink in. "OK, let me rephrase… counselor…"

Jack nodded. "Arrrrghh, sibling. Proceed."

She wadded up a napkin and bounced it off his forehead.

"Ahh..," he muttered, "now you've assaulted me…"

She smiled. "Actually, counselor… that was a battery…."

Jack nodded. "Hmmmm… ever thought of becoming a shyster?"

She tilted her head. "Only in my worst, fever-wracked nightmares…"

He nodded and grinned. "So… you were saying… before the battery…?"

"I was saying that maybe… just *maybe* the potential exists that, even if the Constitution *itself* does not, in so many words, define what it takes to be a 'natural born citizen,' the framers did. By citing de Vattel's *Law of Nations…*, if that's what the words in Article One, Section Eight are referencing …, they knew that its definition of what it took to be a natural born citizen was the one they wanted to incorporate and *adopt* as a requirement of the new Constitution." He sucked in more Dr. Pepper. "Arrrrghh… stranger things could be deduced…"

Annie frowned. "OK, Jack, enough with the pirate stuff. This is serious here."

He nodded. "OK, OK... sorry. Yeah, I know it's serious. But what can be done?" He paused and leaned toward her. "Remember, sissy... Boalt has never directly responded to the question: 'are you a natural born citizen under the Constitution?' *Never*. Instead.... he always punts. *Always*.

"And if anybody even comes *close* to calling him on it, his team of sycophants..., the mainstream media, the law professors, the blogger-kooks... they all flock together and descend upon them like a plague of locusts. Look, the only thing transparent about this guy is his character. He's a charlatan." Then he frowned. "Worse, he's a charlatan on a mission. And the mission is not to the benefit or good of this nation."

He shook his head and looked down at the remaining disarray that was his pile of fries. "But maybe there is, in fact, hope. A lot of others are starting to ask pointed questions... like some active-duty military officers. Good for them. I mean, if they're willing to voluntarily march into harm's way for their country and even weather being court-martialed, is it too much for them to ask for proof that the guy telling them to start marching and or take up residence at Leavenworth is the genuine article?

"Yet he refuses to do it, making him a usurper. And a cowardly one at that. That's why he has tried so desperately to keep the originals of his records secret, because they would disclose the truth and cook his goose. And with the aid and comfort of the press... with a couple of exceptions... he's pulling off the biggest bamboozle since the place opened for business," he glanced around, "and I don't mean just this burger joint."

Annie nodded. "And that's it?"

He returned the nod. "In 10,000 words or less... yeah." He leaned toward her and grabbed her hand. "Look, this isn't about ideology, race or religion. It's about adherence to the core principles set out in the Constitution. And that 'birther' pejorative is just a juvenile diversionary label calculated to keep people from looking behind the curtain while Boalt pulls and jerks the rods and levers of a big carnival sideshow. People who ask these questions are constitutionalists, not pejoratives. And, they are Americans."

He put the remnants of the Angus burger down into its cardboard box. "The way I see it is this. If the nation is ready, as Boalt hopes, to swallow hook, line and sinker that the words of the Constitution mean nothing or that they can be ignored or cleverly manipulated, without consequence, to suit one's own whims, then the term 'nation' no longer applies to us. What is left is either anarchy or dictatorship. And yet, thanks to our pals in the media who never met a collectivist they didn't like, that's where we're goin'."

He lifted the remainder of the hamburger and took an enormous bite out of what was left, chewing and pausing occasionally to draw additional lubricating Dr. Pepper into the cavity where the meat was being processed. He stared into her eye. "Got it?"

She nodded, putting her Diet Coke down. "If you get a chance tomorrow... get me the citation to that law from the first Congress?"

He smiled. "What's it worth to ya?"

She returned the grin. "'Nother burger?"

He huffed a laugh. "Done. Oh... I almost forgot... Magritte's painting...?"

She nodded. "This is not a pipe?"

"Yeah. But that's not the title. It's just what Magritte painted under the image."

Annie shrugged. "So its real title is...?"

Jack grinned. "The Treachery of Images."

She shook her head and huffed a shallow chuckle. "Ironic."

Jack nodded. "Yeah... ain't it?"

TEN

Steve stood at the door as it cracked open: a blue eye peered out at him.

"So, am I comin' in… or do I hafta force entry?"

The door opened and the one blue eye paired up with another, revealing a whole face. He was in his late 30's, with sandy brown hair jutting out from a New York Yankees ball cap. The plain tan T-shirt, with a print of the Marine Corps logo square over the chest, tumbled down over his Levis. On a shelf by the television sat a framed picture of him in Marine formals, the flag curling behind him. They said nothing, but did that quick don't-let-any-of-the-other-guys-see-us-hug-and-slap-on-the-back thing.

"Sittown," Mike instructed. "Thought we weren't getting' together until Saturday." Mike pointed to the refrigerator. "Want one?"

Steve slouched onto the couch. "Not right now. And, yeah, we're still on for Saturday, if that's OK?"

"Saturday's good. Saturday's good. Rachel still comin' with ya? Still good there?"

Steve smiled. "Yeah, still comin.' Still good." He sat up. "But I need something before then."

Mike nodded. "Name it."

Steve wiped his hand down over his mouth. "And on the QT."

Mike tipped his head to one side. "Dude… maybe you've forgotten, but I haven't. You… ahh… saved my life a while back… remember?" Then he pointed back and forth between them, then down at the prosthesis that had become his left leg. "You and me… we're not even here, if that's what you need."

Steve grinned. "Gotta be," sealed with a fist-bump.

Mike positioned his chair directly facing the couch. "Talk to me."

Steve took out his Droid and brushed it a few times. "Did you watch Boalt's press conference tonight?"

Mike nodded. "You mean the gang-hug? Only way to avoid that was to watch the Sham-Wow channel. More entertainment value. But, yeah, I watched it."

"So you know about this.... this new essay they've found..."

"Yeah. Some new Federalist essay?" He raised his eyebrows. "Ahhh... is that... what this... non-discussion is about...?"

Steve shrugged. "Could be."

Mike grinned. "Really?" He nodded. "So your boss is interested? Onto something?"

Steve nodded. "She's got the blaze in the belly, OK."

Mike's grin matured into a smile. "Cool. What do you need?"

Steve motioned him over to his computer as he held his Droid up. "Pull me up something. Is there not some site where you can find who owns a website? And what the website's... whatta they call it... UM...?"

"URL?" Mike sat down in front of the monitor. "Of course." A few keystrokes later, he was at a directory site. "There. What's the site's name?"

"Tangello25.com."

He typed it in, and up came: "Sorry, page cannot be found."

Mike looked up at Steve, who stood behind his chair. "No soap."

Steve nodded. "OK, here's the fun part. Back in August, there was, in fact, a website with that name."

"A website, or a server?"

"Umm... whatever they use to send and receive e-mails."

"So was it a dual-mode site?"

"Dual mode?"

"Could you access the website on the Internet and also send and receive e-mail messages?"

Steve shrugged. "Don't know. All I know is that an e-mail message was received by a researcher last month and one thing led to another... ending up with this new essay being discovered..."

"OK, the site... the address had e-mail capacity anyway then?"

"Yes."

Mike tapped out a few commands on his keyboard, then moved and right-clicked the wireless mouse: a model metal Humvee painted camo and decorated with Marine decals. "Still no soap. Not there. Gone."

Steve leaned closer to the monitor. "How would it go away?"

Mike glanced up at him. "The most likely way it could go bye-bye is for someone to remove it."

Steve's forehead dove into a frown. "And when might that have happened?"

Mike turned back to the monitor and began another series of commands, interspersed with a move of the mouse, a left-click here, a right double click there... an error message... an override... and up popped a spreadsheet screen with hundreds of numbers and letters scattered across the lined matrix. A few more taps on the keyboard... a positioning of the cursor... a left click..."

"Well, it looks like your tangello25.com was still operating as of last week, but sometime around... ummm... six days ago.... actually, a hundred fifty-six hours twenty-two minutes ago... it was taken down."

Steve frowned. "By whom?"

Mike shook his head. "Can't tell, other than it was apparently by someone... or by some remote activated computer... here in the D.C. Metro area."

"How can you tell that?"

Mike smiled. "I got ways. This search app can do some pretty... cool things, but tracking the exact computer where the kill command originated... especially with the gazillion mobile devices now in use... it gets pretty complicated." Then he pointed at some numbers on the screen. "But the command seems to have originated from somewhere in Georgetown. Like between 4:30 and 4:45 AM last... what... Tuesday before last?"

"You're sure?"

Mike offered that "you're kidding, right?" look.

Steve frowned again. "OK, let's see how good you really are. Any way of telling what the last message was?"

Now Mike frowned. "So... you want me to produce the body of the last message on a server that is no longer up? From this computer here?," he gestured toward the monitor.

Steve nodded. "Yup."

Mike exhaled, then turned back to the screen. Yet another series of mouse/cursor moves, clicks, shift'F4s, more taps, more cursor moves... then another screen appeared: "Enter username: ********; enter password: ********." Mike complied, leading to another spreadsheet with more numbers and dates. One of the entries appeared in turquoise font.

"Whooooo," Mike muttered. "Whatta we got here?" He leaned closer to the screen and magnified the font. "Ummmm... interesting..."

Steve recalled their service in Afghanistan. Tippett had a ton of idiosyncrasies, but one that stuck out was the habit of interjecting "interesting" whenever something really weird or unexplainable appeared.

Steve tapped him on the shoulder. "You know I hate it when you say that, don't you? It makes me nervous."

Mike nodded. "Well... what do you want me to say? All looks copacetic?" He turned and looked up at Steve. "Whatever messages were sent to or received from that site... server... whatever it was... they never went through an intermediary server." He looked back at the screen. "The messages were either direct transfers or hidden parasitic messages that 'rode' on other legitimate messages, then 'hopped' off when they passed the receiving or sending computer."

Steve frowned deeply. "How can that happen?"

Mike looked up again, and paused. "I have no idea," he finally admitted. He started shaking his head slowly. "I do know one thing though. There's no way of hacking into the intermediary server or the crypto-computer itself to extract information." He sat back in his chair. "It's the ultimate firewall." He looked up at Steve. "These guys are good. Really good."

He leaned in toward the screen, squinting at it.

"Now this," he pointed to the turquoise information on the screen "tells me that no traceable intermediary server was used." Mike nodded at the screen, but spoke for Steve's benefit. "There are a lot of details and variations on the theme, but the most common method for transferring e-mail messages between and among computers is called SMTP... simple mail transfer protocol."

"OK," Steve offered, faking his understanding.

"If you are hooked into an internal network... like in an office or a retail store, with no external Internet connection, then direct transfers of e-mail between one computer and another on the network don't need an external server to store and relay the messages. You just do it.... like an electronic intercom."

Steve tilted his head. "And?"

"And this," he pointed at the turquoise data again, "... this tells me that even though the computers were not part of a dedicated network, the e-mails acted like they were, but leaving no SMTP server trail."

Steve pulled a chair up and sat next to Mike. "OK... but... I got a question..."

Mike nodded, but continued concentrating on the monitor. "Shoot."

"You say the site... or server... or whatever... evaporated, what, six days ago...?

"Yeah. Sometime early last Tuesday morning."

Steve paused. "You're sure?"

Mike tipped his head slightly, then offered the "you're kidding, right?" look again.

"OK, OK. But if someone went to the trouble of setting this system up in the first place, then dismantled it last week, and the e-mail to Clark took place last August...."

"Yeah...?"

Steve stared at the monitor. "What happened on the site between last month and last Tuesday...?"

Mike registered the question with a slight frown, then turned to Steve. "Interesting. Interesting question."

ELEVEN

Annie held her iPhone up, pointing it at the speaker on the radio. She watched the screen dance around as the device thought its way around the notes, then up came the answer: "Muddy Water Home by Leftover Salmon (Euphoria)." She thought: amazing. Unbelievably amazing. Want to know the name of that song you're hearing? Don't know the performer? Don't know the title? No problem: let the app find it for you.

She adjusted her chair and tilted the monitor down slightly, so that it was more perpendicular to her line of sight. Where to start, where to start? She typed into the search box: "Antesar O'Hara." The screen went white and the processing box filled with one green bar. Then a second green bar. Then, after perhaps ten seconds, a third green bar. Then.... nothing. Annie moved the cursor over the processing box; the little hourglass appeared, emptied, turned over and repeated its routine. Well, she thought, at least the search is continuing... but why was it taking so long? This was a Justice Department attorney with a turbocharger bolted on, so why wasn't there a quickly revealed trail?

She minimized the screen and opened up another Internet portal. She typed into the search box: "The Federalist" Where is it... where is it...? Her eyes scanned the list down. Thomas dot gov? There it is. She clicked and was whisked to the U.S. Library of Congress legislative website, Thomas.gov. Then a left click on "more historical documents." Then "primary documents" and the "find" box. She typed in "The Federalist." Boom... first one to show up on the search results list: http://www.loc.gov/rr/program/bib/ourdocs/federalist.html.

It had been a long time since she had even thought about the essays, much less read them. Another click brought her to the html table of contents. She reviewed the screen. "Federalist No. 1. Title: 'General Introduction.' Author: 'Hamilton.' Publication:

'For the Independent Journal.' Date: blank. She clicked on the link to Federalist No. 1, and shortly: "To the People of the State of New York: AFTER an unequivocal experience of the inefficiency of the subsisting federal government, you are called upon to deliberate on a new Constitution for the United States of America." And on and on....

She scrolled down, trying to catch important words which could lead to important concepts. Empire. Emolument. Ambition. Avarice. Tyrants. Ooooo... "tyrants," she thought, what's that about? She went to the complete sentence:

"History will teach us that the former has been found a much more certain road to the introduction of despotism than the latter, and that of those men who have overturned the liberties of republics, the greatest number have begun their career by paying an obsequious court to the people; commencing demagogues, and ending tyrants."

Wow, she thought: talk about timely. But there were other tasks; she glanced at the digital time in the lower right corner: 11:56 PM. She minimized the Thomas.gov screen and Federalist No. 1, and went back to the Internet to search for Antesar O'Hara: the screen displayed 1 result out of 1 and asked: "Did you mean 'Antes O'Hara'?"

No, she did not mean that... stupid search engine. She typed it again: "Antesar O'Hara." And waited... and waited. Then... same result. Odd. Well, if the buzz on the 'net was this new essay, the engines will have posted a ton by now... so... she typed in "Federalist 86."

"Whoa," she muttered as the page came up: the first entry prioritized by the search engine proprietors was not the New York Times or the Washington Post, but instead the website for... the White House, and indicating as a new item the existence of "Federalist 86" somewhere on the site. She smiled to herself and wondered how much money and how many phone calls and e-mails it had taken to the ISP maintaining the search engine to get that item driven to the top. A lot, or not many, she thought.

She clicked on the link, which brought up the familiar oval framing the north portico of the building. Then came the posting from the White House press office:

'Today, before a Senate subcommittee convened to delve into the recent discovery of another in the series of our nation's founding documents, The Federalist Papers, testimony was taken revealing that a final essay in that series, Federalist 86, was found last week. While additional testimony is scheduled to take place, the existence of this extraordinary document further completes the historical foundations of the republic. Federalist 86 appears to have been written by Alexander Hamilton and addresses issues which at the time of the republic's founding might have been considered tangential to the creation of the framework of the constitution, but which today shed new light on the intent of the Founding Fathers. The discovery of this essay, and its importance, cannot be overstated. To view an image of the document, click here."

Really? she thought. Here we are, not one day past the announcement of the essay's existence, and already the White House has a digitized copy posted on the Internet? She clicked "here" and was whisked to a JPEG image. Sure enough, right at the top, there it was: 'Federalist 86   June 8, 1788.' Amazing, she thought. She began reading the image on the monitor:

"To the People of the State of New York.

"When last the multitudinous issues attending the completion of the collections of these papers were addressed, through your humble servant Publius, but with the sage counsel and confidences of the like-minded, yet not without the trepidations customarily and normally attendant upon matters of such gravity, the singular issue of the qualifications and eligibility of the Chief Magistrate and President of the United States was considered, a series of later-perceived questions and issues surfaced."

Yikes, she thought: they actually spoke and wrote like that back then? Complete sentences and coherent thoughts are important, but if language is incomprehensible, what good is it? She continued, word after anachronistic word, sentence after convoluted sentence, all discussing the issue of eligibility from the perspective of two centuries ago. Cantor was right, she thought.... this was all starting to look just a little bit too convenient...

She kept reading – more like trying to run in water, the words were so labored, so archaic. "...preliminary observations would appear to be in order... womb of the experiment... vigor of government is essential to the security of liberty... commencing demagogues, ending tyrants...."

Wait a second.... wait... just... one... second.... she squinted at the monitor and frowned at the JPEG image:

"History will teach us that the former has been found a much more certain road to the introduction of despotism than the latter, and that of those men who have overturned the liberties of republics, the greatest number have begun their career by paying an obsequious court to the people; commencing demagogues, and ending tyrants."

She frowned more deeply as she looked up at the address bar for the JPEG: http://www.whitehouse.gov/. She squinted at the title: "Federalist No. 86."

She looked at the bottom of the screen: the minimized address for the Thomas website was still there. She clicked, revealing again the The Federalist text. She peered at the screen: http://www.loc.gov/rr/program/bib/ourdocs/federalist.html, then clicked on Federalist No. 1, and up it popped. She clicked on "edit," and the menu dropped down, ending with "find on this page." Another click produced a "find" searchbox. She quickly mis-typed "tyfants," then clicked "next." Up came "text not found." She clicked OK and quickly saw the error: she slowly typed into the find searchbox "tyrants" and clicked "next" again.

Jackpot, she thought: there it was. "Tyrants" highlighted in blue at the end of the fifth paragraph. She studied the entire paragraph until coming to the sentence beginning "History will teach us... tyrants...." She minimized the site and drew the White House site back up, with its JPEG of Federalist 86. The handwriting was clear and easily read: "History will teach us... commencing demagogues, ending tyrants."

Her eyes bulged at the information and her heart began to race. They were the same, she thought. The two sentences were... exactly... the... same. Her pulse exploded in a rush of adrenaline as she scrambled for her iPhone. She tapped it furiously, then slapped it to her left ear.

"C'mon... come ON," she blurted into the microphone.

"Hey, sissy," Jack's voice finally came through. "That you?"

"Jack... you need... to get over... to my apartment. Now."

"Now?" the iPhone asked. "It's, what, past midnight? Can't it wait until dawn?"

"No, Jack, it cannot wait until dawn. I need you to get dressed and get over to my place as soon as you possibly can."

Jack's voice turned serious. "Annie, are you OK? Is something wrong? Tell me you are OK."

She drew in a deep breath, then exhaled into the phone. The adrenaline was now convulsing her voice. "Yes, Jack... I'm

OK… but please, *please* stop talking and just get over here… I think I've stumbled onto something that… that… just come over… please."

"OK, I'm pulling my shoes on right now, but…. does it have anything to do with what we were talking about last night?"

She paused and looked back at the computer monitor. "It's got everything to do with that. *Everything*."

"Give me eight minutes," Jack asked.

"Make it six," she responded.

"On the way out the door now…" he replied.

She held the iPhone in her left palm and tapped on Steve's speed-dial number. C'mon…. c'mon…

"Annie?" Steve's deep baritone asked.

"Yeah, ummm, Steve…. Where are you now?"

"Crystal City…. over at Mike's trying to figure …"

"OK, please stop what you're doing there and come over to my apartment. Jack's on his way here now. I think I've got something."

"Funny you should say."

"What do you mean?"

"I might have something too."

"Like?"

"Not sure, but Mike's workin' on it. Seems the website address where that Clark guy got contacted from was recently taken down. Gone. Kaput."

"Really," she said.

"Really. And the way Mike tells me the message got sent is even…"

"OK, OK. Look… remember when the senator told us to go deep, but go careful?"

"Sure."

She paused. "I could be wrong… wouldn't be the first time… but I think we may be close to that tangible smoking whatever…"

"What?"

"How soon can you get here?"

"Crystal City to Georgetown… Metro and bus… half-hour, forty-five minutes, tops."

"Well, hop to it. You're not gonna believe what might be goin' down…"

"Any preview of coming attractions?"

She hesitated. "Let's just say tomorrow could be… interesting…."

"OK. Here I come."

TWELVE

Annie looked through the peephole: it was Jack. She disengaged the chain, turned the deadbolt and opened the door.

"Hey," he said as he entered, tossing his cap on the table next to the computer monitor. He looked at Annie, then shrugged his shoulders. "Where is it?"

"What?" she asked.

"Whatta ya mean 'what'? My burger. What else?"

She smiled. "Rain check. Here. I need you to sit down here," she pointed to a folding chair she had positioned next to hers, both facing the computer monitor. He obliged.

She had turned her laptop on and positioned it next to the desktop monitor. On the laptop, she had drawn up the Thomas dot com website and gone to the table of contents for The Federalist. On the desktop, she was at the White House website and the image of the first page of a JPEG image reading at the top: "The Federalist No. 86 June 8, 1788."

Jack leaned forward in his chair, glancing back and forth between the desktop monitor and the laptop. He looked at her. "So... when are you gonna break down and get a Mac...?"

She shook her head. "Someday... not now. Here," she positioned the laptop so that they both could see it better. "OK, follow me here..."

"Don't I always?" he said.

She looked at him. "OK, look, I'm serious here... OK?"

He nodded. "OK."

She looked back at the desktop and the White House JPEG, pointing at it. "All right, this is the image of the new document that they say that researcher... Clark... found the other day at the Library of Congress."

Jack nodded. "OK."

She then pointed over to the laptop. "This," she moved the cursor to the table of contents, then clicked on "No. 1 General Introduction." Up popped: "Federalist No. 1, Hamilton."

She looked at him. "This is the original of Federalist No. 1."

Jack looked back and forth between the two screens, then looked at her. "And?"

She went to the desktop and the White House JPEG of Federalist 86, and scrolled down the image to the bottom of the first page; than maximized the image for an easier read. She pointed at the second paragraph, then slowly continued scrolling down to the last sentence. "There."

Jack stared. "There… what?"

"See the last sentence in that paragraph?"

Jack squinted. "Yes. 'History will teach…'"

"Yes… that one. Read it to the end."

"History will teach… yada yada… men who have overturned… ummm…ahh… commencing demagogues and ending tyrants." He looked up at her.

She said nothing, but directed his attention over to the laptop, where she scrolled down through Federalist No.1 to the fifth paragraph… down… down… then she clicked and highlighted in blue: "…commencing demagogues and ending tyrants."

Jack stared at the highlighted words, then stared back at Annie, then over to the White House JPEG image, then back to the laptop, then back at Annie. "Whoa…. *mama*…"

Annie exhaled deeply. "I haven't had time to go over the whole document… the White House JPEG image… but if my suspicions are correct, what we have here is a… could be… might be a… counterfeit."

Jack kept staring at the laptop and the blue-highlighted sentence; then he looked over again at the JPEG on the desktop.

"Sissy...," he began, "you may have found the answer here...." He looked at her. "But you gotta be sure."

She nodded "That's why you're here."

"So how do we do it?" he asked.

She looked back at the JPEG. "OK, if, in fact this White House image is a combination cut and paste... some original wording by somebody, and some just cut-and-paste sections from the real Federalist papers... there may well be other instances."

Jack nodded. "So, like, maybe they had to bulk up the forgery with actual language from the real essays to make it sound more authentic. Or meet some quota?"

She looked at him. "Or deadline..."

Jack nodded "Could be... who knows?"

She looked back at the White House image of the document on her monitor and Jack squinted at the laptop screen. "So...," he began, "if you were intent on forging something having to do... with proving or supporting your argument that you were, in fact, eligible to serve as president under the Constitution..., but knowing that you weren't... where might you look in the real Federalist Papers... for already existing language...?"

He looked at Annie; she reached over and scrolled down the Federalist table of contents on the laptop to: Federalist No. 67. The Executive Department. Hamilton. She clicked the link, producing the text of the essay. "From the New York Packet. Tuesday, March 11, 1788."

"What's 'The New York Packet'?" Jack asked the screen.

Annie responded. "It was one of the newspapers in New York where the essays were published after they were written."

She looked over to the White House JPEG, then back to the laptop, quickly trying to spot similar words or capital letters as a fingerprint of a cut and paste. Jack replicated her motions. Two minutes later, nothing.

She went back to the table of contents and scrolled down to the next essay "Federalist No. 68. The Mode of Electing the President. From the New York Packet Friday, March 14, 1788."

Both she and Jack again began going back and forth between the JPEG and Federalist 68, looking for cut and paste fingerprints. A capital letter. A peculiar word.

"Whoa…" Jack blurted.

"What?"

"Check it out. In the fourth paragraph down, the word 'several' and the word 'one' are all in capital letters. See?" he pointed to the laptop. "Is that duplicated anywhere in the JPEG image?

She scrolled down the first page. "Nothing." Then the second page. "Nothing." Then the third page. Her head jerked back from the screen; Jack looked over at the image. The words "SEVERAL" and "ONE" stood out like a couple of sore thumbs.

"OK," Jack said, "Go to the beginning of the sentence… or no, beginning of the paragraph where those words appear in the White House image. She scrolled up, and began reading aloud from the image "… it was also peculiarly desirable…"

Jack looked at the laptop image of Federalist 68 and finished the sentence for her "… to afford as little opportunity for tumult and disorder."

Annie continued from the Federalist 86 JPEG image. "This evil was not…"

Jack continued from the laptop "… least to be dreaded in the election of a magistrate…" He paused.

She picked up where he left off "… who was to have so important an agency in the administration of the government…," she looked at her brother.

He finished the sentence "… as the president of the United States."

They looked at each other, the silence growing uncomfortably long. Finally, Annie exhaled as if to avoid passing out. "This is… this is…."

Jack finished. "Spit it out." He pointed at the White House image on the desktop. "This is treason. At minimum it is treasonous." He looked at her. "And if Boalt or any of his stooges are implicated, then if this ain't grounds for impeachment, nothing is."

Annie shook her head. "But we've got to be sure. Not 99.9999 percent sure. We need to be one hundred point zero zero zero sure." She looked at him. "You said so."

Jack nodded. "I did say that. Yes, I did."

"So," she looked at the clock at the bottom of the desktop screen: 1:17 AM. "We've got at least another four… maybe five hours to see if there are other fingerprints here," she gestured at the White House image on the desktop, "to get us… to get my boss to that level of certainty. She will be putting everything on the line here if we're right, and she calls them on it. And if we're wrong, she's toast."

She looked at his right eye. "You with me?"

Jack nodded. "Oh yeah, sissy…. yeah." He dipped his chin. "Can I say 'arrrrgghhh?'"

She shook her head. "Not yet. Maybe later… but not yet."

The two then began pointing back and forth between the two computer screens, highlighting this word or that sentence, typing words into the Thomas Federalist website searchbox, scrolling up and down on the JPEG image and the Thomas Federalist table of contents. To the untrained eye, it could have appeared that they were actually having fun.

THIRTEEN

Brown cracked the gavel down on the strike plate. "Order. Please come to order." The crowd noise faded into a quite pool of whispers and the frequency of the strobes stretched out. "Thank you. Thank you. This continuation of the Federalist 86 select subcommittee hearing which convened yesterday will come to order and the proceedings will begin... after I make a most regrettable announcement..."

The pool of roomful whispers sucked into silence.

"About an hour ago, I received word that one of the witnesses from yesterday's session was involved in a serious automobile accident last night. She has been severely injured and is now in a Metro Area hospital about to go into surgery. Antesar O'Hara will thus unavoidably be unable to attend today's session."

Senator Cantor raised her hand; strobes popped everywhere.

"The chair recognizes Senator Cantor."

Cantor positioned her microphone. "Mr. Chairman, if the chair knew of this event an hour ago, why weren't the other members of the subcommittee notified of this development before now?"

Brown creased his patented gaze of sarcasm toward her. "First, e-mails were sent to all subcommittee members' staff as soon as the news was confirmed. Second, while Ms. O'Hara will not be able to attend, the Justice Department is sending someone equally-versed in the issues surrounding Mr. Clark's discovery... the Federalist 86 discovery... to testify. Third, as you can see, Mr. Clark is sitting at the witness table and will be available to take questions." Brown removed his glasses and stared at her. "So you see, senator, the hearing can proceed. All right?"

Cantor repositioned her microphone. "Mr. Chairman, I am saddened to hear of Ms. O'Hara's injuries. I'm sure she is in all of our thoughts and that she enjoys a speedy and full recovery. But as to her substitute, may I ask who that might be?"

Brown nodded. "If your question is who *will* that person be, yes, you may ask. And the answer is Charles Fitzpatrick. The Attorney General of the United States."

With that announcement, the back door to the hearing room opened, and in strode Fitzpatrick, complete with bituminous coal patent Baker Blacks, an impeccably-tailored deep anthracite and ivory pinstripe Armani two-button and a solid neon scarlet tie. And matching breast pocket square kerchief. He maneuvered down the aisle as if it were his runway.

A fusillade of strobes washed over him as he and his flanking aides walked toward the witness table. He sat down at the table and nodded at Senator Brown, as if to grant the chairman permission to proceed. He was tall and lean, in his mid-forties and had that pasty-bleached look of an academic litigator deigning to offer his testimony for consumption by the serfs of the legislative branch. He could have passed for Ichabod Crane, but without the charm.

Cantor could feel a shallow grin beginning to crease over her mouth; she intercepted it with a sip of water from a plastic tumbler that sat before her.

Brown moved his microphone closer to his mouth. "Given the unfortunate accident that has occurred, and with Ms. O'Hara now hospitalized, the Attorney General has taken time out from his other duties to be with us here today and to offer whatever insight and additional explanations that might otherwise have come from his employee, Ms. O'Hara." Brown paused and glanced at Cantor. "Would that meet with your approval, Senator Cantor?"

Cantor leaned into her mike. "Yes, senator.... it will..." she said, looking over at Fitzpatrick and thinking to herself: 'this will be good.'

"Fine," Brown replied, "then let's get started." He looked at Fitzpatrick and hesitated, trying to decide whether to subject him to the oath – it was common knowledge throughout the District that Fitzpatrick was an agnostic – or not.

Fitzpatrick came to the chair's rescue. "It's fine, senator. Go ahead...," he rumbled in a deep bass, standing up as he raised his right hand.

Brown jumped at the opportunity. "Do you swear... or affirm... that the testimony you give here today will be the truth, the entire truth and nothing but the truth?"

Fitzpatrick nodded and smiled. "I do so..." he tossed a glance at Cantor, "... affirm." She thought to herself: an agnostic is merely an atheist hedging his bets. And, next to Boalt, Fitzpatrick was hedger-in-chief.

Brown looked at the Attorney General. "For the record, would you please state your name?"

"Charles Allen Fitzpatrick."

"And your occupation?"

"I am by training a lawyer. I currently serve as Attorney General of the United States."

"And you were appointed by...?"

Fitzpatrick offered up a puzzled "are-you-serious" look. "President Boalt." Fitzpatrick leaned forward in his chair, toward Brown. "And I am proud to serve him."

Brown nodded; strobes flashed; shutters clicked.

"And Ms. O'Hara is your employee?" Brown asked.

"She is, and a most valued one at that. I am greatly troubled by her accident and I will do all that I can to help with her recovery." He grasped his microphone between his thumb and index finger. "I need her back on the job."

Brown nodded. "And are you familiar with the issue at hand here, and with the testimony Ms. O'Hara and Mr. Clark offered yesterday?"

Fitzpatrick nodded. "I am indeed. In fact, Ms. O'Hara and I worked together on the amicus brief filed yesterday in the *Locke* case. I also met with her on numerous occasions over the past few days following the announcement of the discovery of Federalist 86 as she prepared for her testimony before your subcommittee. Yes, I am quite familiar with the issues and with her testimony here yesterday as well as that of Mr. Clark." He turned and looked at Clark, who was sitting in the audience. "Extraordinary discovery, Mr. Clark. Congratulations," he offered.

"So you've read the transcript of both Ms. O'Hara's and Mr. Clark's testimony?"

"And watched the videotape of the hearing as well," Fitzpatrick responded, turning his attention back to Brown.

"Then let me ask you, Mr. Fitzpatrick, if you would be prepared to answer some questions from other members of this subcommittee?"

"Absolutely." He grasped the microphone. "President Boalt himself told me this morning…"

"This morning?" Brown interrupted.

Fitzpatrick nodded. "Yes. At breakfast. In the White House… he instructed me to come up to the Hill and answer any questions which you… or other subcommittee members might have." He flung another glance at Cantor, then looked back at Brown. "Any at all."

Cantor recalled the old but wise Chinese admonition: be careful what you wish for, as you just might get it.

Brown smiled, then looked at Cantor and bobbed his head. "Senator, do you have any questions of Attorney General Fitzpatrick?"

Cantor returned the smile. "Mr. Chairman, as you might suspect, I do. Yes, indeed…. I do."

"Then please proceed," Brown replied, turning his microphone aside.

"Thank you, Mr. Chairman." She looked over at Fitzpatrick: he had bent his mouth into a cross between a condescending smirk and a slit of contempt. She grinned and took another small sip of water from the plastic tumbler in front of her.

"Mr. Fitzpatrick, I…"

"Yes?" he interrupted.

She began again. "Mr. Fitzpatrick, before we get into the substance of the topic before the subcommittee, I'd like some clarification on a couple of things you said a moment ago, after the Chairman swore you in."

"You mean after I affirmed that I would tell the truth?"

Cantor smiled. "I apologize. Yes, after that affirmation."

Fitzpatrick nodded. "Absolutely. I'm pleased to clarify whatever you did not understand…" he allowed the insult to dribble from his mouth. His grin disappeared.

Cantor nodded. "Yes, thank you so much. You said a moment ago that you chatted with the president this morning over these events… the discovery of this essay," she glanced over at the document in its case propped up in front of Senator Brown, "is that right?"

Fitzpatrick nodded. "Correct. I went over the transcript of yesterday's testimony with him… and, yes, he was pleased."

"Pleased?"

Fitzpatrick fondled his microphone. "Yes… as in 'finally this nonsense over the eligibility question may be over.'"

Cantor nodded. "Apart from the fact that such may be a premature conclusion…" she allowed the suggestion to drift, "can we assume therefore that he is familiar with the contents of the essay?"

Fitzpatrick frowned. "Federalist 86? Is that what you mean?"

Cantor nodded again. "Yes, that…"

"Yes, senator, he is familiar with it. Fact is, it has become an instant favorite of his before bedtime. He keeps a copy on his nightstand."

The ripple of media and staffer laughter splashed around the room, then quickly subsided. Cantor positioned her microphone. "So it would be safe to assume, would it not, that he agrees with the conclusion set out in the essay?"

Fitzpatrick grinned. "There are several conclusions set out, Senator Cantor. Which one... or ones... do you mean?"

"Well, I suspect the one with which he would be most infatuated..."

Senator Brown interrupted "Senator Cantor, please. You are talking about the president of the United States. Please keep that in mind."

Cantor glanced at Brown. "Mr. Chairman... let me assure you... the fact that we are talking about the president of the United States is foremost in my mind. And I thank *you*." She looked back at Fitzpatrick. "The conclusion, Mr. Attorney General, to which I refer is the main conclusion.... the one suggesting that, in order for a person to qualify as a 'natural born citizen' under the Constitution, all that one need do is win the election.

"On the assumption that the candidate's background and qualifications, including his birthplace and the citizenship of his parents, will have been exhaustively examined beforehand, the mere fact that he... or she... has been elected will alone suffice to establish... somehow... eligibility to serve as a natural born citizen." She gripped her microphone between her thumb and index finger. "That one. After all, that is what the document says, doesn't it? Do you agree with that conclusion? Does he agree with that conclusion?"

Fitzpatrick leaned forward in his chair and grinned. "With respect, senator, I don't believe the essay 'suggested' that conclusion. Instead, it stated that conclusion, and, I might add, in fairly plain and straightforward English. And, yes, last time I checked, President Boalt did indeed agree with the conclusion."

"So that would have been at breakfast at the White House... this morning?

Fitzpatrick nodded. "Between the poached Araconda eggs Benedict and the grapefruit sections...yes."

Cantor bobbed her head. "Yes. Thank you. Now..."

Brown interrupted again. "Do you have some questions more pertinent to the issues, senator?"

Cantor looked at him. "Senator, I'm just getting started. And yes, I have a number of additional questions."

"Well," Brown said, "please remember that not only are you talking *about* the president of the United States, you are speaking *to* the Attorney General of the United States. And while you may not agree with everything that he says or even with his politics, please try to maintain the respect owed by the Senate and this subcommittee to him as the nation's chief law enforcement officer."

Cantor again grasped her microphone between her thumb and index finger. "I thank the Chairman for the admonition and can assure both him and the witness, as Attorney General, that I will accord to him all the deference due him and his office."

"Thank you," Brown replied. "Please go ahead."

"Thank you, Mr. Chairman." She brought her new iPad up from her document case and activated it, then looked up at Fitzpatrick. "Mr. Fitzpatrick, you also stated a while ago that, as Attorney General of the United States, and having been appointed by the president to that position and confirmed by the Senate, it was your pleasure to serve... the president."

Fitzpatrick nodded. "I did. I repeat that statement now."

"But you are not the president's personal attorney, are you?"

"Of course not," Fitzpatrick snapped. "He has internal White House counsel and entire private law firms doing that."

Cantor tilted her head. "Well, then, as the nation's chief law enforcement officer, and not the president's personal attorney, is it not better stated that it is your pleasure to serve the people of the United States?"

Brown reached for his microphone, but Fitzpatrick raised a hand to stop him from saying anything in response.

"Mr. Chairman, Senator Cantor," Fitzpatrick droned, "let us try to put this session on a professional level, and agree that we have decidedly different political philosophies and ideas about how laws and the policies behind those laws are effectuated and implemented. But I think we can accomplish more here if we can agree to disagree... and do so without rancor and sarcasm. I hope that puts us... ummm... so to speak... on the same page."

Cantor nodded. "It does indeed."

"Good. So, yes, the answer to your question is that it is my distinct pleasure to serve all American citizens... and all residents too... including President Boalt...." He allowed the response to trail off into silence, but the innuendo was lost on approximately zero people in the room.

Cantor repositioned her microphone. "But just to clarify, to make sure I understand, when you stated earlier that President Boalt instruct.... ummm... asked you to come here this morning after Ms. Antesar's accident, it was with the understanding that you would be prepared to answer any and all questions relating to the issue at hand, that is, his eligibility to serve as president under the Constitution. Is that right?"

"Well," Fitzpatrick replied, "if by 'eligibility to serve' you mean in light of the new essay Federalist 86....?" He waited for a reply.

"Yes. That is what I mean," Cantor responded

"Then the answer is yes. And not only 'yes,' a categorical 'yes.' He is, of course, prepared to await any decision in the *Locke* case which might come from the Supreme Court, but as far as this hearing goes, it is basically 'take your best shot.'" He took a sip of water, then produced a wide grin. "And to that point, I am authorized to tell you, that while he feels absolutely no compulsion to do so, and while he believes that the hounding he has endured up to now over his desire to preserve what small sliver of privacy remains in his life is both childish as well as detestable, it is his intention to release all of his original birth records in the next few days."

With that, Fitzpatrick reached into his left suit jacket inside pocket and withdrew a white envelope. As if on cue, the hearing attendees inhaled deeply and the rattle of shutters and blinking of strobe flashes burst through the room. Fitzpatrick held the envelope up: even from a distance, the White House logo-seal was unmistakable.

"This," he said as he handed it to a subcommittee intern for delivery to Brown "is a letter to the Chairman expressing thanks for the disclosures and revelations that will come from this hearing and, to reiterate, expressing his intent to disclose all of his original birth records – despite the clear weight of authority that he is under no obligation to do so – in the hope that, once and for all, the issue of his citizenship and eligibility to serve as president of this, the greatest nation in the world, can be put to rest.

"And put to rest independently as well as separate and apart from what appears to be clear and convincing evidence that the Founding Fathers would have agreed was required. There are far too many other pressing matters commanding his attention than the adolescent distractions being fomented by some in our society."

Brown looked at him over the lenses of his glasses. "The birthers?"

Fitzpatrick shrugged. "That is what some call them. We in the administration prefer the more clinical term 'misinformed.' In a free county, people can believe what they choose to believe, facts to the contrary notwithstanding."

The intern navigated around the reporters in front of the witness table and dais, and handed the envelope to Senator Brown, who opened it and removed the one-page letter. He scanned it, nodding as his eyes swept through the sentences, downward through the three short paragraphs. He looked up. "Thank you, Mr. Attorney General," he said, "and please convey my thanks to the president for his candor." He turned to the intern. "Please make copies of this for the members of the subcommittee and for anyone else desiring one." The intern disappeared through a door in back of the dais.

Brown turned to Senator Cantor. "Senator?"

"Yes, Mr. Chairman. Thank you." Cantor tapped the iPad, and up came the first message from Annie. She looked back at Fitzpatrick.

"Mr. Attorney General, you've indicated... stated that you've read the essay, as has President Boalt, several times and have concluded that it expresses the intent of the founders regarding a president's eligibility in terms of his status as a 'natural born citizen,' correct?"

"Correct."

"And that the president's eligibility should be, in the end, determined not by whether he is a 'natural born citizen' under standards at that time recognized by legal writers? Like Dr. Vattel, as noted yesterday by Ms. O'Hara, correct?"

Fitzpatrick nodded. "Correct. I believe the intent of the Founders is better articulated by Alexander Hamilton as we now see it addressed in Federalist 86 than by a Swiss legal philosopher."

"I see," Cantor continued. "So I assume you believe that, instead, the issue is better determined by whether someone who is running for the office of the president has received the most number of votes from those who have wanted to elect him, right?"

Fitzpatrick frowned. "Well, no... not exactly. The way I read Federalist 86 is that it *defines* the Framers' intended meaning of the term 'natural born citizen' to be the end result of the examination of the candidate's citizenship status *prior* to being elected and that, if the candidate in fact gets elected, that means that those who have elected him have also declared him to be a 'natural born citizen.' They have, in effect, ratified the pre-existing presumption that he is constitutionally eligible by electing him."

Cantor frowned. "But... isn't that a bootstrap argument?"

Fitzpatrick returned the frown. "Bootstrap? Not at all. If the people, by electing a person after having had an opportunity to fully examine the facts of the person's birth history..." he hesitated and looked down at his folded hands.

"Yes?" Cantor stabbed, before he could amend his words.

Fitzpatrick looked up. "Federalist 86 says that the intent of the founders was to place the ultimate, non-reviewable decision upon who is... and who is not... a 'natural born citizen' into the hands of the electorate, and nowhere else. *Nowhere* else."

Cantor nodded. "Yes. But as you were saying just a moment ago, it also says that this process is based on the assumption that the electorate... *before* any election... has had... I believe your words were '...an opportunity to fully examine the facts of the person's birth history...' Is that right?"

Fitzpatrick paused, apparently sensing what was coming next. "Yes."

Cantor removed her glasses and stared at the witness. "Mr. Fitzpatrick, can we agree that the Constitution requires that one of the unalterable constitutional preconditions to being eligible to serve as president is that the person be at least thirty-five years old?"

Fitzpatrick nodded. "Yes... we can."

"And so if someone, say, twenty-nine years old runs and is elected... can he or she serve?

"Of course not."

"Why not?"

"Because twenty-nine does not equal thirty-five, as required by the Constitution."

She nodded. "OK. So I assume we can also agree that another requirement is that the person, apart from the citizenship issue, must have been a resident of the United States for at least fourteen years prior to taking office?"

Fitzpatrick nodded again. "Yes. Article Two, Section One, Clause Five."

"So if the person running first moved here from, say, London nine years before running and getting elected, that would be a disqualifier too, right?"

Fitzpatrick nodded. "Right."

"And finally, that the person must also be a 'natural born citizen,' right?"

"Correct."

Cantor repositioned her glasses. "And is there anything in this Federalist 86 that would change any of those requirements... like say 'twenty-nine years' instead of 'thirty-five years' or replace the fourteen-year residency requirement with nine years?"

"No. There is not."

Cantor nodded. "So we can agree that the only relevance of this essay to the issues at hand is its discussion of what it says was intended by the words 'natural born citizen'?"

Fitzpatrick nodded. "We can so agree."

Cantor tilted her head. 'So, under this essay, does the cause of action being pursued by Mr. Locke... a *quo warranto* action... no longer exist?"

Fitzpatrick frowned. "What do you mean?"

"I mean that a *quo warranto* action – which seeks a court to order an office-holder to answer the question 'by what authority do you hold the office?' – right?..."

"Right."

"Does your essay do away with that cause of action?"

Fitzpatrick shook his head. "No. First off, it's not 'my' essay... it's Alexander Hamilton's essay. Second, no. All Federalist 86 means is that the question 'by what authority is the office held?' is answered, in the case of the president, by saying 'my election alone is the only authority needed.'"

"Really?"

"Really."

"Absent voter fraud, of course..."

Brown raised his gavel; Fitzpatrick raised his hand. "Of course, absent fraud..."

"And so," Cantor continued, "speaking hypothetically, if a candidate for president affirmatively, but *falsely* asserted... prior to the election... that he or she was eligible as a natural born citizen, and was elected, but later it was discovered that he or she was *not*, in fact, a natural born citizen... this essay would not change that fact... would it?"

Fitzpatrick shook his head. "As I said, no court in the land would uphold that election, with or without this essay. Courts should not be complicit in the perpetration or perpetuation of frauds, especially those committed upon the electorate." He leaned toward her, nearly swallowing his microphone and boomed the words into it: "Because that would be *wrong*...."

Cantor glanced at the iPad, then back at him. "Well, is it then your opinion that, against the backdrop of what you say this new essay...."

Fitzpatrick interrupted. "It is an old essay. It is only newly-discovered."

Cantor grinned. "Semantics aside, is it your opinion that, prior to Mr. Boalt's election, the electorate was afforded an opportunity to fully... let me emphasize that word... your word... *fully* examine the facts underlying his birth history?"

Fitzpatrick repositioned his microphone. "Yes. Yes, I do."

A deep crease bent Cantor's forehead. "Had he released his original birth certificate prior to the election, so that all could examine it?"

Fitzpatrick smiled. "His birth certificate is posted on the Internet. More people have seen that birth certificate than the ones of all of the other presidents combined."

Cantor persisted. "Perhaps you did not understand my question, so I'll repeat it."

"Thank you," he sneered.

Cantor dipped her gaze at him. "Would it help you if I used simpler, smaller, words?"

Brown discharged a crack of the gavel. "Senator... remember my admonition... this is the Attorney General of the United States."

Cantor nodded. "Oh... I'm well aware of that, Mr. Chairman. *Well* aware." She turned her attention back to the witness. "Prior to the election, had the president released the *original* of his long-form Missouri Department of Vital Records birth certificate, as opposed to offering up a picture of an abstracted document posted as an image on the Internet? Yes or no?"

Fitzpatrick smiled again. "Well, if you mean..."

Cantor interrupted. "Let me help you. The answer is no. He did not."

Fitzpatrick shook his head. "He did not believe that was necessary, because all of the information needed to establish his status as a 'natural born citizen' was available on the certificate that he broadcasted to the world on the Internet."

Cantor raised her eyebrows. "Really?"

Fitzpatrick bobbed his head. "Really."

Cantor tilted her head. "All right, let's test that contention."

"Let us do that."

"All right. Where was the president born?"

"St. Louis, Missouri."

"Let us assume that is correct."

"Thank you."

"OK. Who was his father?"

"Abraham Boalt."

"Correct again."

"Thanks again."

"And who was his mother?"

"Chelsea Chandler-Boalt."

139

"Good. Three out of three…"

Fitzpatrick smiled. "Not bad for a beginner, huh?"

Cantor grinned. "Not bad at all. And all of that information can be gleaned from the certificate posted on the Internet?"

"Yes." He reached into his inside coat pocket and extracted a folded piece of paper, which he held up. "It's where I got it. Would you like a copy?"

Cantor shook her head. "Not really… but I have a couple of other questions."

"Of course." He dropped the folded copy to the table.

"Where was Abraham Boalt born?"

Fitzpatrick frowned. "Pardon?"

She spoke slowly, as instructed. "Where… was… the… president's… father…, Abraham Boalt…, born?"

Fitzpatrick picked up the copy from the table, opened it, and began scanning it. "It doesn't say."

Cantor nodded. "And what was his father's citizenship?"

Fitzpatrick frowned again. "Ahhh… I'm not sure…" he scanned the copy of the birth certificate he had brought to the hearing. "Ummm… the United States. He was a United States citizen."

"And how do you know that?"

"Well, it's… it's… ahh… common knowledge…"

"But I thought it was common knowledge that Abraham Boalt was born in Madras, India."

"And where do you find that?"

Cantor smiled. "In the autobiography written by the president. Before he ran for office."

Fitzpatrick shook his head. "Well, even if he was born in India, he was probably later naturalized as a U.S. citizen."

"Let's assume that happened too. When did it happen… before or after the president was born?"

Fitzpatrick stared at her silently. "I don't know... but my staff will get that information for you."

"Thank you. So, just to be clear, would you agree that neither his father's birthplace nor his citizenship can be determined from the image of the abstract of the president's birth certificate that he put on the Internet? Is that correct?"

"Well..."

"And if I were to ask you the same questions about his mother, Chelsea-Chandler Bolt, you'd give me the same response, correct?"

"Ummm..."

"And are you aware, Mr. Fitzpatrick, that an original, so-called 'long form' birth certificate from the State of Missouri from the time when the president says he was born there will reveal not only the birthplaces of the child's parents, but also the names... and even the signatures... of the delivering physician and attending nurse? And the parents' occupations? And whether they were married? Are you aware of those facts?"

"No... I was not aware of them. But I don't believe any of that now has any relevance."

"Mr. Fitzpatrick, is it not true that no one... not you... not Chairman Brown... not me can, by just examining the copy of the president's abstracted birth certificate you have there in front of you tell, where his mother or his father was born or what *their* citizenship status was when he was born. Can you?"

Fitzpatrick shifted slightly in his chair. "As I just said, no... but to elaborate, it doesn't matter if the president's parents were citizens or whether they enjoyed that status before or even after he was born. And, by the way, I think you are doing a marvelous job establishing the relevance of Federalist 86, which moots and thus answers all of those questions.

Cantor frowned again. "Mr. Attorney General... I'm not a lawyer... mercifully... but... how does the 'mooting' of a question 'answer' it?"

Fitzpatrick took a sip of water. "Yes, perhaps the word 'answered' is too strong. A better word would be 'resolved.'"

Cantor nodded. "You mean 'resolved' as in 'no further questions allowed'?"

Brown started to raise his gavel, only to lower it as, yet again, Fitzpatrick visually intercepted and restrained him.

Fitzpatrick stared at Cantor. "No, senator. 'Resolved' as in 'no further questions *necessary.*' One is always allowed to *ask* questions, no matter how irrelevant... or inane... they might be. It is still a free country."

Cantor kept nodding. "And so, under your interpretation of the essay, it is *because* the voters have made a decision at the ballot box that, retroactively, the constitutional eligibility of the person winning the election is determined. Right?"

Fitzpatrick shrugged. "Apart from the fraud exception we've discussed, yes, under the seemingly clear language of Federalist 86, I suppose you could jump to that conclusion, yes." He paused. "But I will leave that question to the Supreme Court."

"So the actual birthplace and citizenship status of the winner, as well as the birthplaces of the parents and their citizenship... would no longer matter?"

Fitzpatrick grinned and took his microphone between this thumb and index finger. "Did they ever?"

Cantor leaned forward in her chair. "At one time, they did."

Senator Brown glanced at Cantor. "Do you have more, senator? Is this going anywhere?"

Cantor fired a glance back at him. "Oh, yes, Mr. Chairman.... yes..., I have more."

Brown huffed a sigh. "Well, before we do that, let us take the mid-morning break. This hearing is adjourned for twenty minutes." With that, he slapped the gavel down, stood from his chair, and disappeared through the door behind the dais.

FOURTEEN

Senator Brown cracked his gavel down, producing a room full of quiet anticipation. He looked at Senator Cantor. "Senator, you may proceed."

Cantor directed her attention back at the Attorney General. "So let me get this straight, Mr. Fitzpatrick. According to your testimony here this morning, you now believe that the new... newly-discovered essay articulates the idea that, actual birthplaces and citizenship of the candidate and the candidate's parents aside... and conceding the exception for voter fraud... the mere fact that the person gets elected trumps other notions of what constitutes a 'natural born citizen.' Is that right?"

"No, not exactly. I would not use the word 'trumps.' That term conveys a contentious and adversarial tone. I prefer the term 'ratifies,' because, as Federalist 86 states, the ultimate proof or ratification of the concept of eligibility as a 'natural born citizen' comes as a result of the election itself."

He leaned forward. "And, as I have already stated, even though he is under absolutely no compulsion to do so, the president intends to order the release of all... repeat... *all* of his original birth records in the near future. That is what the letter he gave to me this morning for delivery to Senator Brown states. And it is what he intends to do. And however you want to characterize it... mooting.... resolving... ratifying.... those documents, coupled with what I believe to be the clear expression of the intent of the Founding Fathers, will put an end to these... these... foolish 'eligibility' distractions."

Cantor nodded. "So the president says he will be releasing these papers soon?"

"Yes."

"Why 'soon' as opposed to 'now'?"

Fitzpatrick leaned forward. "Because he is the president. And since he is under no compulsion to do *anything*, my guess is that he alone will decide when he wants to do *something*."

Cantor took a sip of water. "And so, as you read it, if the voters had elected... say... Elvis Presley president, that would mean, under your interpretation of the essay, without anything else, we could have concluded that he was a 'natural born citizen'?"

Fitzpatrick smiled widely. "Well, apart from the fact that the entire world knows he was born in Tupelo, Mississippi... also located within the United States...yes, that's right." He paused. "Although there might be a problem at the inaugural swearing-in..." A smattering of media chuckles rippled through the room.

"So, if I were to tell you that *only* where both the mother and father of a future candidate to the presidency are, at the time the child is born, themselves citizens of the country where the birth takes place... only then can the child be deemed a 'natural born citizen,' would you disagree?"

Fitzgerald lowered his head, glanced at Senator Brown, then fixed his gaze on Cantor. "Before the discovery of Federalist 86, I might have agreed that such a conclusion was not unreasonable. It's what de Vattel contended and even what the Supreme Court suggested in *The Venus* and other cases. But following the discovery of Hamilton's essay, the final one in the Federalist Papers series, yes, I would disagree with that conclusion. The citizenship of the parents is no longer the controlling issue."

Cantor shook her head, then tapped the iPad. She read the text message streaming in from Annie.... then looked up at Fitzpatrick: he was whispering to one of his aides and smiling.

Cantor cleared her throat. "Mr. Fitzpatrick..."

"Yes, senator?"

"I'd like to direct your attention to your copy of the essay. I believe you said you had one?"

An aide handed him his own iPad, which he tapped once, twice, swipe... swipe... "Yes, I do."

"I see that you are viewing an image of the essay on that device, yes?"

"Yes. It is the same as the paper copy. In fact, it is the copy that was posted on the Internet yesterday."

"Ah, yes... on the White House website...?"

He squinted slightly at her. "Correct... as well as everywhere else."

Cantor allowed a small grin to crease over her mouth. "Something like looking at an image of a document posted on the Internet....?"

Fitzpatrick frowned. "I'm not sure I see the humor in that question, senator."

Cantor nodded. "Humor was not intended. Nonetheless, fine. I too am looking at the image from that website... the White House website. So, just to make sure we are... so to speak... 'on the same page'..., does your image show the first page of the document? Are you there?"

"Yes."

"OK. Now, before we get into it, let me ask again... as part of your preparation for today, did you read Mr. Clark's testimony from yesterday? The part where he was confirming the examinations of the document performed by the FBI and the CIA?"

Fitzpatrick looked up from the iPad. "You mean when he testified that the FBI and CIA had confirmed.... as I recall, with absolute, one hundred percent certainty... the authenticity of Federalist 86... is that what you mean?" He smiled.

Cantor returned the smile. "Actually.... no, that's not what I mean."

Fitzpatrick's brow vee'd. "Oh? Then what *do* you mean?"

"What I mean... and the question I'm asking... is whether you remember Mr. Clark testifying that the FBI and CIA had confirmed, with 100% confidence, the authenticity of the *parchment*, as opposed to the text. Do you remember that testimony?"

Fitzpatrick dipped his chin with a derisive 'duh' shrug. "Of course. He said that both agencies had concluded that the document... the parchment... absolutely dated to between 1788 and 1789. Yes."

"And you remember him stating that they also concluded that there was a..., what?... 98-plus percent likelihood that the handwriting was that of Alexander Hamilton? Remember that?"

"Yes. Yes I do. Ninety-eight point eight... say... ninety-nine percent."

"And that there was a 95-plus percent likelihood that the ink used on the parchment originated between 1785 and 1788?"

"Again... yes." Fitzpatrick's frown deepened.

Cantor nodded. "And all of these circumstances, you believe, confirm that this essay is, in fact, a newly-discovered statement by one of the Founding Fathers... Alexander Hamilton... setting forth what they, or at least Hamilton, believed was intended by the term 'natural born citizen' in the new Constitution... yes?"

Fitzpatrick again repositioned his microphone, took a long drink of water then produced an exasperated exhale. "Senator, I think I've been patient here. Actually, more than patient. And I don't mean to sound quarrelsome... I really don't." He leaned forward in his chair. "But I cannot see what more you want from me. Or for that matter, what more you want from the president. He and I are both, as you say, 'on the same page' regarding Federalist 86. And from what I can tell so far, so are millions of other Americans. All of your innuendo and intimations suggesting that, somehow, the president is ineligible to serve this nation as its duly-elected leader are, with respect, going down the drain with the discovery of the essay."

Cantor looked down again at her iPad as it buzzed receipt of another message from Annie, then looked back at Fitzpatrick.

The Attorney General rattled on. "I can understand your disappointment. I can understand the disappointment of the 'bir...' the 'misinformed' and willingly 'uninformed' folks out there who... again with respect..., are more interested in believing what they *want* to believe than in believing what is, in fact, the reality of the situation."

He paused for another sip of water. "But as they say, facts are stubborn things." He sat back in his chair. "So, yes, it is my belief that Federalist 86 stands for the proposition that, in this instance, the president is, by virtue of his election alone, eligible under the Constitution as a 'natural born citizen.' Moreover, I can assure you as well that such is his belief too. Along with the vast majority of rational, thinking Americans."

The camera strobes popped and shutters chirped, then a semblance of quiet returned to the room. Cantor positioned her iPad in front of her. "Mr. Fitzpatrick, I agree. Facts *are* stubborn things and sometimes, reality doesn't quite match up with what we want it to be. But as they say, such is life." She lowered her head and stared over her glasses at the Attorney General. "Accordingly, could I ask you to scroll to the first page of the essay on your iPad? Please?"

Fitzpatrick twitched a quick series of blinks, then glanced down at the iPad and swept his finger up. He looked up at Senator Cantor. "Yes?"

"Directing your attention to the second paragraph... see it?"

Fitzpatrick looked at the iPad image and began reading aloud "It will be forgotten..." He looked up. "That paragraph?"

"Yes, that one. You began reading it... please continue, for the record here."

He looked back down at the device. "It will be forgotten, on the one hand, that jealousy is the usual concomitant of love, and that the noble enthusiasm of liberty is apt to be infected with a

147

spirit of narrow and illiberal distrust." He paused. "Shall I continue?"

Cantor nodded. "Yes... please."

Fitzpatrick looked down at the iPad text. "On the other hand, the vigor of government is essential to the security of liberty; that, in the contemplation of a sound and well-informed judgment, their interest can never be separated; and that a dangerous ambition more often lurks behind the specious mask of zeal for the rights of the people..." he paused, but did not look up, then started reading again "than under the forbidden appearance of zeal for the firmness and efficiency of government."

He paused again and reached for his bottle of water, taking a short sip, then looked up at Cantor. "Would you like me to continue?"

Cantor nodded. "Please."

He looked back down to where he had left off. "History will teach us that the former has been found a much more certain road to the introduction of despotism than the latter, and that of those men who have overturned the liberties of republics, the greatest number have begun their career by paying an obsequious court... to the people; commencing Demagogues, and... ending Tyrants." He stopped and looked up.

Cantor stared at him. "Strong language, would you not agree?"

Fitzpatrick nodded. "Sounds a lot like what Hamilton believed in."

Cantor grinned. "And the passage you've just read, you believe Hamilton wrote it?"

Fitzpatrick nodded again, more forcefully. "Yes. Yes, I do. And I believe the rest of Federalist 86 only fortifies that conclusion."

"Really?" Cantor asked.

"Yes... really," he responded.

Cantor smiled. "Mr. Fitzpatrick, are you familiar with the Library of Congress?"

He frowned and thought: that's a dumb question. "Of course."

"And are you familiar with the Internet legislative service maintained by the Library... Thomas dot com?"

"Yes I am."

"Do you use that site?"

"I have used it frequently, as have the attorneys who serve under me."

"And you consider it accurate? Authoritative?"

He nodded. "Of course. It is maintained by the Chief Librarian himself. Absolutely it is accurate and authoritative."

"Would you please access that site now... on your device?"

Senator Brown interrupted. "May I ask the senator why? This seems to be about as far afield as I am comfortable allowing...."

Fitzpatrick – for the umpteenth time – enjoined further help from the chairman and tapped away at his iPad. "Yes," he muttered to the device, looking up at Cantor. "Got it."

"Good," Cantor said. "Could you please now access the Federalist Papers on that site?"

He tapped and swept and tapped and swept, then looked up at Cantor. "Yes?"

"On the table of contents, how many Federalist essays are listed?"

"Eighty-five... for the time being," he replied.

Cantor smiled. "Please go to Federalist No. 1."

Fitzpatrick nodded, ran his index finger over the screen, then looked up again. "And?"

Cantor leaned forward, repositioning her glasses on her nose. "All right, then. Please scroll down to the... ummm... sixth paragraph of Federalist No. 1."

Fitzpatrick produced a combination frown-grin, but then swept his finger up, up, up..., then stopped. "The one beginning 'in the course of the preceding observations... that one?"

"Yes, that one."

"Do you want me to read that one too... for the record...?" More snickers rattled around the room.

Cantor smiled. "Actually, no, not that one. But I would like you to look up into the preceding paragraph... the fifth paragraph... and find the last sentence in that paragraph... the one that begins 'history will teach us...' Could you please do that for me... and, yes, could you please read *that* sentence aloud... for the record...?"

Fitzpatrick shook his head slowly. From behind and to his left, an aide who had been replicating Cantor's instructions on her own iPad began frantically tapping at Fitzpatrick's arm. Startled, he turned and positioned himself so that she could whisper information into his ear. When he turned back toward the dais, minute beads of perspiration had begun to sparkle on his broad forehead. He took his handkerchief, dabbed the moisture away, then looked back down at the iPad.

"For the record, please, Mr. Fitzpatrick?" Cantor asked.

"History will teach us... that the former has been found... a much more certain road... to the introduction of despotism than the latter... and that of those men who have overturned the liberties of republics, the greatest...." He stopped.

"Mr. Fitzpatrick?" Cantor asked.

Another aide handed Fitzpatrick a piece of paper onto which had been scribbled some frantic advice. Fitzpatrick nodded.

Brown interjected. "Mr. Attorney General, would you wish to take another recess?"

Fitzpatrick shook his head. "No... no... that won't be necessary." He looked back up at Cantor. "The language appears to be the same."

Cantor nodded. "Not only the same…. it is identical… is it not?"

"Well, I've not read the whole sentence, so…"

"Then please continue… for the record…"

Fitzpatrick looked down at the glowing iPad. "… the greatest number have begun their career… by paying an obsequious court to the people; commencing Demagogues, and ending… Tyrants."

Cantor looked over the top rim of her glasses. "Identical, yes?"

Fitzpatrick ran a pale pink tongue over his lower lip, then looked up at Cantor. "That… that would appear to be the case…. But of what possible significance is that? There are probably many instances throughout the Federalist Papers where similar or identical language is used. And since Federalist No. 1 was written by Hamilton, why should it come as a surprise that he may have used the same language in Federalist No. 86?"

Cantor slid her glasses farther down on her nose. "Mr. Fitzpatrick, you are the chief legal officer of the United States. The Attorney General of the United States. Can you cite to me one single other instance… even *one* instance… throughout the eighty-five essays comprising the *original* Federalist Papers…" she allowed the emphasized word to linger, "…the documents which we all concede are the roadmap to what the Founding Fathers intended when they drafted the foundational document for the nation, the Constitution… where the *identical sentences* … word for word… term for term… are repeated? Anywhere?"

Fitzpatrick gripped the red pocket square and blotted his mouth. "Well… ahhh…. I suppose…. I'd have to research the…"

"Let me help you again. The answer is 'no.' There are *no* other such instances." She removed her glasses altogether. "Zero. None."

Fitzpatrick tilted his head. "Yes… but… but again, this newly-discovered essay, written by the same man who wrote

151

Federalist No. 1, could well be... ahhh... *sui generis*... an entity unto itself. The fact is that Hamilton could have simply lifted the language from the first essay and repeated it in the last in order... in order to unify the theme... to tie everything together, first into last ... so to speak."

Cantor frowned; even Senator Brown was squinting at Fitzpatrick. "So to speak?" she asked.

Fitzpatrick nodded slowly.

Cantor put her glasses back on. "All right, then. Mr. Fitzpatrick, let me ask you to scroll down again into the table of contents for the Federalist Papers on the Thomas website."

Fitzpatrick swept his finger up on the iPad, then tapped it, then swept his finger down once, twice." "Yes?"

"In the table of contents, do you see Federalist No. 69?"

He nodded. "I do."

"Please go to that essay."

He swept his finder down, tapped twice, then looked up. "Yes?"

"Could you please read the second paragraph, both sentences... for the record?"

He looked back down at the screen. "The executive authority, with few exceptions... is to be vested in a single Magistrate. This will scarcely, however,... be considered as a point upon which any comparison can be grounded; for if, in this particular, there be a resemblance to the king of Great Britain,... there is not less a resemblance to the Grand Seignior,... to the khan of Tartary,... to the Man of the Seven Mountains, or to the Governor of New York." He looked up at Cantor. "Is that what you mean?"

Cantor nodded. "Yes." She manipulated her own iPad. "Now would you please go back to the White House website, where we find posted the image of the new essay... I'm sorry... the 'newly-discovered' essay?"

Fitzpatrick replicated her manipulations on his device. "I am there."

"All right. Please scroll down to the second page, about three-quarters down the page... and begin reading where Mr. Hamilton starts by saying 'The executive authority, with few exceptions...'"

Fitzpatrick stared down at the words, then shot a quick glance at Senator Brown, and then at Cantor. He looked down. "You'd like me to read that paragraph as well?"

Cantor positioned her microphone between her thumb and index finger. "For the record... yes, I would..."

Fitzpatrick hesitated, then took a long sip of water: the whole room saw his Adam's apple jerk as he swallowed. "The executive authority, with few exceptions... is to be vested in a single Magistrate. This will scarcely, however,... be considered..." he looked up, then back down, "... as a point upon which any comparison can be grounded; for if, in this particular, there be a resemblance to the king of Great Britain,... there is not less a resemblance to the Grand Seignior,... to the khan of Tartary,... to the Man of the Seven Mountains, or to the Governor of New York."

Cantor squinted at him. "It is also... is it not... identical to the two sentences you quoted a moment ago from Federalist 69? The passage from the White House website image of the new... newly-discovered essay... is, once again, identical to a passage from Federalist 69?"

Fitzpatrick swept his finger up and down across the iPad screen, confusing the software. He sucked in a deep breath, then exhaled. "Yes... it would also appear to be the same."

"The same?"

He shot a contemptuous glance at Cantor. "The same, yes."

"As in 'identical'?"

Fitzpatrick lowered his head slightly "Yes... but, once again, I fail to see the relevance. Everyone *knows* that Alexander Hamilton also wrote Federalist 69. So, as was true with regard to Federalist No. 1... also written by Hamilton... and the language used in Federalist 86, he could have also taken language from Federalist 69 and repeated it in Federalist 86."

"And is that what you think happened?"

Fitzpatrick scowled at her. "How would I know? I wasn't there at the time."

Cantor lowered her head, but fixed her gaze on him. "My question was whether now... *today*... you think that is what happened as Hamilton labored over this essay...?"

Fitzpatrick nodded. "Based on what I know, yes, I do."

Cantor again removed her glasses. "Mr. Fitzpatrick, if I were to tell you that there are other even *more* extensive segments of your 'Federalist 86'" this time, Cantor produced two, over-gesticulated air quotes around the essay's working title "which appear to have been 'repeated' or 'replicated' from other Federalist Papers essays and seemingly cut and pasted... almost like a word-processing exercise... into the document we now see on the White House website... would you disagree with me?"

Fitzpatrick slapped his hand down on the table, producing a fusillade of camera strobes and shutter chatter. "*Yes*, as a matter of fact, I *would* disagree with you!" His voice began to betray his growing discomfort. "And even if there *were* such repeats, again, as with the others, Hamilton could have for *whatever* reason deemed it appropriate to repeat verbatim in the final essay certain relevant passages from his prior essays... particularly in a matter as critical as the theretofore unexplored issue of what it meant to be a 'natural born citizen.' So, *yes*, senator, I *would* disagree with you!" His voice approached soprano. "How many different ways can I *phrase* that for you... I mean, is English your second language? Or, as you've asked me, should I use smaller words? Or speak more *slowly*?"

Cantor nodded. "Mr. Fitzpatrick, American, a close dialect of English, is my first language. And, as opposed to smaller words, I think I'd be satisfied with precise and responsive words... spoken at whatever velocity you'd like." She paused. "All right then, please go to the Federalist table of contents again and click onto the link for Federalist 68, then go to the fourth paragraph."

Fitzpatrick slapped the iPad down and began rubbing and jabbing at it, as if it were a pet being punished. "It was also peculiarly desirable,..." he paused, then looked up. "Is that where you mean?"

"It is."

"Do you want me to read it now... for the record...?"

"Well, let's do this the easy way. Go ahead and read it silently to yourself, then read the next paragraph silently to yourself."

Fitzpatrick's eyes darted back and forth across the screen, left to right, *back*, left to right, *back*; Evelyn Wood would have been proud. "All right." He looked up.

"Now please go back to the White House website and the essay at hand, and go the third page, the last one, near the top... where there's a paragraph that begins with the words..." Cantor looked down at her screen, "It was also peculiarly desirable..." She paused. "Do you find that paragraph?"

Fitzpatrick nodded, "Of course."

"Please read that paragraph silently... and the next one too..."

Fitzpatrick scanned the screen even more rapidly, then looked up. "Yes. Again, they are the same."

"Identical?"

"I suspect you already know the answer to that..."

"Your suspicion is correct. They are, in fact, identical."

Fitzpatrick pushed the iPad to one side. "But senator, again, I ask. What does it prove? Alexander Hamilton wrote Federalist No. 1, Federalist No. 68 and Federalist No. 69.

Everyone *knows* that. So *what* if he took some passages from his prior writings and repeated them? You cannot commit plagiarism by copying your own words."

Cantor dipped her chin at him. "Sir... plagiarism is not my concern."

Fitzpatrick produced a shallow frown, as if trying to identify what Cantor's concern actually was.

"Mr. Fitzpatrick," Cantor said, "please then go to page three of the White House image of the essay we're discussing here and find the paragraph beginning 'As part of the process...'" She paused. "Do you see that?"

Fitzpatrick swept and tapped the device. "Yes, I do."

"Midway through that paragraph, do you see a sentence beginning 'By excluding men under thirty-five... see that sentence? It's long, but well-reasoned."

"Yes."

"Would you please read it... aloud... for the record...?"

Fitzpatrick swallowed again. "By excluding men under thirty-five from the first office, and those under thirty from the second, the Legislative body, it confines the electors to men of whom the people have had time to form a judgment, and with respect to whom they will not be liable to be deceived by those ... brilliant appearances of genius and patriotism, which, like transient meteors, ...sometimes mislead as well as dazzle." He looked up. "Yes?"

"Do you agree with that sentiment?"

Fitzpatrick nodded. "I do."

"Including the parts about 'misleading' and 'dazzling'?"

"Especially those parts. Hamilton was critically concerned about the integrity of the office of the president."

"But there's a problem."

Fitzpatrick produced another combination grin-frown. "And what might that be, senator?"

156

Cantor removed her glasses. "Those words originally were written by John Jay, who, along with Hamilton and Madison, were the acknowledged authors of the essays. Jay's words, which you have just quoted from the White House image of this newly-discovered essay, first appeared in Federalist 64. In March 1788. Authored by John Jay."

Strobes sparkled, shutters clicked. Fitzpatrick again licked his lower lip, then swallowed hard.

Cantor continued. "Mr. Fitzpatrick, assuming for the sake of argument that you are correct in your assumption that Alexander Hamilton lifted and replicated entire passages of prior Federalist Papers essays he authored into his final essay, ... the one here being discussed... why would he have lifted this passage from an essay authored by John Jay, not him?"

Fitzpatrick swallowed again and ran his handkerchief across his forehead. "As I have said... I wasn't there... so I can't answer that question." He took another deep drink of water. "But still, the overwhelming evidence still shows that Hamilton wrote Federalist 86, and..."

"Mr. Attorney General, hold up a second..." Senator Brown interrupted. The fact that Brown, instead of Cantor, was taking up the interrogation produced, again, the firing of strobes and rattling of camera shutters.

Fitzpatrick, startled, looked up at Brown. "Yes, Mr. Chairman...?"

"Ummm... you keep referring to the document here," he gestured toward the case in which the parchment was protected, "as 'Federalist 86.' And indeed, that is what it says on its title page. However... in view of what seems to be developing here, ahhh... I wonder if it might not be better to refer to it as 'the essay' ... just for the time being... and the record.... ummm.... you being under oath."

Fitzpatrick swallowed hard again and nodded. "Certainly, Mr. Chairman..." He applied his handkerchief – now a deep scarlet-purple from absorbed sweat – and looked back at Senator Cantor. "The overwhelming evidence still supports the conclusion that the essay... this essay..." he held up his iPad, "was written by Alexander Hamilton. In June 1788. And the fact that verbiage he used in other of his Federalist essays, or verbiage he ... he may have borrowed from one of his compatriots... after all, they all published under the same, single pseudonym *Publius* ... doesn't change that." He leaned forward in his chair. "That's what the FBI concluded and that's what the CIA concluded, so I'm not sure what else you want."

Cantor shook her head. "Actually, Mr. Fitzpatrick, that's *not* what the FBI concluded, nor is it what the CIA concluded."

Fitzpatrick frowned. "And upon what facts do you base that conclusion?"

"Mr. Fitzpatrick, the FBI and the CIA concluded only that the parchment upon which the essay was written dated from the period you state. They also concluded only that the handwriting was, with a high degree of likelihood... but less than 100 percent... that of Alexander Hamilton using ink that, with a similar likelihood... as well as uncertainty... was from that time period too." She removed her glasses. "But what they did *not* conclude was that the text of what was being said in the essay was authentic."

More strobes; more shutter chatter; more muffled inhaling across the room.

Brown cracked the gavel once. "Senator, I would admonish you to be very careful here. *Very* careful. Because if you are suggesting what I think you are suggesting...?"

"And what would that be, Mr. Chairman?" Cantor asked.

"That this document... the essay ... is fraudulent ... a counterfeit?"

Even more strobes popped around the room, and the chatter of camera shutters and high-speed miniature servo motors coupled to zoom lenses whistled through the gathering. A low murmur of reportorial mutterings began to fill the room, triggering another crack of Brown's gavel.

"Mr. Chairman," Cantor began, "I do not know the answer to your question. I do not want to believe that the essay is a fraud or a counterfeit, because that would implicate far more ominous problems for this subcommittee and, potentially, the nation than I am now prepared to deal with. *Far* more ominous." She turned toward Fitzpatrick. "But I do know this. This subcommittee... this senator... you as Chairman, as well as the American people... are entitled to the truth. That is all I am seeking here... nothing more..., but let me assure you,... I'm seeking nothing less."

Brown nodded. "Proceed."

Fitzpatrick's head was tilting back and forth – right, left, right, left – as two aides were alternately whispering to him, one in each ear. He motioned them away.

"Mr. Fitzpatrick," Cantor began, "I understand your argument that Alexander Hamilton could well have determined, when writing the essay, that it made sense to him at the time to repeat certain passages which he had previously included in others of the Federalist papers series. And perhaps even that he had John Jay's permission to ... as you say... 'borrow' Jay's language from Federalist 64."

Fitzpatrick nodded. "Yes." His Adam's apple jerked as he swallowed.

"On the other hand," she tacked, "I have some additional concerns about the essay which I would like to bring to your attention and ask for your response and clarification. Would you be willing to do that?"

He glanced back at one of his aides, who was busily texting on an iPhone. He held the screen closer to his face, then looked up at Fitzpatrick and produced a slow, hesitant affirmative nod of his head. Fitzpatrick looked back at his tormentor. "Yes."

"Good," she said. "I'd hoped that would be your answer." She tapped her iPad. "Could you please go back... unless you are already still there...?"

"Back where?" Fitzpatrick asked.

"Back to the White House website, where the essay is posted."

"Yes," he looked down, "I'm there."

"Good. On the second page, third paragraph... the one starting after the paragraph ending with the word 'Tyrants' is a paragraph starting with the words 'That such pernicious temptations...'" Do you see that?"

"I do."

Cantor nodded. "Would you please... for the record... read *that* paragraph?"

He swallowed again. "That such pernicious temptations... have proved the undoing of innumerable prior experiments of like character as here proposed... is a matter of common knowledge, giving birth to the famous recognition by Sir John Dalberg-Acton, Lord Acton, *viz.*, that 'power tends to corrupt, and absolute power corrupts absolutely' ... peculiar relevance to the matters at hand." He looked up, but said nothing.

Cantor nodded at him. "Please go on."

Fitzpatrick looked down again at the text. "For ever since in the Year of Our Lord 1774, when first the Liberty Bell rang out in proclamation to the world the independence...." He stopped and looked up. "Is that enough?"

Cantor dipped her chin slightly. "Mr. Fitzpatrick, would Alexander Hamilton have said such a thing? And if so, why would he have said such a thing?"

Fitzpatrick offered a shallow shrug of his shoulders. "As I've told you... repeatedly... I wasn't there, so I don't know. But I would agree, as I assume you would too, that the quote he used was particularly relevant to the question of the constitutional eligibility of a president. What I do know is that the... *essay* you are attack… that you are questioning says what it says. The FBI and the CIA have authenticated, with virtual certainty, that the handwriting is Mr. Hamilton's and that the parchment and ink of the essay are similarly, with high if not absolute certainty, authentic." He tipped his head toward her. "Those are the facts."

Cantor nodded her head. "And one of the facts you've assured us of today is that the president agrees with you on these matters as well? And that Federalist 86, including its textual conclusions about eligibility and 'natural born citizens' is authentic?"

Fitzpatrick again leaned forward in his chair, his mouth mere millimeters from his microphone. "One… hundred… percent…" He removed his glasses. "In fact, senator, I am authorized to tell you, from the president himself, that if you can prove otherwise, you'd better do it soon, because the people who elected you might not take kindly to baseless innuendo…, the elections being just under a year away."

Cantor nodded again. "I see," she paused and took a slow sip of water. "Then perhaps, Mr. Fitzpatrick, you can explain to me… and to Senator Brown and to the other members of the subcommittee… and finally, to the American people watching this hearing, including the voters of Tennessee who sent me here… how Alexander Hamilton… in 1788… could have known, for example," she looked down at the e-mail from Annie on her iPad, "that the bell to which he refers in the sentence following his quote from Lord Acton was not called 'The Liberty Bell' until 1835, it being known before that date as 'Old Yankee's Bell'?"

Fitzpatrick's eyes widened. "Pardon?"

"Would you like me to repeat the question?"

Fitzpatrick sat mute.

Cantor continued. "Or that," she looked down at the iPad again, "Hamilton's reference elsewhere in the essay to Blackstone relies for its 'eligibility' conclusions on a legal doctrine… *res ipsa loquitur*… not recognized or defined as such until 1863 in a lawsuit from England, like, seventy-five years *after* Hamilton supposedly referenced it in this essay?"

Fitzpatrick's Adam's apple did another quick, frantic spasm.

"Or *most* curiously," Cantor looked down at Annie's e-mail again, "how Hamilton could have known, in June 1788, when you and President Boalt claim this essay was composed... about the quote from Lord Acton you have just recited from the essay... at a point in time nearly a full century *before* Acton actually composed the quote... in 1887... and, in *fact*... at a point in time over sixty years *before* Acton was even *born*."

She paused and removed her glasses, then stared directly at Fitzpatrick. "Do you... or for that matter does President Boalt contend that Alexander Hamilton, in addition to being one of the Founding Fathers, was also clairvoyant? Or perhaps that Acton, in 1887, was himself plagiarizing from this undiscovered 'Federalist' essay..." she twitched two air quotes "that you and the president contend Hamilton wrote in 1788? Can you explain these facts to me, Mr. Fitzpatrick? Or perhaps better stated: can you explain them *away*? Or are they too stubborn for you?" She tilted her head at him. "Should I repeat the questions... with smaller words... or spoken more slowly?"

Fitzpatrick looked up: a deer in the headlights would have shown more emotion.

"Isn't it true, Mr. Attorney General..."

Brown cracked his gavel down rapidly three times, startling the crowd. "Senator, you are *out* of order. Those questions are *over* the line. This hearing is..."

Cantor grabbed her microphone. "This hearing is *what*, Mr. Chairman?" she shouted. "Is *what*? Is it simply a forum for the perpetration of a *fraud* upon the Senate as well as upon the people of the United States? The perpetuation of the very species of fraud

Attorney General Fitzpatrick here today has condemned? Is *that* what it is *?*"

Brown cracked the gavel down three more times, trying to silence her.

"Mr. Chairman," she persisted, "you can try to bang this hearing to order as much as you want, but I will *not* be silenced. Not *this* time. You can adjourn the hearing right now. That's your prerogative. But I guaran*tee* you that I will simply re-convene my own press conference off-site on my own turf to pick up where you cut me off! I'll even throw in some coffee and donuts for those who want to come and hear what's *really* going on here! And you can *count* on that!"

The strobes and shutter chatter approached Category Three intensity.

"And at that press conference," she continued, "you can also count on me disclosing what my staff has uncovered and answering each and every question posed to me by the press about what I have learned about this 'document' that the Attorney General," she tossed a glance at Fitzpatrick, who was again mopping his mouth with his now deep purple handkerchief, "and, yes, all the way up the food chain to the president have told us about the essay's 'authenticity.'" She paused. "Is that what you want?"

The day's most robust detonation of strobe flashes, shutter chatter, mini-servo motors driving and focusing zoom lenses and startled gasps from the crowd puffed through the room. Category Four. The rising tide of whispers quickly became a wave of exclamations and shouted questions from the reporters strewn around the room. Brown stared at Cantor silently... then, slowly, he lowered the gavel to the desk and stood up.

"I..." he stammered, "I'm sorry, but... I've been called away to another... urgent meeting," Brown lied. "The chair is turned over to the vice-chair, Senator Ortiz."

Senator Barbara Ortiz, a petite, deep auburn-haired Hispanic looked up at Brown as he stood next to her; she accepted the gavel Brown tendered to her. Brown then abruptly turned and headed for the door behind the dais. As the door closed, Ortiz looked over at Cantor and brought her microphone in front of her mouth.

She focused her gaze on Fitzpatrick, then ceremoniously released the gavel to the floor behind her chair. An aide started to pick the gavel up, thinking it had been accidentally dropped; she stopped him with an upraised hand.

"Leave it," she said.

She then took possession of the encased essay, then turned to her right. "Senator Cantor," she began, still staring directly at Fitzpatrick, "please proceed with your questions."

Cantor nodded her appreciation at Ortiz, then turned toward Fitzpatrick.

"Mr. Attorney General," she began, "do you remember the last question I posed to you... or would you like to have it read back? Slowly?"

Fitzpatrick stared straight ahead, not looking at Cantor, not looking at Ortiz, but fixing his eyes on the mahogany of the dais and breathing slowly. His aides stopped texting and tapped their Bluetooth units, activating voice connections with their cell phones. They tried to camouflage their discussions with their hands, like football coaches on the sidelines trying to frustrate opposing team lip-readers by holding playcards over their mouths. The aides exchanged panicked stares until one of them began batting Fitzpatrick's left shoulder and muttering into his ear. Then, almost as if by cellular cue, the entourage rose from the witness table and flanking row of chairs, gathered their papers, iPhones, Droids and iPads, and retreated out of the hearing room.

Senator Ortiz grabbed the microphone. "Let the record reflect," she began, silencing the growing chatter of astonished discussion in the room "that the witness has failed to answer

Senator Cantor's questions and has now left the hearing room. Let the record also show that a citation for contempt of the Senate will be and issued to the Attorney General, with a copy to be delivered to White House legal counsel." Ortiz turned her attention toward Cantor. "Let the record also reflect that, since the Attorney General has forced the adjournment of this hearing, I, for one, intend to be present at the press conference that Senator Cantor has promised us," she nodded in Cantor's direction, "because I believe that she will have a lot more to reveal about what we have just witnessed here. A *lot* more. And I'm looking forward to the coffee and donuts too. Thank you. This hearing is now adjourned."

The roar of the media crowd poured from the outer hallway back into the hearing room. Category Five. Senator Ortiz stared at Cantor; she stared back. Cantor again nodded appreciation to Ortiz, who returned the gesture, then looked back toward the hallway beyond the back of the room, where Fitzpatrick had retreated: a dense jungle of reporter's microphones, digital tape recorders and video-camera lenses were pointing at her as the herd of reporters began screaming their questions.

FIFTEEN

Annie tapped her iPad and navigated to the WiFi live stream from the White House press room. The scarlet red crawl across the bottom of the screen announced the upcoming event:

"The president will deliver his comments regarding the revelation today that the document dubbed 'Federalist 86' is a fraud. *** Attorney General Fitzpatrick has tendered his resignation and the president has accepted it. *** The president will deliver his comments regarding the revelation..."

She looked up: Senator Cantor had entered the room and was staring at her.

"Senator?" Annie asked.

Cantor kept staring, then managed: "Annie?"

Annie put the iPad down on the floor in front of her chair. "Senator... are you OK?"

Cantor nodded. "I'm OK... now... I think." She took in a deep breath, then blew it out and headed for the couch, where she collapsed into its leather side-back-seat corner. She shook her head slowly as Steve entered the room, trying to gauge the atmosphere to decide whether to remain stone-faced or whether to smile. Undecided, he sat down in the chair next to Annie.

Cantor darted looks back and forth between the two of them as the intercom on her desk chirped. "Senator?"

Cantor looked at the desk. "Yes, Ellen?"

"Senator, the phone is ringing off the hook out here, there are... maybe... seventeen hundred reporters and media types in the reception area and out into the hall... what do you want me to do...?"

Cantor sat up. "Tell them… tell them that I will be issuing a press release within the hour and scheduling a conference later this afternoon." She looked back at Annie. "Right now, I just need to catch my breath a little."

"I'll try," the intercom voiced.

"Annie," Cantor said, "could you please turn the TV on?"

Annie grabbed the remote and aimed it at the Sony. "Sure."

The reporter, from the customary photo-op spot on the northwest lawn, with the White House in the background, was talking. "… and the next big bombshell… like we needed any more… came about thirty minutes ago, when White House press secretary Holloway announced that Attorney General Fitzpatrick had tendered his resignation to the president, and that it had been accepted."

The reporter held his hand up to his left ear, pushing his earpiece in a bit to better hear the information being fed to him from his producers offsite. "And now… yes… I'm getting word that Senator Beth Cantor, the one who has blown the lid off this town today, will be issuing a press release soon and will be holding a press conference later today. And you can rest assured that we will be there live to bring it to you," he assured, staring into the camera.

Cantor looked at both Annie and Steve. "Blown the lid…?" she mouthed, grinning.

Annie nodded. "Big… time…."

Steve added. "Mega-big… time."

They looked back at the Sony and the reporter. "So, to recap for you, today, before a subcommittee chaired by Senator Craig Brown, testimony was delivered by Attorney General Fitzpatrick confirming that both he and President Boalt were personally vouching for the authenticity of the new essay discovered last week, this new 'Federalist 86.' That essay, of course, seemed clearly to suggest that the Founding Fathers believed that whether one was eligible or not under the Constitution to serve was a matter to be decided at the ballot box, not in the courts and not in the Congress.

"That's a hot topic in this town, of course, given that the issue is pending just a mile or so up the road from us here at the Supreme Court. Everything seemed to be going fine for that theory and everyone was buying into the story until Tennessee Senator Bethany Cantor suggested... and rather persuasively, I'm told..., that in all likelihood, the document... Federalist 86... was a fake. A fraud. And not just any fraud. A fraud concocted by the Boalt Administration, if not by President Boalt himself."

Suddenly, from behind and to the left of the reporter, the Sony HDTV showed two White House security police jogging toward him, their distant shouts becoming more clear as they neared him. The reporter turned toward them, then turned back to his cameraman. "Jake... *whatever* you do, keep the camera *on*. Keep it *on*...."

"Ten-four...," a voice off-camera replied.

"Sir!" the taller of the two officers shouted a deep baritone at the reporter as he jogged to a stop behind him, "I'm going to have to ask you to stop what you're doing here and leave the grounds." The camera image began shaking as the other officer approached and left the field of view, the image of his left hand rising up toward the lens, then cupping over it.

"Why? I don't understand," the reporter's voice asked. There was no cupping of the audio microphone.

"Sir," the audio continued, "all I know is that your presence here is no longer authorized and both of you must leave. Now!"

With that, the camera began showing the ground, oscillating back and forth as the photographer walked. Occasionally, one of the officer's pants leg and shoes would enter the field as the escort off the premises continued. Jake had done as he was told: the camera, and the audio pickup, was still on, although still pointing at the ground.

"Officer, I don't understand," the reporter's voice repeated.

The officer's baritone voice responded. "I don't know either. We just got word that you were to be immediately escorted off the White House premises. And I'm going to need you to surrender back to me your White House press credentials and press passes."

The shaking image of the ground and trudging over the ground continued. Cantor looked at Annie; Annie looked at Steve; Steve was shaking his head. "This thing," he said, "is starting to unravel..."

They looked back at the Sony. "But why us? We were just reporting..."

"Not just you," the officer's voice interrupted. "All press credentials and passes are being confiscated and all reporters are being escorted off the grounds."

"All of them?" the reporter asked.

There was a pause, with only the trudging of the audio and jerky image of the ground as they walked coming over the TV.

"Yes. All of them," the baritone said.

"This might be getting old," the reporter's voice began, "... but why?"

Another trudging pause. "You're right, it is getting old. All I know is that we got an order directly from the Oval Office to escort you off..."

"Oval Office?"

"Right."

"As in, 'Boalt' himself?"

Another pause. Then they stopped; the camera had auto-focused on an acorn from one of the mature oak trees on the grounds that was partially hidden in the deep green ryegrass. Then the reporter's voice came over. "What are you listening to? In your earpiece... officer? Is someone giving you...?"

Abruptly, both the picture of the ryegrass and acorn and the audio evaporated, to be quickly replaced by an in-studio talking head. "Well," the studio reporter began, "we seem to have lost our feed from the White House...." He paused and turned to his co-anchor. "So, Bev... what do you make of all this...?"

Again, Cantor looked at Annie; Annie looked at Steve; Steve looked at... his buzzing Droid, which he answered. "Mike..." he spoke into the device, "yeah.... yeah, we just finished watching it... weird, huh? Yeah. Yeah.... say *what*...?" He looked at Cantor, but kept listening to Mike on the Droid and nodding his head... seconds, seeming more like minutes, passed. "OK, hang on a second..." He lowered the device and darted quick looks at both Cantor and Annie. "You're not gonna believe this..."

He activated the Driod's speakerphone function and placed it on Cantor's desk.

"Mike?" Steve asked.

"Yeah?"

"You're on speaker with Senator Bethany Cantor and an aide, Annie Armstrong... and me." He looked at Cantor. "Senator, this is Mike Tippett, my bud from the Marines... I spoke with you about...?"

"Yes, of course," Cantor said. "Hi, Mike."

"OK. Hello to all," Mike's speakerphone greeting came.

"Mike?" Cantor asked.

"Yes, ma'am? ... I mean..."

"Ma'am is fine, Mike," Cantor interjected. "Just fine. And thank you for your service to the country."

"My pleasure... ma'am."

Steve looked back at the Droid. "Mike, I need you to repeat for the senator and Annie here what you just told me a second ago."

"OK. Well, when Steve came over here and started walking me through these things... the disappearing e-mail addresses and what-not..."

Cantor frowned at Steve, who held up a finger, but also pointed with another finger at the Droid.

Mike's voice continued, "After Steve left, I became really curious about this whole constitutional eligibility issue. And so I started doing some instant research on the Internet."

Cantor and Annie both rolled their eyes.

Mike's Droid voice continued. "I know, you probably just rolled your eyes and thought 'oh good, Internet-based research... now *that's* authoritative...' "

Cantor, Annie and Steve all laughed simultaneously.

"So I was right.... Right?"

Steve nodded at the Droid. "You were indeed."

"OK. Well, stay with me here. What I just told Steve a while ago was that I think I just stumbled onto something more. I mean, I watched the live feed of the proceedings this afternoon where you, senator, were asking some pretty good questions of Attorney General Fitzpatrick."

Cantor leaned toward the Droid. "How did it look?"

"By the end, before he walked out, the guy was sweating like a pig.... What a piece of work that guy is."

"Was," Annie added.

"Yeah, right. I heard he resigned," Mike said.

"He did," Cantor replied. "But what is it you think you've found, Mike?"

"Well," Mike continued, "after you cut through all the stuff you brought out, senator, regarding the counterfeit essay... Federalist 86... I ran across a couple of websites that made reference to something not mentioned at the hearing. An old statute enacted by the first Congress in 1790... one that defined a natural born citizen exactly the way you explained it in the hearing."

"Wait," Annie blurted. "That's what Jack was telling me last night..."

"Jack?" Cantor asked.

"My brother. He's a second-year at Georgetown Law."

Cantor sat up on the couch and looked at her. "And?"

"He was saying that there was an old statute.... Actually, not a 'statute' that got assigned a place in the U.S. Code, but a law enacted by the Congress in 1790... a 'Public Law' that dealt with the issue of what constituted a 'natural born citizen.'"

"Yeah," Mike's voice replied, "that's it. It was enacted by the first Congress in 1790. As far as I can tell, it showed up in the books... I think it's called 'Statutes... something...'"

"Statutes at Large," Cantor offered.

"Right," Mike confirmed. "It showed up in Statutes at Large as, literally, 'Statute II,' the second law Congress ever enacted."

Silence. Finally, Cantor asked "And?"

"Statute II, and all of the other statutes that later repealed, amended or altered it... were themselves all repealed by Congress early last year. They had to do with immigration and uniform rules of naturalization. Gone. So it's as if the original Statute II ... not only got repealed ... it never even existed in the first place. The repealer was buried in... you ready...?"

Cantor frowned at the Droid on her desk. "Yeah.... I guess..."

"It was buried in one of the financial bailout bills."

Cantor stood up. "You mean the seventeen-hundred pager... that no one read?"

"Ummm...," Mike replied, "yeah... that one."

Annie stood up. "And the one that Boalt himself lobbied the Congress for on the Hill?"

"That too...," Mike added.

Cantor hunched over the desk directly above the Droid. "And can you prove this?"

"Not only that, anyone with access to a computer can do it. The bailout bill that did the repealing is now posted on the Internet. The repeal of Statute II and its later versions is found on page...

172

ummm...1698. Buried in a string of, maybe, eighty-five to ninety statutes being amended, re-numbered or repealed along with it. And, making it even more juicy... the only section of the bailout bill that is declared to have retroactive effect is...?"

Cantor looked at Annie, but spoke to the Droid, "The one repealing Statute II and its relatives?"

"Bingo," replied the device.

Annie joined Cantor leaning on the desk. "Mike, how on *Earth* did you find this...? And on such short notice... without even being asked...?"

There was a long pause. "Well, it's this way... when Steve said he needed some help and there was something I could do to respond,... hey... once you get the hang of it, navigating around the Internet without falling into a punji pit or tripping an IED, you can find some pretty interesting stuff. And as for why.... well... because Steve needed help... and it seemed like the right thing to do. So... semper fi...."

Steve stared at the Droid silently, then swallowed hard. "Thanks, bud..." he said.

"Oooo-rah..." replied the Droid.

"Mike," Cantor began, "I cannot thank you enough for this information."

"Well," he continued, then paused. "Like the commercial says... 'but wait... there's more.'"

"More?" Cantor asked.

"Yup."

"OK?"

"While tracking down the source of the e-mail that this Clark fellow ... the guy who says he discovered this Federalist 86...?"

"Rod Clark?"

"Yeah, that guy. The e-mail he said he got from some distant relative of Alexander Hamilton... or Hamilton's friend.... I finally tracked the source of that e-mail back to a computer in...

get this… a tailoring shop on Connecticut Avenue, Northwest. Up by the zoo."

All three in the room stared at one another, saucer-eyed. "And?" Cantor asked.

"Shortly after I had located it there… I got an e-mail *through* that computer, but not *from* that computer. The electronic trail indicated the message actually originated off site and was merely relayed to me through the computer."

"Really? You can track that stuff?"

"Like I said, once you get the hang of navigating cyberspace, you can find out a whole bunch of useful things."

"Where did the e-mail come from?"

A pause, then, "Dubai, U.A.E."

"And it was from?"

Another pause. "Somebody named 'Charlie' at a 'tangello25.com.'"

Cantor went erect from leaning over the Droid. "That was the e-mail address that Clark said this Allison Hardesty used to tell him about the diary he found."

Cantor stared at Annie; Annie stared at Steve; Steve stared at the Droid. "Mike?" Steve asked.

"Yeah?"

"What did the e-mail say?"

A pause, then, "You want to see it?"

Cantor began rapidly bobbing her head. "Yes, yes… oohhhh yes…"

"OK. Her ya go, Steve."

A moment later, the Droid e-mail alert beeped. Steve went to Cantor's upper right desk drawer, looking at her. "May I?"

"Of course."

He extracted a connector cable, jabbed one end into the Droid and the other into the Sony USB port. He clicked the remote, changing inputs, and up came:

"Hello, whoever you are. First off, you're pretty good. Not superstar…, but still, pretty good. Too bad we couldn't have met under different circumstances… I can always use talent.

"But I'm good too, so forget trying to catch me because, as you must know by now, I am gone. The shop is shut down, all prints and traces are removed and all of the accounts are secured offshore. So, sayonara. Oh… and if you think this e-mail originated in Dubai… think again… amateur…. But since you've gotten this far, it's pretty clear that you'll soon discover the rest, so you win the prize. It's been a ride, but all rides must eventually come to an end, right? Your reward for bringing the ride to an end is something I suspect that you… and some… but not all… will value: the truth.

"First, of *course* Federalist 86 is a fraud. The whole Saberjet Onyx *gambit* was a fraud. Stevie Wonder could have seen that. But sometimes, political ambition and thirst for power is even more sinister than terminal blindness. And remember what that guy from Germany said a while back: if you're going to tell a lie, tell a big one, because people won't believe a small one, especially from a politician. And for best results, tell it early, and tell it often.

"In concept, F-86 was a really *good* fraud…
but still a fraud. When Boalt's chief of staff,
Ross Ellis, first brought the proposal to me
last summer, I knew it was doomed to fail.
And, yes, I told that directly to Ellis *and*
Boalt. In the Oval Office. They didn't care.
All they wanted was an end-around run
safety-net in case everything else they had
used to stonewall the truth failed.

"They thought they had it all covered… from
parchment used for the original Articles of
Confederation to the best cursive handwriting
forgers in the world. And planting the forgery at
the Library of Congress was a snap. That guy Clark
could have found it blindfolded.

"But the reality that the gambit was doomed was
sealed in concrete when Boalt insisted on
outsourcing the text to one of Mrs. Boalt's wannabe
nephews instead of letting me do it. Blur the trail.
Stooooopid…

"And then they go post it to the Internet… on the
official White House *website*? Wow. Dumb…
imbecile dumb. By the time you read this, there's
probably an 'Error 404: page unavailable'
message up on whitehouse.gov after they saw things
starting to go south and they scrubbed it off.
Nobody would ever confuse these guys with rocket
scientists… par for the course in D.C., though. But
for what they were paying me, they could be as
lunatic dumb as they wanted.

"Second, you can bet they will now be trying to cover their tracks. The guy who supplied the parchment for the document? Grant Kaplan? Gone. A Volvo 18-wheel semi took him and his 'Vette out on 495 north of Bethesda yesterday.

"And the guy they tasked with writing the counterfeit? Ella Boalt's nephew? That was Neal Graves. He worked for me at OLRC too, but was even crazier than Kaplan, so I booted him too. But like the proverbial bad penny, one day he showed up in Ross Ellis' inner circle of drinking buddies... and the next thing ya know: boom. Ellis has him assigned with drafting the biggest bamboozle in the history of the republic. Anyway, Graves disappeared last Sunday... no trace... along with all of his computers. I think he saw it coming and hit the road.

"Third, you and Senator Cantor and people close to her are safe, ... for now. These guys are Jersey crazy, but not so crazy as to whack a sitting U.S. senator. But they are dangerous. And if you want to make sure the truth finally prevails, don't let up on the pressure, because the only thing these guys understand... is force.

"Remember, you don't stop a cobra on the attack by cutting off its tail... that'll just get it... more irritated. And trust me, this F-86 gambit is the tip of the iceberg... and the upper portion at that.

"Finally, if you ever decide you want to make some *real* dough... shoot me an e-mail. You wouldn't *believe* the amount of money out here available for… these kinds of projects. Seriously. It's like a casino… they don't count the money. They weigh it. Then they just multiply by the denominations per pound. Usually Bennies.

"Ciao."

Cantor stared at the Sony screen slack-jawed.

Annie tapped her on her shoulder. "Senator?"

The senator closed her mouth and looked at the aide. "Yeh?"

Annie held up her iPhone screen for the White House website: "Error 404: page unavailable."

Cantor nodded and looked at her. "We should probably get started on the press release." She looked at Steve. "Steve, you need to secure and preserve that message. Copy it, print it, burn a CD… whatever. That message cannot be lost."

Mike's voice emanated from the Droid. "Senator?"

"Yes, Mike. I'm sorry, I forgot you were there."

"All I wanted to say was… not to worry. I've already printed a screen-shot copy and burned a CD. The e-mail is secure." He paused "But I have a question…."

A pause. "Yes? What?" she asked.

"Can I post it to the Internet? Anonymously? No trail back to you?"

What a great and delicious thought, she savored, then replied. "Mike… I can't tell you what you can and can't do… but until all of this sorts out a bit more, I'd appreciate it if you'd not do that. Not yet. Please, not yet."

"Ten-four," he acknowledged.

SIXTEEN

"Good afternoon," Cantor began. The brass-trimmed oak podium was flanked by two American flags in the main auditorium of the Hart Senate Office Building. A jack-straw bouquet of microphones – each logo colorfully vying with all the others for prominence – poked up at her. The auditorium quieted and the strobe-flashes and electro-chatter of the still cameras was replaced by the nearly silent, mosquito-pitched mini-motors and electronics of the digital video equipment.

"Good afternoon," she repeated. "Well... to say that today has been a roller coaster ride for me would likely be the understatement of my career. But my career... such of it as may remain after today... is not the issue. The issue, of course, is this document called 'Federalist 86,' which purports to be a newly-discovered essay... the last essay... in the series of documents we know as The Federalist Papers.

"I won't dwell on those original, eighty-five essays by Alexander Hamilton, James Madison and John Jay. You already know about those... or if you don't..., you should. Seriously... you should... you could learn a lot about your country and what the people who constructed the Constitution for us intended this country to be. Trust me, it is much different now than what was originally intended by the Founders.

"This document," she held up a paper copy of the counterfeit, "is fraudulent. It is the concoction of people who would stop at nearly nothing to stay in power, going even so far as to counterfeit another brick in the country's foundation, and pass it off as genuine. It is not genuine. It is a fake. I will not point fingers in the direction from where this counterfeit essay may have come... that will be for others to do." She paused and swept her eyes across the roomful of eyes. "But as they say..., if you can't connect the dots, you need a sharper pencil. And, to grossly understate the matter, those who are responsible for this give new meaning to the term 'treason.' And to 'perfidy' too... look it up.

"On the other hand... and I mean no insult, but the truth is emerging... a pretty good argument can be made that all of you," she swept her index finger, left to right, over the sea of reporters sitting in the auditorium, "and more specifically your stratospheric Beluga, brie and Chardonnay employers... with very few exceptions... have been complicit in this fraud. Your acts and omissions were those of an enabler giving aid and comfort to the counterfeiters. In a way, you were all what Lenin was thinking about when he coined the term 'useful idiots.'

"When President Boalt's... and I use that title advisedly... when his constitutional eligibility was first raised, even before his election, you ignored the story. When the rumors persisted and he hunkered down in his foxhole of elected-office intransigence, you ran cover for him by trivializing and lampooning his critics. And when the issue just wouldn't die and the Supreme Court looked as if it was going to render an important decision on the matter, you pulled out the long knives to defend him and slashed away at the heretics with ink and word processors.

"You called them 'birthers,' 'traitors' and worse." She paused. "You should be ashamed of yourselves... and those of you with a remnant of a conscience will silently... in your own minds... agree with me. You have betrayed your profession. Worse, you have betrayed your country."

The silence in the auditorium was, yes, deafening. And long.

"It now appears, however," she resumed, "that a turning point may be at hand. As you know, I asked some very pointed questions of Attorney General... *former* Attorney General Fitzpatrick today regarding the authenticity of this..." she held up the copy again "this... counterfeit. He did not answer those questions. Maybe *you*," she leaned forward over the podium and swept her gaze around the room, again, left to right, "would have better luck getting him to answer." She paused. "That is, of course..., if your employers *allow* you to even pose those questions."

More silence.

"Remember when all of you went after the Bush administration over the WMD's that were thought to be Saddam Hussein's next gambit and which were part of the reason for going to war in Iraq? You said they needed a lie in which to believe to justify the invasion? This is no different. Except that the country under attack is your own. You needed a lie to believe in to justify keeping Boalt in office. Well, it looks like you got one." She held up the copy of the counterfeit again.

"You know," she continued, "it's really sad. Under our Constitution, there are four professions... and maybe a better word is 'trustees'... of the public good... that are identified by name in that document. The presidency, the Congress, the judiciary... and the press. That's why your profession is sometimes called 'the Fourth Estate.'

"At one time, all four of these trustees were held in high esteem in this country. Now, it's different. But if you in the press think that only the first three trustees have breached their fiduciary duties to the people and ignored their duties... and, trust me, they have... and that you are blameless in all of this... think again." She paused. "You are not. And if you care for your country, ditch your denial. Then reassume your duties under the Constitution."

Silence.

She paused. "OK... the flogging portion of this press conference is done... for the moment. Now, here's what my staff has uncovered in the past thirty-six hours regarding this fraud. And, by the way, if Mr. Fitzpatrick... or the president himself has answers to these questions, now would be a good time to cough them up.

"From what we've found... so far... it seems that people at the highest levels formulated a plan to counterfeit a fake additional essay in the series of papers by three of the Founding Fathers, the Federalist Papers. They even stooped to desecrating and vandalizing the Constitution's original precursor document... the Articles of Confederation to get the paper... parchment for their counterfeit. And why? Not only to hide the truth regarding the president's eligibility, but also... worse... seemingly to try to perpetuate his illegitimate grip on power.

"And you need to also know that there is growing evidence that although former Attorney General Fitzpatrick did not know of the fraud... I'm gonna guess that was pretty obvious from his performance earlier today..." she paused as a wave of nods undulated over the group, "the same cannot be said of Chief of Staff Ross Ellis. We have information that he was well-aware of the plan and, in fact, was one of the prime architects of the plan and in the decision to implement it." She took a sip of Dasani.

"You know, there are some pretty good quotes coming out of this fraudulent essay, although they were originally used in other genuine essays... I especially like the one where it notes that the greatest number of rulers who have started out good have done so by paying, this is a quote, '...an obsequious court to the people; commencing Demagogues, and ending Tyrants.'" She stared out across the room. "Sound familiar?"

A reporter in the front row raised his hand.

Cantor looked at him. "Yes?"

"Senator... I'm Jim Pratt, Channel Two here in D.C."

"Sure, Jim. I recognize you."

The reporter shook his head. "This is all pretty overwhelming..."

"Tell me about it," she interjected.

"Anyway, are you and your staff aware of the televised statement to the nation the president has called for tomorrow night?"

Cantor shook her head. "Been too busy.... What statement?"

"Well," Pratt continued, "we just got word that he's called for a prime-time half-hour television address to the nation tomorrow...."

Cantor nodded, then frowned slightly. "Half an hour? That's barely enough time for him to clear his throat." She shrugged. "But as long as he occupies the White House, and as long as your bosses fear his wrath, he'll probably get his request."

Pratt nodded again. "Oh, he has. He has. 8:00 PM D.C. time. But the added attraction is that it will be a joint address. With Vice-President Chambers participating."

Cantor frowned. "Really?"

Pratt nodded. "Yeah. Really."

"Why?"

"Got no idea." Pratt held up his cell phone. "But I'm told that they've also invited one other person to attend the broadcast..."

Cantor tilted her head. "C'mon, Jim... enough with the tease..."

Pratt nodded. "They've requested that House Speaker Simpson be there too...."

Cantor produced a deep squint-frown. *"What?"*

A rumble of conversation began surging through the assembled media; Cantor glanced over at Annie, who could only offer up an "it's-news-to-me" shrug as she began tapping out text on her iPhone to try and get more information.

Pratt continued. "Yeah, apparently the president wants both the vice president and the Speaker of the House there in the Oval Office. For the broadcast." He paused. "And there's a lot of speculation already starting about why."

Cantor was still frowning. "But Adam Simpson's not even a member of the president's party. In fact, since he switched parties two terms ago, I wasn't even aware Simpson and Boalt were even on speaking terms."

Pratt shrugged as well. "Go figure. All I know is that the speculation is that Boalt wants him there an hour before the broadcast to brief him on what's up."

Cantor glanced over at Annie, who was motioning for her to step away from the podium, which she did.

"What is it, Annie?" Cantor asked.

"I think I might know why they want Simpson there…" she whispered into Cantor's ear. "I just got hold of Craig Talton, Simpson's chief of staff. He tells me that when the White House called, they would not tell him the reason they wanted him there… but that it involved… these are his words… 'Simpson's future… and the immediate future of the nation.' And remember… Simpson's third in line…"

Cantor's eyes bulged. "You can't mean…." She held up her hand. "Don't say any more…."

SEVENTEEN

Ellen's voice came over the intercom. "Senator?"

Cantor muted the Sony from her desk chair. A pile of phone messages cluttered the work surface. "Yes, Ellen?"

"Ummm... Congressman Simpson would like to talk to you."

"The Speaker?"

"Yes."

Cantor looked at the desk telephone: line 1 was blinking "hold."

"Put him through."

The phone chirped; she picked up the receiver. "This is Beth Cantor."

"Thank you, senator, for taking my call," Simpson's bass sounded in her ear. "With all that's going on, it would have been easy to say you were busy and put me into voice-mail. I really appreciate it."

"Mr. Speaker, under all of the circumstances..."

"Yeah," he interrupted. "Circumstances will get you every time, won't they? Ahhhh... I hate to sound cryptic and all cloak and dagger... but..., do you have time to see me? I mean in person?"

"Of course. When?"

"Actually, I was hoping it could be now... or as soon as you could meet me. And somewhere off-site." He paused. "It's quite important that I see you. In private. Soon.

Cantor paused. "Well, given the press carnival that's going on, I'm not sure how easy that will be. What do you suggest?"

There was a pause. "Well, I'm here in the Speaker's Office at the House... and you're just a few blocks away at Hart Senate. Umm... there are some private study carrels over at the Library of Congress... next to the Supreme Court... would that do?"

"Yes, I know where those are, off the lobby.   Fine. When?"

"I could be there in fifteen… maybe even twelve minutes. Alone."

"Done."

***

Carrel A-17 was not much bigger than a walk-in closet, with a study-weathered metal desk, a typical green plastic and brass study lamp and two battered metal chairs.   The door had a chicken-wire reinforced window panel and the ceiling fluorescent fixture showered the enclosure with light.   But it was private.   She tapped on the glass and a tall, full silver-haired man in his late 60's stood up and opened the door.   They sat across from one another.

"Thank you for coming on such short notice," Simpson said.

"Candidly, Mr. Speaker, given all that has taken place… and seems to be continuing to unfold… I'm not sure what to make of your request.   And I'm not even sure why I've agreed to meet with you, given some of our past differences when I was in the House.   But I'm here… so, how can I help you?"

Simpson nodded.   "I understand your concerns.   Believe me, I do.   There are a lot of folks who would be very curious knowing that we are even talking.   Especially in private."   He placed is left palm on his forehead and slowly dragged it down over his face, past his nose, over his mouth, off his chin.   "But the things I've learned in the past two days… and the things I hope to learn from you here now… will be very important… critical to me… to you… and to this country."   He nodded again.   "I know, that sounds very melodramatic, and I regret that.   But it is the truth. And I don't know how to otherwise state it."

Cantor swallowed.   "Mr. Speaker, I've had a rough couple of days here too.   I've learned things that in my wildest dreams I never thought could have been conceived… much less put into

186

motion… by the people who we've elected to run our government. I am sickened and saddened at what seems to have taken place here."

"Senator," Simpson replied, "I'm old school. I actually believe that this nation's founders knew what they were doing when they drafted and signed the blueprint for this nation. Some folks don't like what it says. Too bad. I believe that the Constitution means what it says. But given the battering that it's taken over the years and the morphing of its words by…. well, many folks, from judges, to politicians on both sides of the aisle… to pontificating law professors… it's a wonder the republic has survived as long as it has."

"Amen," she added, "… if I may say so…."

Simpson smiled. "You certainly may." He glanced out the window of the door; seeing no one, he turned back to her.

"All of this political wrangling and posturing we have to go through each day… each week… each term… is just that. Posturing. Wrangling. Static. You know it and I know it. I know we don't share identical political philosophies, but I suspect we both value something far more important that those philosophies."

"Truth?"

"Truth. At the end of the day, if we don't care what any of these laws we write and pass say or do against the backdrop of the blueprint… then we're as good as done. Toast. And if what you exposed today at the hearing is any indication of what lies ahead, then I am gravely concerned that toast is all that we might be eating from now on."

Cantor leaned forward. "Do you mean that?"

Simpson leaned forward. "On my grandkids' life."

Cantor sat back in her chair; Simpson mimicked the move.

"All right, then," she said. "Tell me what I can do to help."

Simpson nodded. "Before we get to what I need from you, there are a couple of things you need to know. First, after the hearing this afternoon and your press conference, I received a phone call on my cell. Actually, it's not a cell. It's a satellite unit. My private... very private satellite phone. Very few people in this world know I have it... and even fewer have the number..." He patted his left front inner coat pocket.

"Yes?"

"It was from the Vice-President."

"Chambers?"

"Yes."

"And?"

"He wanted to meet and discuss the events of the day as well."

"With you?"

"With me."

"But...," she paused. "He's one heartbeat away from Boalt... and, by the way, you're two heartbeats away...."

Simpson grinned. "Well, speaking of heartbeats... not many people know this either, but, when Chambers and I were in college together... yes, we both attended and graduated from college together. When we were at Auburn, there were more than a couple of times when we were your... how shall I phrase it...? typical college goofs."

Cantor allowed a small grin. "Been there. Done that. I have a son at Vandy right now. Love him to death... but there are days...."

Simpson smiled. "Anyway, one afternoon... on a dare from a frat brother that he could not eat a hamburger in one gulp... actually, it was a bacon cheeseburger... your vice president... William Carson Chambers... nearly ran out of heartbeats on the floor of the main cafeteria. He took the dare and tried to down an entire burger in one bite. He got it all in, but in the process of trying to chew and liquefy it so he could swallow it... go figure... he started to choke. Most of us were laughing our socks off... until he blew one of the buns... more like mush... out of his mouth, but then fell to the floor with the rest of it still blocking his throat and airway."

"Urg…" she muttered, with a frown.

"Well, when we finally stopped laughing and saw what was going on… me, being the jock I thought I was, I picked him up and started doing the Heimlich thing on him. First couple of jerks did nothing… but the third one… I really laid into it… did the trick. Not a pretty sight…"

"Ya think…?"

"But it worked. Saved his hide… and he's never forgotten it. We don't really speak about it publicly… I mean, we're on opposite sides of the political fence and, oh yeah, it's a bit of an embarrassment to him… but he's never forgotten it. Kinda one of those life-altering events you go through from time to time? Ever since then, on St. Patrick's day, he sends me something green to commemorate the event. I'll let you guess why it's green… He never acknowledges that I saved his life on St. Patrick's Day at Auburn… but I always know what his card means when I get it."

Cantor tilted her head. "And this story has relevance to….?"

"The relevance is that, despite our political differences, Chambers and I have remained personal friends. Close personal friends. His satellite phone number is in my speed-dial, and mine is in his. No one knows that… and you should forget it. We don't share the same political beliefs… although current events may be changing that… but we still respect one another. And we're friends. Listen, if you ever get a chance to save someone's life, do it. It can pay off *big* in the long run."

Cantor squinted slightly. "Meaning?"

"Meaning that…," he hesitated. "Are we having this conversation?"

Cantor stared into his right eye. "Not if you would prefer otherwise."

"That would be my preference."

"Not sure why I'm OK with that..., but I am. Go."

Simpson nodded. "The Vice President called me right after Fitzpatrick high-tailed it out of the hearing this afternoon, but before your press conference. He had watched the entire hearing on C-SPAN. When he called me... he was shaken. We've had a lot of private discussions over the years as our political careers have blundered along... but this was different. It was like a mixture of fear and rage... yeah, rage would be the word..."

"Over what? Rage over what?"

"Over what for all the world appeared to be a colossal fraud and treasonous attempt by his boss to manipulate the strings to stay in power... no matter what. And desecrating the Articles of Confederation for his own counterfeit ends? Get a grip. That was the last straw. So when you sliced and diced Fitzpatrick and he ran away... Bill... Vice President Chambers knew that the time had come for him to do something. He felt he'd been duped and deceived... punk'd... and he was *not* happy.

"I'm still confused."

"When he called me... right after the hearing... it was to tell me that he was considering resigning. I urged him not to do that."

"Good advice."

"As it now turns out, great advice."

"Because?"

"Because as he was talking to me on his satellite phone, he got a landline call from Boalt."

"I'm listening."

"The call was to tell him that Boalt intended to resign immediately, which would make Chambers president."

"Just like the Constitution says...."

"Speaking of which, how certain are you... how certain is your staff and the ones who have helped you gather all of this information... that your findings are accurate? That, in fact, a fraud has been perpetrated? That the Federalist essay 86 is counterfeit? That Boalt, even if he *was* born in Missouri as he claims, is nonetheless ineligible under the Constitution? And that he was part of the fraud? On a scale of one to ten?"

Cantor leaned forward over the table. "Twelve. On *all* of those issues."

Simpson nodded. "Boalt told Chambers that he wanted him, and me and Chief Justice Phillips at the Oval Office by 7:00 PM today to discuss... to discuss... Bill... the vice president... quoted Boalt as identifying the topic to be the 'transfer of power.'"

"So he *is* going to resign?"

"Yes... he is. But there is a string attached. A big string... more like a gallows noose...."

"Which is...?"

Chambers leaned forward in his chair. "Before I go there, I need to know again. Scale of one to ten? And especially on Boalt's involvement?"

Cantor drew in a deep breath, then exhaled. "Twelve... and rising... my staff is still on it.... There's an eyewitness who's talking...."

Simpson nodded. "I suspected as much. And so does Chambers."

"The vice-president knows that the essay is a fraud?"

"He didn't before now. But like two or three million people per hour as time goes by and the news on the Internet goes viral, he is being forced to acknowledge that it is a counterfeit." He hesitated. "Are you at liberty, senator? Who is the eyewitness?"

"I'm not sure I *am* at liberty. But if you or your Auburn alum have some names in mind, I might be able to say whether I recognize them or not... and you can draw your own conclusions."

"Fair enough. Elvis Presley?"

"Nope."

"Bart Simpson... no relation...?"

"Nope."

"Charlie Hardin?"

Cantor squinted at him. "Like I said, I don't know if I'm at liberty…"

"I thought so. That's who Bill… the vice president suspects that he's the one who is spilling the beans. And is now very much on the run. He'd better be…. he's on their 'to do' list…, if you get my meaning. Before I called you at your office this afternoon, I had just finished a satellite call with Bill. From his personal quarters at the Naval Observatory… from inside the bunker… linked to a surface antenna."

Cantor's forehead rippled upward. "So let me ask you: are *you* at liberty? What did he say?"

"He confided that for the past four… maybe six months, he's been frozen out of virtually all of the high-level policy discussions that have taken place between the president and his closest confidants. Ross Ellis. Some 'K' Street lobbyist named Rossiter. His personal lawyer in the *Locke* case, somebody Cassini. He knew something was up. But following the Supreme Court's acceptance of the *Locke* case for review, no one would confirm to him what it was. 'Better that he didn't know' was always the between-the-lines explanation. But when news of the new essay… maybe the better term now is counterfeit…?"

Cantor nodded. "'Counterfeit' works for me. 'Fraud' too… maybe even 'treason'.…"

Simpson tilted his head. "Funny you should use that last term… it came up a couple of times in my conversation with Bill… with the vice-president."

"But where is he going with it?" she asked.

"He isn't sure. All he needed from me, he said, was lead-pipe confirmation that the Federalist 86 essay being peddled by Senator Brown and Attorney General Fitzpatrick… was not genuine. That it was a fraud they had concocted and perpetrated in order to influence the decision in *Locke* and keep Boalt in office.

That's why I called you. Then he said he would… take it from there…"

Cantor frowned. "I hope that didn't mean he was going to try to down another cheeseburger whole."

Simpson smiled. "No, not likely." He paused. "But he said 'epiphany' a couple of times. Odd. He's not a religious guy."

Abruptly, out of the corners of their eyes – Cantor's right eye, Simpson's left eye – a figure moved in front of the chicken-wire window in the door. A middle-aged woman – she appeared to be with library personnel – was pointing at her watch. Cantor and Simpson both glanced at their own watches: 4:46 PM.

The two people in the carrel both looked at her and the librarian thought: these two folks don't look like students or researchers. *Way* too well-dressed. They looked vaguely familiar, but she couldn't quite place them. The man was holding up his index finger and nodding at her, visually communicating that they were just about done and would vacate the carrel shortly. The librarian nodded at them and walked back to a stack of books, as if searching for a particular volume, but still watching the two as they continued their discussion in the carrel. The study rooms were well insulated from noise, so she could not make out any of the words being spoken. Where were the lip readers when you really needed them?, she thought.

The man said something that caused the woman to jerk back in her chair, then lean forward as if asking him a question. He answered. She asked another question. He nodded slowly and mouthed a response. She was no lip reader, but she thought his response was "no." The woman started shaking her head back and forth signaling the negative; the man began nodding his head up and down, signaling the opposite. Then they both stood up, opened the carrel door, and quickly walked away toward the exit.

And the librarian wondered: what on earth was *that* all about?

EIGHTEEN

Steven felt the Droid vibrate and looked down at the caller-ID displayed. He tapped it.

"Hey, Mike. 'Sup?"

Mike's voice went up to the Bluetooth in Steve's right ear. "Hey back, dude. You're not gonna believe it."

"Seen and heard a lot of things today, Marine. Try me."

"How about I just received another e-mail from Charlie."

"Oooo…. OK… that's got my attention. You want me to conference in the senator?"

"Not yet. I mean, if you want to, that's OK, but this is just a reality check for me. I want to bounce his latest message off you first."

Steve nodded to no one in particular and took another sip of coffee as he sat in one of the overstuffed chairs at the Georgetown Starbucks.

"OK. Whatta you got?"

"Awright, I succeeded… don't ask me how… I was able to get a direct message link to him. I mean, live text, ya know?"

"Yeah. Facebook… Twitter networks."

"No no, not through them… but like them."

"OK."

"So when he sent the original message to me... the one you showed to Senator Cantor?"

"Yeah?"

"He had run that message through Dubai, but he was actually at that time in Modena."

"Italy?"

"Italy."

"OK."

"So.. again, don't ask… I was able to link up directly and engage him in some really… *really*… interesting discussions." He paused. "Even scary…"

"I'm listening."

"So, remember when he said in his first message that the F-86 thing was just the tip… the upper portion of the tip… of the iceberg?"

"Yup. So does Senator Cantor."

There was another pause. "He wasn't kidding."

Steve put his coffee cup down. "You mean like in, we shouldn't be discussing this on a cell phone?"

"You're, what, at the Washington Harbor Starbucks… on 'M' Street… right…?"

Steve frowned. "How… do you do that…?"

Mike huffed a laugh. "GPS is a cool tool… I'll bet you could be back at my condo in twenty minutes, by cab. Forget the Metro… you need to get over here *now*."

Steve gulped the last of the warm coffee and put the cup down. "On the way."

***

Steve exited the elevator, turned right and headed down the hall. He stopped at 705 and knocked. The tiny video camera in the "0" blinked on, then the door latch clicked and it cracked open.

"C'mon in," Mike instructed.

Steve complied and headed for the chair that had been stationed beside his in front of the computer monitor.

"Check it out," Mike said as he maneuvered the wireless mouse – the Marine Corps model Humvee – to bring up a text instant message exchange. "This is what I'm talkin' about."

The image filled the screen; Mike drilled down through the thread, pulling the Humvee's hood-mounted scroller wheel into a series of reverse jumps. "It's long." He looked at Steve. "But compelling." He went back to the top. "Start reading here, then go down through the thread." He handed the Humvee to Steve, who parked it on the mousepad: a miniature Marine Corps logo, the eagle gripping in its beak a ribbon with "semper' on one side, and 'fidelis' on the other. He scrolled to the beginning of the message.

CH: "So, you're better than I thought you were. I assume you tracked me down with one of the new Isis GPS apps... yes?"

MT: "Yup."

CH: "Slick. So... let's see how good you really are."

MT: "Go."

CH: "OK. Where am I now?"

MT: "Modena, Italy."

CH: "Big town."

MT: "Not that big. Hang on... Isis app puts you at ... umm... the Hotel Rafaello... probably outside – strong signal – at one of the poolside tables near the back of the property."

CH: "Ahh... not bad... but... what am I drinking...?"

MT: "I'm good..., not clairvoyant... but I'm workin' on an app for that... But since it's morning there, I'm goin' with coffee. Black. Probably a doppio."

CH: "Ouch. Very close. Ristretto."

MT: "Yeah... that would have been my second guess..."

CH: "Ahh... humor too. Good. Humor's good. The world is such a humorless, unhappy place these days... don't you think?"

MT: "Could not agree more."

CH: "So, now that you've found me, you realize, of course, I could turn this thing off, drop it in the trash and disappear again... don't you?"

MT: "Of course."

CH: "So why shouldn't I do that? Right now?"

MT: "Good question..., why haven't you done it already?"

CH: "Excellent response. I guess it's because I'm intrigued by ingenuity and cleverness. You seem to have both."

MT: "That I do."

CH: "But why have you contacted me?

MT: "Because I'm intrigued too. By your prior message about F-86. Actually, that message has already become the catalyst for an upheaval this nation not seen since... well, ever... I mean, it was nuclear...."

CH: "Not surprising. I warned them. I mean, I almost refused to help them, they were so dumb. It's like that John Wayne poster on the Internet... he's staring out at you, and the caption reads 'Life is tough. It's even tougher when you're stupid.' Nothing can bite you harder than a stupid client, especially one who gets his mail at 1600 Pennsylvania.

"But, like I said before, given what they ended up depositing into my accounts, they could have been blind, mute imbeciles and I still would have taken the money."

MT: "So Boalt was the actual client?"

CH: "OK..., that's a direct question. At this stage, I prefer indirect questions, assuming I decide to even entertain **any** more questions..."

MT: "Oh, I think you will..."

CH: "That's bold… why so presumptuous?"

MT: "Well, we're still talking, aren't we…? and you went back to specifically **bold font** the 'any' two responses ago…"

CH: "So gimme more reasons to keep this going…"

MT: "For openers, one, I am not a threat to you. Other folks… folks with fears, bad intentions … and most likely some pretty lethal weaponry… are probably scouring the globe for you right now… maybe even trying to monitor this communication link…."

CH: "Which you have prevented…?"

MT: "Let's just say, there's an app for that too. Wasn't born yesterday…."

CH: "Isis-based?"

MT: "Isis 4.0. Only the best. And this link is beyond secure. As far as their capability goes, it doesn't even exist. We're not even talking."

CH: "***Man***, I wish I could have recruited you back then…. We could have doubled… maybe tripled the take…. Still probably could, if you're interested."

MT: "Nah. I got other priorities right now. But since I don't begrudge you yours, don't begrudge me mine."

CH: "So what, **exactly**…, note the **bold**… is your priority in this mess?"

MT: "You identified it in the nuclear e-mail."

CH: "?"

MT: "Simple. The truth. Nothin' more… but nothin' less…"

CH: "Deal. So what do you want to know?"

MT: "Lots. Like, is all of this for real? Not some charade or diversion?"

CH: "Nope, no charade. It's as real as it gets... as dangerous too."

MT: "So, how did you get the parchment for F-86?"

CH: "Boalt's chief of staff... Ross Ellis. He's always skated on the edge. Sometimes over the edge. He knew some 'git-er-done' people from back when Boalt was running for the Senate, so he recruited one of them. A guy named Grant Kaplan. Like I said before, he had worked for me back at the OLRC... but he was *waaay* too careless. And greedy... so I fired him. But he convinced Ellis he could 'get it done,' so he hired him."

MT: "To...?"

CH: "To actually cut pieces from the original Articles of Confederation at the National Archives. Got no idea how he gained access, but he did. My guess is that either Ellis or Boalt himself authorized it. Dead of night. Just do it. Cut a bunch of strips from each page, then one big section from the last page.

"We replaced all of the missing sections with color-corrected linen content paper that was epoxy laser-welded back into place. Used our mobile lab parked in a lot across the street from National Archives one night... took us four hours... then we gave it back to Kaplan and he got the document back into the vault at Archives.

"It's an amazing job. To the casual eye, it looks exactly the same now as it did before. And the fading and visual differences between the paper and the parchment won't show up for years, maybe decades. As long as that didn't happen until after Boalt had left office, they didn't care. Then we brought the real strips back to the shop and did the same epoxy laser welds, and… presto: parchment from 1787."

MT: "Amazing…"

CH: "Not really. But thanks anyway…."

Steve looked away from the screen at Mike. "They… went and actually cut pieces… out of the original Articles of Confederation… to perpetrate their fraud?"

Mike nodded. "It looks like. But…, remember what Acton said. And keep reading… like they say, 'you ain't seen nothin' yet….'"

Steve returned his gaze to the message thread where he had left off.

MT: "And the ink?"

CH: "Much easier than the parchment. We had some really good chemists on contract… even one who in his prior life had received a Nobel Prize. Guess those stipends don't go near as far as they used to. All we needed was a stray dot of ink from the Articles for spectroanalysis… which we got from the last page… and a bunch of chemicals under a gradient ultraviolet light. Next thing you know… aged ink from 1788."

MT: "Unreal…"

CH: "Actually…, very real."

MT: "But you said…, you wrote in the original message… the nuclear e-mail… that all of this was just the tip… actually, the 'upper portion' of the tip of the iceberg."

CH: "Yes, I did…."

MT: "So are we far enough down the yellow brick road….?"

CH: "I think we are. Soooo, what do you want first? The upper point of the tip…, the tip… or the iceberg itself…?"

MT: "I'm gonna go for curtain number three… the whole enchilada…"

CH: "I would have guessed that…."

MT: "And you would have won."

CH: "You sitting down?"

MT: "Yeah. You think I should lie down?"

CH: "Well, if you pass out, you'll do less damage to your head if you're closer to the floor."

MT: "Try me."

CH: "OK. The iceberg is… the calculated breakup and dismantling of the United States of America as a functioning nation. From within."

Steve looked at Mike again. "Sweet mother of …." Mike nodded, then pointed back at the screen. "Keep goin.'"

MT: "OK…, yeah… that's big. But it could mean anything from a super volcano under Yellowstone to another San Francisco earthquake… not that that would be a *bad* thing…."

CH: "OK, look. I'm not joking here. Forget about volcanoes and earthquakes. What I'm talking about is…"

MT: "What…?"

CH: "Done for now… gotta go… re-establish later."

Steve looked up again at Mike. "So that's it? He just quit?"

Mike shrugged. "Not sure. The message sounded more like he was forced to stop… either he saw something, or he was attracting too much attention… don't know…"

Steve nodded. "And so how long ago did that happen?"

Mike looked at his Seiko. "About three hours ago."

Steve frowned. "So… what…, now, we just wait?"

"I guess."

"OK." He stood up. "Got any Henry's in the fridge?"

Mike smiled. "There's Weinhard's and a couple of Stella's. Help yourself… and you could bring me one too…."

"Any preference?"

"Yeah. A Stella."

***

The soft ping of the instant message link opening startled both of them. Mike looked at his watch: 10:15 AM. "OK, here we go…" he grabbed the model Humvee and maneuvered it into place between "semper" and "fidelis" on the mousepad.

CH: "You there?"

Mike typed: "Yes. With a friend…, a trusted friend."

The screen remained in limbo for seconds that seemed more like minutes.

"CH: "OK. Where do you show me now?"
"MT: "Bologna. At or near the Hotel Mercure…, yes?"
CH: "Yep."

Steve hunched over Mike's right shoulder as the two exchanged communications in real time.

CH: "Sorry about the abrupt departure before… just felt it better to hit the road again, if you get my drift…"
MT: "Sure."

CH: "So who's your friend?"

Mike looked up at Steve with that 'is-it-OK-to-tell-him?' look. Steve nodded.

> MT: "Steve McCracken. We served in the Marines together... Afghanistan. Steve works for Senator Beth Cantor. The one who blew the lid off things yesterday. He roped me into this at his boss' request, one thing led to another, and so... here I am."

Again, the screen seemed frozen. Then,

> CH: "OK... cool. Actually, really cool... Does she know we're talking? Senator Cantor?"

Mike looked at Steve, who slowly shook his head, left, right. "No. Not yet."

> CH: "OK... probably better... for now..."
> MT: "So when we left off, the topic was the breakup and dismantling of the nation. I gotta tell ya, that's grabbed our attention. Big time."
> CH: "Good. It should."
> MT: "I'm sure there's a whole bunch of details and background..., but like the contingency moon sample they grabbed on the first landing, what's the short version... just in case we get... interrupted again...?"
> CH: "Sure. And for preservation purposes...?"
> MT: "Yeah?"
> CH: "You should probably take periodic backup screenshots of these texts."

Mike nodded and moved the Humvee around on the pad to accomplish an automatic screen backup every twenty seconds. "Done."

CH: "OK, buckle up… this will be the strangest tale you've heard in a long time… maybe ever. Trust me."

MT: "Shoot."

CH: "OK… short version. First off, the folks in power now are thugs. And that comparison trivializes real thugs. No other way of describing them. They may sport $500 manicures and $300 haircuts, but they're still thugs. They do not care who they hurt, they do not care the cost of their actions. All they care about is power… power focused on one objective.

"They care most about making sure that the United States of America… at least as we have known it for the past couple hundred years… is no more. They want to cripple it so that it cannot remain standing on its own, so that only they can rehabilitate it…, but according to their own design. Without the constraints of the Constitution. The election of Boalt, for the first… and probably only time… has given them the opportunity to actually pull it off."

MT: "So there are others…. above and beyond Boalt?"

Another motionless screen. Then,

"CH: Oh… yes… definitely yes."

MT: "Go on…"

204

CH: "At first, they believed that Boalt's election alone would ensure that the plan could be implemented. I mean, he won by a sizeable, if not compelling, majority. And the voters were so sick and tired of the preceding administration, they would have voted in *anyone*.

"In fact, that was the whole tail-wag-the-dog theory underlying F-86... the results of the election alone self-authenticated Boalt's status as a 'natural born citizen.' Goofy... but who cared? Machiavelli. The ends justified the means. And besides, with the media in Boalt's pocket, who would dare to say otherwise? And all of Boalt's handlers knew that."

MT: "Handlers?"

CH: "Handlers. The ones with the money... the ones with the plan...that 'global' thing...."

MT: "And?"

CH: "But they had not done their homework. All they saw was someone who could get elected and lay the foundation for the implementation of the plan. They never looked deeper into Boalt's past and the implications of him not being even eligible to serve as president."

MT: "The 'natural born citizen' thing?"

CH: "Right. That issue wasn't even on their radar screens until it was *far* too late. They had invested too much in him to shift course, so the strategy was to trivialize and marginalize his ineligibility. Didn't matter. What's done is done. Get over it. And it worked like a charm, right through the campaign, through the election, and after the inauguration. Until the Locke case wouldn't die in the lower courts. So the whole F-86 Project was concocted... a fake Federalist Paper essay purporting to bolster his claim of eligibility and nailing the coffin shut on those challenging him."

MT: "But this is already…. I mean, is this the iceberg?"

CH: "No… no. This is the ocean where the iceberg is floating… backdrop. The real peril here is why they needed to keep him in office to begin with. You ready?"

MT: "Yes."

CH: "The real objective was to make sure that he had a vice-president who would toe the line in order to become himself president… and that he had a majority of the Senate who would unquestionably approve his nominations… to the Supreme Court."

MT: "OK, I'm lost…. You just lost me there."

CH: "Pay attention here. The biggest problem with being a president is that you have to deal with 535 *other* politicians. Some of those 535 may be competent, but the vast majority of them will be *completely* incompetent. Worse, they will be venal, incompetent and ego-maniacal… never a good combination.

"But if you only have to deal with nine other people… nine arguably capable and intelligent people, four of whom you can't stand because of their philosophy and view of the Constitution, but four of whom share your philosophy and view of the 'living' Constitution… then there is only one person… usually called the 'swing-vote'… who might present an impediment to, as they say, 'running the table.' Especially if your objective is nation change."

MT: "OK, hang on… so you're suggesting that Boalt's objective was to stay in office long enough

to appoint enough Supreme Court justices to…
to…. what…?"

CH: "To run the table. Remember, under the scheme laid out in the Federalist Papers and carried forward into the Constitution, there is… supposedly… a separation of powers among the executive, legislative and judicial branches. But it is the Supreme Court that has the *final* say on what the Constitution actually requires… or permits… or forbids. And so if five out of the nine justices say the Constitution provides for 'A', when the other four would scream at the top of their lungs that it says 'B' or 'anything but A,'… guess who wins?"

MT: "The five."

CH: "Mama didn't raise no fool… It is far easier to deal with and persuade… and if needed, to bully and threaten… five people to a particular way of thinking than it is to try that with 535 prima donnas. Recent history should confirm that, don't you think…? Especially against the backdrop of those pesky restrictions of the Constitution.

"And even if you can't bully or threaten *all* of them to your way of thinking… all you need is four of them on your side… the ones you already had…, then you can just roll over the others. Let them draft and sign on to their dissent. Let them rant and rave. So what? You win. They lose."

MT: "But that still doesn't…"

CH: "Stay with me. As originally planned, Boalt would serve out his first term and be re-elected to a second term. During the second term, he would have free rein to appoint whoever he wanted to the Court, especially if he retained his grip on the Senate. But the combination of the eligibility issue and the reaction of the electorate to the policies he tried to ram through during his first term strongly suggested... even compelled the conclusion that he was going to be a one-termer.

"And by the way, did I mention that while a president can dabble in his mischief for four or eight years, absent impeachment..., a Supreme Court appointment is for life? So when the Locke case actually made it to the Supreme Court on certiorari, they knew the handwriting was on the wall... so 'Plan B' got triggered."

MT: "So we're getting closer to the iceberg?"

CH: "Much closer. The Federalist 86 gambit... they coded it 'Onyx' to make sure those who knew of it understood it was to remain a deep black operation... the project got placed on a fast-track in an effort to make sure the Court didn't do anything in Locke before the 'discovery' of the essay. That is to say, the counterfeit.

"The hope was that the essay would give the four justices who favored a denial of standing for Locke the needed ammunition to persuade the swing vote justice... Justice Montgomery... to agree. That would deep six for good... or at least until after the next election... the eligibility question. It would also allow the time needed for the next part of the scheme to be implemented."

MT: "Iceberg up ahead...?"

CH: "Starboard bow..."

MT: "Can't quite see it yet..."

CH: "It's coming. Since the F-86 ruse has now been exposed, and there is a high likelihood that the wheels are starting to come off... they really should have taken Fitzpatrick into their confidence and at least briefed him… poor sap… hung out to dry. They should have let Chambers in on it too, but they didn't. It's that 20-20 hindsight thing. Anyway, seeing that this might happen, they planned ahead. The prime time television window to address the nation Boalt has requested…?"

MT: "Yup. 8:00 Eastern…"

CH: "The smart money is that he will announce that, for the good of the nation and to remove the cloud of suspicion over his eligibility as an issue…, illegitimate as he will persist in calling it…, he is resigning the office immediately…. not tomorrow or the next day… immediately… at the conclusion of the telecast. Even faster than Johnson did.

"At that time, Vice-President Chambers will then be sworn in as President, with all the powers of office that entails…, including the power to nominate and… get set… get set… actually appoint to the bench *without* Senate approval… Supreme Court Justices."

MT: "But… there's no opening… no vacancy there now."

The screen remained motionless again. Then,

CH: "Trust me… by 8:00 PM Eastern tonight…. there will be…."

Mike's eyes bulged at the information; he jerked a glance up to Steve, whose expression was no different.

MT: "Are you saying what I think you're saying…? Justice Montgomery is going to resign?"

CH: "Let's just say… there will be a vacancy on the Court soon… really soon. Not only that… do you really believe Montgomery's stroke was from natural causes? Do you? I told you this would be the strangest tale you've ever heard. And scary… did I mention scary?"

MT: "But we all know that it takes the approval of the Senate to have a nomination to the Supreme Court ratified and approved. Remember what happened to Bork?"

CH: "Ahhh… as they say… timing is everything. Silly man, go read your newspaper… the Senate is in recess until after the first of the year. That means the president can make what they call a 'recess appointment' that installs the justice on the Court until the end of the next session of the Senate after it reconvenes."

MT: "Are you kidding me?"

CH: "Nope. Check the Constitution… plain as day. In fact, Washington did just that when he made a recess appointment of a Chief Justice of the Supreme Court… Justice Rutledge… in the 1700's. So the precedent is there."

Mike stared at the monitor and shook his head. "Unreal," he muttered to no one in particular. Then he typed:

MT: "But even if Boalt were appointed immediately to the Supreme Court… even if this goofy 'recess appointment' thing were used… he couldn't participate in deciding his own case… the *Locke* case… could he…?"

CH: "Not legally, no. He would have to recuse himself."

MT: "So what's the point?"

CH: "The point is that, if the Court is evenly split... four to four on Locke's standing... with no ninth Justice to break the tie, Boalt having opted out of the review of the case for the sake of appearances... then the lower court of appeals decision stands.

"And since *that* decision found that Locke had *no* standing, then no decision of the Supreme Court affirming or reversing happens, the lower court decision denying standing remains in place... and the eligibility case goes away.

"Then Boalt's free to opine whatever the heck wants to opine, along with his soul mates on the Court..., for life. Unless Congress has the courage to impeach him... yeah... like that's gonna happen...."

MT: "And that's it? The iceberg?"

CH: "You wish."

MT: "What's that supposed to mean? You can't mean it gets worse... can you?"

CH: "It means that this would be a lot easier if that were, in fact, the iceberg."

MT: "So it's not?"

CH: "No."

MT: "OK, you're going to have to draw me a picture."

CH: "It finally dawned on them that the lid was blowing off, so if the real objective here – getting Boalt appointed to a lifetime position on the United States Supreme Court – was to happen, radical steps needed to be taken. And quickly. Because with all of the walls caving in, if Boalt were not nominated and seated on the Court almost immediately, before the truth of his complicity in the F-86 fraud were revealed, then the final goal would likely become unattainable."

MT: "Not Locke?"

CH: "Not Locke."

MT: "The iceberg?"

CH: "The iceberg. There are a slew of contrived and concocted projects and cases out there in the pipeline that Boalt would have salivated over deciding... ranging from the one seeking reparations for the survivors of Dresden, Nagasaki and Hiroshima... there are still a few of them... as well as their descendants.

"Another project..., not a 'case' as such..., sought to invite and actually precipitate a military coup d'état against him while he was out of the country... kind of a 'Seven Days in May' thing, but with a different twist... so that he could call upon the United Nations and the Security Council to intervene and reinstall him with even greater powers after the military had been defanged. And what they had planned for the Electoral College would curl yer hair...."

MT: "Seriously? A coup d'état? "

CH: "They were seriously discussing it. My personal favorite was the case advocating the confiscation of all private *weapons*... not just guns... but knives, swords, slingshots, bows and arrows... pitchforks... and declaring the Second Amendment itself... get this... unconstitutional."

MT: "You're kidding, right?"

CH: "Well, yeah... I'm kidding about the pitchforks... but not the rest. They're dead serious here. Crazy... but dead serious. And some could easily argue... plain old dangerous. But there's reason to believe the first case they were going to select to run with was the most radical one.

"A decision of the United States Supreme Court in a case of original jurisdiction… no need for lower court appeals or such time-consuming nonsense… to these people, if it is worth doing at all, it is worth doing *now*.

MT: "Yeah?"

CH: "An original lawsuit will be brought between two states… Connecticut and New Mexico. A concocted, bogus dispute, of course… like F-86. But it will be super-fast-tracked. And with the governors and attorneys general of those two states also all in Boalt's pocket… and five justices… including Boalt… magically finding 'standing' in the parties and agreeing to hear the case, the dispute would be allowed in the front door immediately. And here comes the scary part.

"This particular case… and remember, there are other projects in progress still being refined in the pipeline… it would draw into question the continued viability and validity of each and all of the treaties entered into over the past two-plus centuries between the United States and as many as 300 Native American Indian tribes. "If those treaties were to be declared void… or as will be held '*void ab initio*'… that is, 'void from the beginning,' … then each of those tribal nations can… and *will*… be retroactively restored to full and *independent nation* sovereign status.

MT: "And?"

CH: "Right now, Indian tribal entities are treated as 'domestic, dependent nations' whose continued existence and viability depends almost exclusively on the sufferance of the United States. Which means, basically, the Congress and the president. Contrary to popular belief, they are not like France. Or Kenya. Or Ecuador.

"But if those treaties are voided and the tribes are restored, retroactively, to their status an independent aboriginal nations, complete with all of the sovereign powers possessed by independent nations, then... they could... for example, lay claim to the lands they 'exchanged' for federal reservation 'protection.' Or seek reparations. They could exercise full jurisdiction over people... not just tribal members... found within those lands. Which is basically everyone everywhere between Maine and Maui or Alaska and Florida. Passports. Visas. Deportations.

"California would look like it came down with a bad case of acne and Arizona would look like Swiss cheese. And there would be a huge hole in the nation north of Texas where Oklahoma used to be."

Mike sat back in his chair and took a long draw from the bottle of Henry Weinhard; Steve repeated the exercise... twice.

CH: "It gets worse."
MT: "How much worse than that?"
CH: "How about this?: if 300 newly-established, completely sovereign nations are carved out of the various states in which they previously existed as 'reservations' and were suddenly free to, say, enter into treaties with other foreign nations... not just other new Indian nations... like France. Or Kenya. Or Ecuador."
MT: "Or Iran...?"

CH: "Or North Korea? Or Cuba? Maybe Venezuela, for 'mutual defense' purposes?"

Mike could only shake his head.

MT: "That's ludicrous. Even *if* that were possible, Native American tribes would never buy into a scheme like that. They may have been taken to the cleaners in the past, but they are still Americans. They would never do that. Never. And if you think the Congress... even *this* Congress would stand by and do nothing, you're crazy. *Never* gonna happen."

CH: "'Never' is a big word... it's so... absolute. And, by the way..., not that it matters, I told them the same thing. But do you think that had any effect or changed their plans? Forget about it.

"Look at it this way... these people plan ahead. *Way* ahead.

"Even if 99% of the tribes do exactly what you say and re-up with new treaties and agreements with the United States... more 'equitable' ones, shall we say... with healthy infusions of foreign aid and grants..., ninety-nine percent of 300 is still 297... leaving three tribes out there who might... just *might*... for the right reasons or the right payoff... decide to change partners and go it with France. Or Ecuador. Or Iran.

MT: "Still never gonna happen."

CH: "And get this, there are at least eleven tribes out there with borders shared either with Canada or Mexico, and over a dozen with seafronts on the Pacific or Atlantic coasts. So if any one of them decided to cozy up to..., say..., Iran... or North Korea... you could well have, in a worst case scenario, a foreign military base well within the former geographic boundaries of the United States, and without the need for aircraft overflight or sea corridors to get there.

MT: "This is getting surreal. You are actually saying that they were laying plans that would allow for the establishment of foreign power military bases within the United States? Even foreign powers hostile to the United States?"

CH: "I'm not exactly saying that. *They* are saying that."

MT: "You lost me again. Where are *they* saying that?"

CH: "You still sitting down?"

MT: "Yes."

CH: "In the opinion in *Connecticut v. New Mexico.*"

MT: "What are you talking about?"

CH: "I'm talking about the Unites States Supreme Court decision… yet to be handed down, of course, because the case hasn't even been filed yet… but it will be… and an expedited determination will be sought and granted, of course. The decision laying the foundation for all of this has already… been… written."

MT: "You have got to be kidding now…."

Steve motioned to Mike to keep the conversation going as he took his Droid out and tapped the address book and speed-dial for Senator Cantor.

CH: "Do I sound like I'm kidding? Look, we both know that sooner or later, they're going to track me down and… do what needs to be done. They give new meaning to the term 'ruthless.' So I've got nothing to lose. I got enough money on deposit and

electronic access to it to stay on the run indefinitely. Or at least for a while… it just depends on how much more clever than their henchmen I can be."
MT: "My money's on you…"

The screen went motionless for a while, then:

CH: "Thanks. And the reason I know the decision doing all of this has already been written is because…" He paused, with an ellipsis…
MT: "Because…?"
CH: "Because…."
MT: "Because you wrote it?"
CH: "Like I said… mama didn't raise no fool. Actually, one of our contractors wrote it. We gave her…"

The words appeared on the screen, then stopped mid-sentence. Then:

CH: "The assignment and overall thesis of the project was given to the contractor based on instructions from Boalt. Actually, the thesis and schematic of the opinion and what it needed to say came from Ross Ellis. But Boalt signed off on it."
MT: "And how do you know that?"
CH: "Because Boalt told me so. In the Oval Office. He was behind his desk, I was on the couch. Anyway, the opinion in the case… a 5-4 split decision… will set the stage for just what I have described. We don't know what the dissent will say since, obviously, they haven't yet seen what the majority opinion is… but you can count on a

dissent. Then again, who cares? Five is bigger than four. Five wins. Four loses."

Steve motioned for Mike to continue the exchange with Hardin, then spoke into the Droid. "Senator?"

Senator Cantor's voice radioed into his Bluetooth. "Yes, Steve... where *are* you? I need you."

Steve nodded. "Yes, m'am... I know... but trust me, this thing is still unfolding..."

"I know that, but what do you mean?"

"I mean there's a lot more going on here than just the bogus Federalist essay."

"You need to explain that for me."

"Well, the short version is that, one, Justice Montgomery's safety or continuation on the Supreme Court may be at imminent risk. Imminent. Two, the president's address tonight will likely be to announce his resignation."

"Steve, Steve, Steve... slow down."

"Senator," he exhaled, "I'm as serious as a heart attack about this. I've been here with Mike Tippett... the computer guru...?

"Yes?"

"He's established a direct line of communication with Charlie Hardin... the guy whose e-mail we read in your office... the guy who can confirm that Federalist 86 was and is a fraud. He knows.... he's had direct conversations with Boalt and Ross Ellis about *all* this stuff.... and more that he hasn't even gotten to..."

"Go on..."

"Hardin is telling us that the whole object of all of this has not been only to keep Boalt in office as president. On top of that, if things went south on the eligibility front... as they are now ... the additional fall-back 'Plan "B"' proposal was to get him appointed to... to a position as a Justice of the Supreme Court after he resigns tonight..."

"What?'

"That's what Hardin says. And the resignation will be immediate... at the conclusion of the address."

Steve listened for a response; none immediately came. "Senator? You there?"

"Yes, Steve. Some of this is now beginning to make sense. I just had a meeting with House Speaker Adam Simpson. He was, in fact, asked by the president to be at the White House for the telecast tonight. But he also found out that there would be a fourth participant."

Steve nodded to himself. "Let me guess. The Chief Justice."

"How did you know that?"

"Hardin said that Boalt would resign at the end of his address. That would mean the Chief Justice could be called upon to immediately swear in the new president. Administer the oath of office."

"Speaker Simpson?"

"That's what they *want* you to think."

There was a pause. "Well, that would make sense if Chambers were implicated in the F-86 fraud, especially if he knew of Boalt's ineligibility during the campaign and before the election, there's a pretty good argument that he would be ineligible too."

Steve responded. "Well, that might tend to disqualify him... but I'm not sure it would make him constitutionally ineligible. And anyway, I'm not sure Chambers *is* implicated."

"Steve," Cantor interrupted, "he's implicated... but after what I've learned from Speaker Simpson, Chambers is not implicated in the way you think."

Steve peered over Mike's right shoulder as the information exchange with Hardin continued.

> MT: "My bud here, Steve McCracken, has Senator
> Cantor on his cell phone."
> CH: "Say 'hi' to her for me...."

MT: "You know about the meeting at the White House tonight? For the address to the nation?"

CH: "Of course. It's all over the news… except maybe in Antarctica… I'm not sure they get satellite in Antarctica…"

MT: "So you know that both Boalt and Vice President Chambers will be there?"

CH: "Yes. And so will Speaker Simpson… right?"

MT: "Correct."

CH: "Well, if they stick to their plan… and it sounds like they are… Simpson's presence there is strictly for show… a sucker punch, juke-move."

Steve was reading the text from the monitor into the Droid for Cantor.

MT: "Huh?"

CH: "Sure. Inviting and having Simpson there is a ruse… they're good at concocting ruses. It's a move calculated to keep people… and more importantly, the media… thinking that, because of the wheels falling off the Federalist 86 ploy, *both* Boalt and Chambers… for the good of the nation… will simultaneously resign, thereby dropping the presidency into Simpson's lap with… how convenient … the Chief Justice already there to administer the oath of office. Badda bing…. badda boom. Seamless transition. Boalt gone. His lackey Chambers gone. The dawning of a new day…."

MT: "I sense some cynicism…."

CH: "Nothing wrong with your senses. The Chief Justice will not be there to give the oath of office to Simpson. He will be called upon to swear in *Chambers* as president… not Speaker Simpson."

MT: "Even if Chambers is ineligible?"

CH: "That's the beauty of it. Chambers *is* eligible, because he is a natural born citizen. That was one of the first things they confirmed when they vetted him for vice-president, knowing that Boalt was not. And, completing their fraud, they made sure that Chambers knew absolutely *nothing* about F-86. Plausible deniability. That way, if the ruse blew up, he could truthfully say that he knew nothing. He'd pass any lie detector test they wanted to administer. Truth is, even on his best days, Chambers knows next to nothing, so there's usually no occasion for him to fake ignorance.

"On the other hand, Chambers wants to be president just like any other vice-president, so in return for promising to Boalt that he would do the recess appointment thing and appoint *him* to the Supreme Court if the whole thing went south… like it is…, Boalt resigns the presidency, but is rewarded with a lifetime membership in a smaller group of folks who can do just as much mischief, if not more, than the gang across the street on Capitol Hill."

MT: "So Boalt resigns because he's now implicated in a fraud?"

CH: "Nope. Boalt resigns because, as he will tell the people, he's innocent and had nothing to do with the essay fraud. *Nothing.* But for the good of the nation, and put behind us… meaning 'him'… all of this 'distraction' so that the important business of governing can move on, he's stepping aside.

"But in reality, he knows, like I said before, that it's a *whole* lot easier to swing four other people to your way of thinking than it is to have to contend with 535 egocentric Congressmen and Senators. And since only five members of the Court will be needed

221

to sign onto the decision in *Connecticut v. New Mexico,* or for that matter, any of the other cases still brewing in the cauldron, the task of reforming the nation into something quite different than that which we have known for the past 230-plus years... will be far easier to pull off. *Far* easier."

MT: "So you really think Boalt's objective is the fracturing and dismantling of the United States? Seriously?"

CH. "Yes... I do... and so do a bunch of other folks around the world who'd like to see the same thing. Birds of a feather..."

Steve tapped Mike's right shoulder. "Tell him you need to take a break and you'll get back to him. We gotta call Cantor."

MT: "I need a break. Let me get back to you."

CH: "Do what you gotta do, but understand... you may not be able to get back to me.... I just got a message from the guy who drafted F-86... Ella Boalt's nephew... the cowboy they trusted over my warnings. He's nearing Mexico over back roads, but thinks they may be closing in on him. Those Predator drones are sneaky.... And really deadly."

MT: "Closing in...?"

CH: "Yeah... like, in, cover their tracks. Erase the trail. Take him out."

MT:" Where is he now?"

CH: "Southern Arizona, 'bout fifteen miles from the border... on the Goldwater Gunnery Range. Goin' it alone in a pickup truck."

MT: "Right...I'll get back... take care..."

CH: "I intend to, but like they say... you can't tell a lie forever..."

NINETEEN

The Oval Office was bathed in the glare of the White House halogens: the CFC corkscrews had been discarded because they weren't bright enough and they made his skin look pasty. He sat behind the Resolute Desk and glanced at the teleprompters, first left, then right…. then back left. He was always more comfortable looking left.

On the sofa sat Vice-President Chambers and, next to him, House Speaker Simpson. Both had worn their dark blue HSM suits, Chambers with a mid-blue and silver striped tie; Simpson with a red and blue striped tie. Across from them, Chief Justice Phillips sat in his black formal robes. The cameraman held up five fingers… four fingers… three fingers… two fingers… one index finger that immediately pointed at Boalt.

"Good evening. I have asked that I be allowed into your living rooms, onto your computers and your mobile devices tonight in order to deliver to you what will be for me the most important message of my presidency. I won't take a lot of your time, but the time I will take will be very important.

"On a sad note, however, I must first bring bad news to you. Following a brief and valiant struggle after the massive stroke he suffered, I have been informed that Supreme Court Justice Montgomery has quietly passed away earlier this evening. He was a respected and towering intellect on the Court, and his presence there will be sorely missed. The thoughts and prayers of the nation, and this president, go out to Justice Montgomery's family."

Senator Cantor looked away from the Sony in her office and made eye contact with Steve and Annie. "So Hardin… called it…." she said. They slowly nodded, then looked back at the Sony. Boalt shifted slightly in his chair.

"My fellow Americans, over the past few months and weeks, it has become increasingly clear to me that the nation is at war, and not only with foreign powers and nongovernmental entities. No, sadly… the nation has been for some time at war with itself. Large and intractable segments of our society, and the subcultures and groups within that society, have become polarized and alienated, one from another, and from mainstream America.

"While there are many issues over which the polarization has spread, at the heart of the discontent has been the notion… the claim… that I am not qualified… not even eligible, under our Constitution… to serve as your president. To be perfectly honest, that hurts. I have done everything in my power to earn the trust and confidence of all Americans, not just the ones who voted for me… but *all* Americans.

"I failed. Indeed, there were some on one side of the battle-lines who openly advocated that I be impeached because they did not believe I was eligible to serve as required under the Constitution. Never mind that I showed the world… and if there is Internet reception on Mars, there too… my Missouri birth certificate, nothing would satisfy them.

"And on the other side of the battle-line, in a misguided, blundering and wholly rogue attempt to bolster my claim to being eligible, other people, thinking they were helping me, only made matters worse by forging a document purporting to show that the Founding Fathers intended at the beginning of the republic to establish principles that would assist me on the question of my eligibility. Not a good idea.

"But I will not lie to you. Like many of you, until I learned it could be fraudulent, I had sincerely hoped that the discovery of the long-lost Federalist essay would put an end to the controversy and allow me to put one more major distraction aside. The burden of presidential responsibilities is enough as it is without the added weight of irrelevant distractions. But now that the essay has been seemingly discredited... and the jury is still out on that issue... I can no longer simply hope that the issue will just go away."

Senator Cantor stared at the Sony, her mouth agape and silently mouthing "jury... still... out?" She again turned slowly toward Steve and Annie, who were sitting on the couch watching the delivery as well: not only were their mouths opened wide, their eyes bugged at the deception coming over the airwaves. Boalt shifted in his chair again.

"Let me assure each and every one of you watching and listening to me: while I still believe that I am constitutionally eligible to serve as your president... I was, after all, elected by you to the office... and while I would have welcomed the confirmation of my eligibility with a genuine document such as the one now cast into doubt as having the potential for being a forgery, I cannot and will not condone or be a party to any ruse or deception calculated to trick or fool the American people. The people mean too much to me. And this nation means too much to me. And I trust Justice Montgomery would have agreed."

Cantor could only slowly oscillate her head...right....left... right...

"The point, however, is that the damage has been done and the bell cannot be 'un-rung.' No quantity of facts, no volume of explanations and no collection of realities can now reverse the damage done by the false and baseless allegations made against me. I wish it were not so, but..., as they say, it is what it is. Such is life. Moreover, I have concluded that the continued litigation of these issues before the Supreme Court has become counterproductive and corrosive to the structure of the nation. That litigation needs to come to an end... and I intend to facilitate that result.

"Accordingly, for the good of the nation, I have determined that it is time to move on. It has been my distinct honor to serve you as your president. However, as of the end of this address, I am immediately resigning the office which I hold. As my last official act, I have signed this letter of resignation" he held up three pieces of letterhead, "done in triplicate original, one for Vice-President Chambers, one for Speaker of the House Simpson and one for Chief Justice Phillips."

The camera angle pulled back as Boalt handed the three pieces of paper to each of the others in the room.

"The letter announces my resignation. Immediately. And because I will allow no interruption in the continuity of our government, the letter requests that Chief Justice Phillips immediately administer the oath of office to Vice-President Chambers, making him your next president. That is why I have asked him to join us here in the Oval Office. I also thank Speaker Simpson for being here to ensure that, if for any reason, Vice President Chambers knows or believes himself to be disqualified or ineligible to serve, that he would say so, thus alternatively making Speaker Simpson, upon administration of the oath by the Chief Justice, your next president.

"Thank you... and good night."

With that, Boalt stood from behind the Resolute Desk and motioned for the Chief Justice and Chambers to stand in front of it, which they did. He pulled what appeared to be an old Bible from one of the desk's drawers and placed it within Chambers' reach.

In her office, Senator Cantor, Steve and Annie continued staring at the Sony, speechless. History was unfolding in 1080-pixel high definition before them, as well as before everyone else in the world watching or listening.

Chief Justice Phillips looked directly at Boalt as he stood behind the desk with his arms folded across his chest, a shallow grin on his mouth and the high density crystal face of his Rolex glinting in the camera lights, his right White House presidential cufflink twinkling in support, then shifted his attention to the vice-president. "Vice-President Chambers, to say the least, these are unprecedented events and proceedings."

"They are, indeed, Mr. Chief Justice," Chambers intoned.

The camera angle was just right, framing Justice Phillips on the right, Chambers on the left and Boalt standing in the middle, behind the desk.

Justice Phillips nodded at Chambers. "You have read President Boalt's resignation letter, have you not?"

"I have," he replied.

"So you are aware that one of his concerns regarding your succession to the office of the presidency is that of your eligibility under the Constitution, correct?"

"Yes, I am aware of that."

"That being so, do you know of any reason or are there any facts of which you are aware which would render you ineligible under the Constitution?"

"No, I do not. And, in fact, I have sought my own legal counsel on the question and have received a legal opinion that I am, in fact, eligible under the Constitution... although as in the case of President Boalt, both my legal counsel and I concur that the Supreme Court would have the last say on that question should it ever be raised."

Phillips nodded. "All right, then let me ask you the next question. Are you willing and prepared to succeed to the office of President of the United States following President Boalt's resignation?"

Chambers nodded. "I am."

The Chief Justice motioned to Speaker Simpson. "Mr. Speaker, would you please join us here?" Simpson stood and walked over to stand beside Vice President Chambers.

Justice Phillips glanced over to the Bible on the desk. "Mr. Speaker, while it is customary for someone selected by the one to be sworn in to witness and hold the Bible, under the circumstances, and with Vice President Chambers' permission, might I ask you to do that here?"

Simpson nodded. "Of course." He grasped the Bible and positioned it before Chambers' front left hand. To the rear, Boalt's grin was evolving into a toothy smile; but his arms were still crossed, and the glitter from his watch and cufflink still made a periodic flash into the television lens.

Back in Senator Cantor's office, the mood had metastasized to that of a funeral parlor. Or maybe a morgue. Cantor looked over at Annie; Annie looked over at Steve; Steve looked back at Cantor and produced a fullback's shrug. On the Sony, the Chief Justice raised his right hand. Chambers placed his left hand on the Bible being held by Simpson.

"Mr. Vice President, please raise your right hand and repeat after me..."

Chambers complied, raising his right palm just to the side of his cheek. "I, William Carson Chambers...," Justice Phillips began.

"I, William Carson Chambers..."

"Do solemnly swear or affirm...," the jurist continued.

"Do solemnly swear...," Chambers said, pausing for the Chief Justice to continue.

"That I will faithfully execute the Office of President of the United States...,"

"That I will faithfully execute the Office of President of the United States...," Chambers repeated.

"And will to the best of my ability, preserve, protect and defend...,"

"And will to the best of my ability, preserve, protect and defend...," Chambers echoed.

"The Constitution of the United States."

"The Constitution of the United States."

Justice Phillips reached out with his right hand, grasping Chambers' right hand. "Congratulations, Mr. President."

"Thank you, Mr. Chief Justice." He shook his hand firmly, then offered his hand to Boalt, who also shook it firmly, sealing the congratulation with his left hand as well. Boalt then turned the presidential chair to one side and offered it to the new president, who immediately accepted the gesture and sat down.

"Please," he gestured to Boalt, Simpson and Justice Phillips. "Sit down with me for a few moments. On this momentous occasion, I have a number of important things to say to everyone, including each of you here in the Oval Office. Please," he gestured to the sofa and chairs.

Simpson and the judge sat together on the sofa; Boalt allowed a shallow crease to race over his forehead, sort of like that "this-isn't-what-we-rehearsed-so-what's-going-on?" look when things don't look exactly like they are developing as planned. Or like when a teleprompter goes rogue during a live broadcast or pep rally. He sat into an upholstered occasional chair to the left of the desk.

Chambers looked at each of the others in the room, then looked directly into the camera. "My fellow Americans, you have just witnessed one of the most solemn events contemplated under our Constitution... the seamless and peaceful transfer of power from one president to another. I cannot express to you how proud and humbled I am to now have the honor of representing you as your president and this, the greatest nation on the planet.

"I congratulate President Boalt for his decision to moot and make irrelevant the pending case in the Supreme Court questioning his eligibility. That case was, as he stated a moment ago, corroding the very structure of the nation. His resignation has, indeed, mooted that litigation."

Chambers leaned forward slightly in his new chair and folded his hands on the Resolute Desk.

"However... the mooting of litigation does nothing to resolve or answer the issue in controversy. It merely puts it aside for another day. The question doesn't go away... it just hibernates... like a mama grizzly in winter."

Boalt was becoming visibly anxious; much as had Attorney General Fitzpatrick at the hearings on the F-86 counterfeit essay, his forehead began to slowly glisten with micro beads of fluid.

"In order to rectify all of the wrongs that have led us to this point, I now deem it necessary to level with you." He stared directly into the center of the television camera lens.

Cantor and her staffers focused on the Sony, each, in their own way, sensing something big on the approaching video horizon.

"First, all of you need to know that I have experienced over the past few days... an extraordinary transformation and realization... an epiphany, of sorts. Not a spiritual awakening or religious revelation... but a moral, political and intellectual one. And, yes, a personal one. And I suspect others involved have also had similar experiences lately."

He paused, dipped his chin, then looked back up at the camera. "An epiphany brought about by the painful realization that there is now compelling evidence... and therefore good reason to believe... that former President Boalt did, in fact..., have prior knowledge of the ruse that was the Federalist 86 counterfeit. And, in fact, that along with others in his administration... he participated in and facilitated the execution of that fraud upon the nation. And, in the process, he also authorized the desecration of one of our nation's most hallowed artifacts... the Articles of Confederation."

Boalt started to rise from his seat and turn for the door.

"Mr. President," Chambers barked, shifting his gaze to the former president, "... I wouldn't do that... if I were you. You need to stay and listen to me."

Boalt froze as two Secret Service agents – one a Black with a BMI like Steve's, the other the prototypical image of a Viking warrior, but with what could have been the world's last flat-top haircut – stared him down; he retook his seat and removed a handkerchief from his pocket. Chambers looked back into the camera.

"In addition, I refuse to take my first steps as your president in furtherance of a charade and fraud. You need to know that earlier today, I met with and spoke with certain other people in our government and learned a number of things I had suspected... but not known... before. Scary things. Bad things. Things which would have given any one of the Founding Fathers a stroke or heart attack... or both... had they known of them.

"I also shared with them what President Boalt and his Chief of Staff, Ross Ellis, told me this afternoon in preparation for his resignation and this broadcast. That in return for President Boalt's resignation and my swearing in as your next president, I would agree to immediately appoint him... to the Supreme Court... replacing Justice Montgomery... who at that time had not even left us. I can tell you, it is not a pretty picture. In fact, once you learn... as you will in time... all the details, you will feel like the subject in that painting we've all seen at one time or another ... 'The Scream.'"

Boalt was now feverishly mopping his forehead; he had disengaged the top collar button on his shirt and loosened his tie. While the TV camera stayed focused on Chambers, Boalt's growing panic jerked at the side of the frame. The two Secret Service agents' arms could be seen in the far left portion of the screen.

"For now, the important things for you to know are these. One, I will not lie to you. If you catch me in a lie, I too will resign. No need for talking heads speculating or senatorial calls for impeachment... I will resign. And..., I'm not kidding.

"Two, I offer my deepest sympathies to the family of Justice Montgomery, who served the Court and this nation with skill and, of equal importance, dignity for over twenty years. But we are in the most perilous of times. And so as my first official act, I deem it essential that the Court be restored to its full membership, and that means immediately. Accordingly, earlier this afternoon, I requested that Speaker of the House Adam Simpson... himself a distinguished lawyer in private practice before becoming a congressman... agree to his appointment as a Justice to the Supreme Court."

Cantor looked over at Annie and Steve, who each were firing astonished glances right back at her; she nodded at them.

President Chambers continued. "Since the Senate is in recess, the 'recess appointment' means that he will serve without the need for Senate confirmation until that body returns from its current holiday and takes up the question of whether to retain him on the Court, or remove him. And since the Chief Justice is already here, as soon as I am done speaking to you tonight, I will request that he administer the oath to Speaker Simpson."

He nodded at the camera. "Third, because I just told you I would resign before lying to you, I need a solid vice-president. I need someone who will both *tell* the truth as well as *fight* for the truth. I need someone who is not afraid to take a stand and defend this nation, its institutions and its Constitution, no matter what the talking heads on cable say or what those who would undermine what this nation stands for want. I need a vice-president who refuses to 'go along to get along' or blindly march in lockstep with those in leadership positions who have nothing but their self-aggrandizement and personal agendas on their minds. Because that is what has led this nation to the perilous cliff we now stand beside.

"I need a vice-president who is all of these and much more, and... hang on to your hats... whether belonging to my party or not. If things are going to get better... and I have *great* confidence that, given time, they *will* get better..., then true cooperation and... I hate the term 'bipartisan' because it has been so perverted and slaughtered in this town... bipartisanship will help to lead us there. So, to repeat, I need a solid vice-president. I have someone in mind... but the person does not yet know it."

Senator Cantor slowly... *very* slowly... turned her gaze to Annie. Annie, just as slowly turned her gaze to Steve. Steve looked at both of them and produced a gigantic smile, then said: "Can he be ... is he saying... what I think he's saying?"

Chambers continued. "Soon, however, that individual will be receiving a request from me to join me as we try to fix the mess we now find ourselves in. I'm going to need all the help I can get... so I hope the request will be accepted. And, no, I will not identify that person until we have spoken directly."

Cantor said nothing; Annie said nothing, but produced a smile almost, but not quite, as big as Steve's. They looked back at the Sony. President Chambers had turned in his seat and was staring at Boalt.

"Finally, Mr. President... when first you asked me to run and serve as your vice-president, I was honored. Deeply honored. Throughout the difficult days of the campaign and your first year in office, I did everything I could to support you, ignoring all of the warning signs that should have alerted me to your true character. Like millions of others, I bought into the propaganda. Because I believed what I wanted to believe... instead of what was the reality of your character.

"But following the revelations of the past few days and the falling into place of scores of puzzle pieces, one after another after another... and yet again after another... I can no longer ignore reality. Shame on you. And shame on all of your sycophants and enablers, including until now, me, both inside as well as outside the formal organizations of government... who have facilitated and lubricated your slide through this office.

"Foolishly, I put party and politics ahead of country and reasoned analysis. But after learning the truth of what you and those in your inner circle have done, it finally dawned on me... the epiphany I referred to... that being an American means doing what is right for the nation, rather than winning 'no matter what.'"

He looked directly at Boalt. "Those days are gone. Done. So, my suggestion to you now is that you leave this building and go find the very best lawyers you can who are willing to represent you. I am confident you will have no problem at all finding a lawyer or two in this town still willing to do just that. Start with your campaign donor list. And you might think about suggesting that your chief of staff do the same thing. Both of you should choose your lawyers wisely... because I think you are *really* going to need them."

With that, Boalt slowly rose from his chair – almost disheveled in a now sweat-soaked Armani *Collezioni* shirt and blotched blue *Forzieri* necktie – and started to exit the Oval Office, the two Secret Service agents taking up positions beside him.

"Oh," Chambers blurted, "I almost forgot. I'm going to need you to surrender your passport too as soon as you get your personal things gathered."

Boalt had turned slightly and glanced back at his successor over his left shoulder; the president tilted his head slightly at the poseur. "I'm sure you understand." Boalt shrugged, turned and disappeared out the anteroom door with the agents.

Chambers faced the camera. "My fellow Americans, I do not yet have a clear picture in my mind of where all of this will actually lead. But I do have a clear picture in my mind of where we have been and where we need to go. I ask for your support, your patience and most of all your abiding faith that this nation is, with all of its warts, blemishes and faults, still the greatest nation on the planet and worthy of preserving. Because if this nation fails... what next?

"I will keep the faith if you will. I will also get back to you in the next few days. But right now, I've got a *lot* of other things to do... some of which, I will tell you, are already under way... and including witnessing the appointment of the next United States Supreme Court Justice. So, if you will excuse me, I will for now say good night. Stay safe, and God bless you and this, the United States of America."

The Sony screen went to an exterior shot of the White House, bathed in lights, the rooftop flag undulating slowly in the crisp December night. Cantor sat back in her chair; Annie sat back as well; Steve stood up. "Sooo… now what?" he asked no one in particular. The uneasy silence persisted until:

"Senator?" Ellen's voice came over the intercom.

"Yes?" Cantor replied.

Ellen allowed a brief pause. "You have a call on line one." Another pause, then: "It's the White House."

TWENTY

Neal yawned as the morning chill began to dissipate with the flow of warm air from the propane heat exchanger. He sat up – still in the flannel padded sleeping bag – and looked out the side window of the F-250's camper shell. To the southeast, the accelerating dawn lit the bottoms of the far horizon's stratus clouds a pleasant peach-grey. To the southeast, a distant range of desert mountains chewed at the brightening sky. The sky to the west, out the camper-shell window, was still dark, lit only by the setting full moon: the disk looked gigantic against the sporadic saguaros and mountain peaks, although it was farther away than when overhead.

He opened the rear hatch and stared out at the moonset, then glanced at his GPS unit: he was around 15 miles north of Monument Bluff, and so maybe another two miles more from the border. He lifted a can of Dr. Pepper and took a full swallow, savoring the irony of fleeing the bad things happening to him in his country for the safety of northern Mexico.

***

He adjusted the scope to compensate for the wind, the temperature and, of course, the euler force. The target lowered a can of soda pop and stared out toward him, apparently at something behind him... perhaps the setting moon.

He positioned the crosshairs in the scope on the bridge of Neal's nose, then began the rhythmic respiration to coincide with his heartbeat, all to ensure one shot, one kill.

***

She centered the crosshairs of her scope just above his left ear and made her final adjustments for the breeze, the chill and the coriolis force. In her head, she sang along with her iPod "... *where the skies are so blue*... *da da da da dat da*... *Lawd I'm comin' home to you*..." She inhaled... exhaled... inhaled... exhaled... and fired. The sniper's iPod fell to the ground, its dislodged earbuds serenading early morning insects foraging the desert floor with the final bars of Lennon's *Imagine*. And she closed her eyes.

***

Neal jumped as the sharp, hard crack of a large caliber rifle shot boomed out over the terrain. A pair of hawks that had been sleeping in a cluster of mesquite trees rocketed into the sky and spasm-flapped through the chill, away from the noise. He could not tell where the shot came from, but that was of no concern: it came from somewhere. He quickly scrambled through the camper shell's window into the pickup's cabin and fired the engine.

The F-250 lurched forward, bounced past several shrapnel scarred target cars, then bore south toward the border. He never stopped to look back, but only forward as the primitive road cut by decades of immigrants and smuggler's vehicles pouring north snaked back and forth through the desert, leading him to safety and asylum to the south.

But out of the corner of his left eye he could see the growing bump of Monument Bluff poking into the accelerating pastels of the dawn. The radio reports from last night about Boalt's resignation and the collapse of his world around him rattled in his mind... perhaps that rifle shot had been meant for him. After all, he thought: they rolled the dice... and lost. And that could not have pleased them. Not Boalt. Not Ellis. And certainly not his aunt. Nobody at all.

On the other hand, he thought as he aimed the vehicle toward the equator: it looked like it was going to be a promisingly nice, new day. High, thin wisps of snow white cirrus ice crystals raced above the disappearing stratus.

And to boot, he grinned, Christmas was just around the corner. He thought to himself as the truck wobbled and bounded over the muddy road high-centering its way south: Ho... ho... ho....

www.ingramcontent.com/pod-product-compliance
Lightning Source LLC
Chambersburg PA
CBHW070608130626
46556CB00001B/309

9 780615 571096